Case File:

UNION
PACIFIC

Paul Colt

Durban House

Printed in the United States of America.

For information address:
Durban House Press, Inc.
5001 LBJ Freeway, Suite 700
Dallas, Texas 75244

Library of Congress Cataloging-in-Publication Data

Schmelzer, Paul

Case File: Union Pacific / Paul Schmelzer

Library of Congress Control Number: 2008925726

ISBN: 978-0-9800067-8-0

First Edition

p. cm.

10 9 8 7 6 5 4 3 2 1

Visit our Web site at
http://www.durbanhouse.com

Author's Note:

While certain characters and events of these stories have a basis in historical fact, the author has taken creative license in characterizing the individuals and events to suit the story. Where there is any conflict between historical fact and the author's interpretation of the characters or events, it is the author's intent to present a fictional account for the enjoyment of the reader.

ONE

How in hell could this happen? The cost overruns alone run to tens of millions of dollars. The breach of public trust is inexcusable.

Ulysses Simpson Grant tossed the report on his desk in disgust. He stood and clasped his hands behind his back. Hunching his shoulders forward, he paced the Oval Office trailing a cloud of blue cigar smoke. The President still carried his modest frame with a burly military bearing despite his civilian suit and the formal trappings of the Oval Office. In truth the structured chain of command over at the War Department suited him better than the political subtleties surrounding the presidency. Much of that remained an unfamiliar and uncomfortable mantle. His eyes burned with the intense concentration of a field commander as he reflected on the report. His features hardened under the salting of gray beginning to fleck his neatly trimmed moustache and beard.

Grant had discovered the financial troubles of the transcontinental railroad project within days of being sworn in as eighteenth president of the United States. He ordered Grenville Dodge, the Union Pacific Chief Engineer, back to Washington for a briefing. The meeting with Dodge that morning had done little to reassure him or answer his questions.

The damn railroad is important. It will bind the nation together in an economic union never to be shaken again as it was by the war of secession. Reconstruction was proving to be a slow and painful process. The country needed economic growth to speed the healing of the nation's wounds. The railroad would bring lifeblood to that growth.

1

The transcontinental railroad would be an achievement of historic proportions, though tainted it seemed by mismanagement, fraud, corruption or worse. The situation called for an investigation.

Grant would call on his new federal law enforcement agencies to investigate the troubles plaguing the Union Pacific. This case provided the perfect opportunity for his Justice Department to prove its worth under the leadership of Attorney General Ebenezer Rockwood Hoar. Justice would oversee a thorough audit of the project and the investigative field work of the U.S. Marshals Service.

Grant had long held that the nation needed a federal law enforcement agency to deal with cases that reached beyond the jurisdiction of local law enforcement, or rose to the level of national interest. The Union Pacific mess looked like just such a case. It would prove the merit of his policy. He'd ordered Chief Marshal Bryson to create a Special Services Section within the U.S. Marshals Service and attach it to Hoar's Justice Department.

He'd made sure Special Services got off on the right foot by insisting on the appointment of Jedediah Rutherford Chance to the section. Chance had served under Grant during the war, first as a young cavalry officer and later as a staff officer when Grant assumed command of all Union forces. Grant gave him the nickname Lucky after he led his cavalry troop on a sweep around rebel lines to silence the batteries supporting a hotly contested piece of dirt at a place called Shiloh Church. That raid and the victory that followed began to turn the tide of victory in favor of the Union. The general found a warrior that day. A bond formed between the two men that grew through the rest of the war.

A knock at the door brought Grant back to the moment. "Attorney General Hoar, Chief Marshal Bryson and Marshal Chance are here to see you, sir," Administrative Secretary Orville Babcock announced.

Grant motioned them in, his head wreathed in the ever-present cigar smoke. "Good afternoon, Rockwood," Grant boomed, gesturing for the droll former Massachusetts judge to take a seat on the settee at the side of the office.

"Chief Marshal, good to see you as always." Grant valued the officers and men with whom he served. The chief marshal had earned the President's confidence riding with Fighting Phil Sheridan during the war. A bull of a man, Bryson fought with the same dogged determination he brought to the Marshals Service.

"Lucky, my boy, how the hell are you?" Grant wrapped an arm around the young man without waiting for a reply. At twenty-eight, Chance attracted no particular notice by his average height, sandy cropped hair and dark blue suit. Alert blue eyes spoke of experience beyond their years. The jut of his clean-shaven jaw suggested the quiet confidence of a competent man with an instinctive head for command. He made an effective investigator in the Marshals Service.

Grant guided him to a wing chair across the coffee table from the one he took for himself. "How are things over at Special Services, son?"

"Just fine, Mr. President. Thank you for askin'." Chance flushed over the President's familiarity in the presence of his boss, never mind the attorney general.

"Just the other night Julia was saying that we haven't seen you in ever so long. I swear she is planning to get you fixed up with that Amanda Bellaveau woman over in Maryland. You'll have to come to dinner before you leave on the assignment I've got for you." At that Grant caught himself and got down to the business at hand.

"Gentlemen, I've been reviewing the records of the Union Pacific railroad project. That railroad is important work, as you know. It will bind this nation together for the greater good of all our people. That said, the project is awash in cost overruns and losses that run to tens of millions of dollars. It's an inexcusable disservice to the country.

"I had Colonel Dodge, the Union Pacific chief engineer, in here last week to get his report on the situation. The man had as many questions as answers and freely admits that some of what has happened out there doesn't make sense to him either."

Grant flicked a long white cigar ash into the crystal tray. "Gentlemen, this is either a case of the shoddiest management of any human endeavor in the annals of recorded history, or we are the victim of high crimes, corruption or fraud. I'm not prepared to exonerate Colonel Dodge from the charge of shoddy management, but my gut tells me there's more at work here than that. Rockwood, I want a complete investigation starting with an audit. You can get some help on that from George Boutwell over at Treasury. Chief Marshal, I'm hoping you can spare Lucky here to do the field work in Cheyenne."

"Certainly sir, Special Services is at your disposal."

"Splendid. Now Lucky, when you get to Cheyenne I suggest you start with Colonel Dodge. Any questions?"

"None, sir," Chance said, rising.

Grant rose to shake his hand. "Good luck then, son."

TWO

Chance arrived in Cheyenne a week later, traveling the Union Pacific line that would become the eastern trunk of the transcontinental railroad. The train rumbled into the station south of the boom town growing up beside the tracks. He stepped down from the train to a rough-hewn plank platform. Bright sun lit a clear early spring day. A cold gusty wind cut through his dark blue traveling suit and duster like a knife. He tugged on the collar of his duster, turning his back to the wind as he headed down the platform to the stock car. The roof lines of the rough-cut log depot stair-stepped toward the cobalt blue sky in three distinct sections. The smaller original structure now served as the U.P. offices. The larger passenger lounge stood between the office and the two-story U.P. Hotel.

He collected his horse and tack from the stockman who unloaded him. Salute gave him a warm nuzzle, plenty happy, it seemed, to be done with the swaying of the train. Chance had drawn the big sorrel as a remount before Appomattox. General Grant requisitioned the string from a man named Morgan somewhere in Vermont. General Sheridan swore a Morgan-bred horse had the strength, endurance and heart for cavalry service, heart being horse talk for courage, if a horse were to have such a thing. Chance had named the proud-cut gelding Saber Salute for the strut of him. He had an attitude about him like he was always on parade. Chance had paid the quartermaster twenty dollars for him when he mustered out. They'd been together ever since.

Chance threw his saddle up on the big Morgan's back and slipped the hackamore over his ears. He hadn't put a bit in the horse's mouth since he finished with cavalry tack. Salute took his leads from gentle cues with no need of a bit. Chance led him around the depot to the U.P. Office hitch rack. He looped a rein over the silvered rail and climbed the worn platform step to the depot.

Cheyenne Station stood on the south side of Fifteenth Street near the center of town. Chance clumped up the plank step to the office door and went in. He looked around the dusty, rough-planked room that had once served as the passenger lounge. The old ticket counter now served as a Western Union office and post office.

Chance stepped up to the counter. A shriveled little man, with garters holding up the sleeves of a once-white shirt that could stand the sight of a washtub, looked up from his desk. He frowned, annoyed at being disturbed from the press of his business, which seemed to be reading the weekly edition of the *Rocky Mountain Star*.

"Where can I find Colonel Dodge?" Chance asked.

The man jerked a thumb toward a door at the end of the ticket counter. Chance found the chief engineer huddled over a small rolltop desk covered with stacks of ledger paper, telegraph foolscap and rolls of blueprint. Gray sunlight spilled through two dirty corner windows, lighting the desk and a small side table.

Chance knocked on the door frame. "Colonel Dodge?"

Dodge looked up absently and blinked behind a pair of smudged spectacles.

"J.R. Chance, U.S. Marshal, sir." He pulled his duster and coat open to reveal the shield stamped "U.S. Marshal" pinned to his shirt. "I've been sent to look into the troubles you recently reported to the President."

"Come in, come in, Marshal," Dodge replied, waving him in. "I've been expecting you." Dodge cleared a stack of paper off a chair beside his desk and piled it on top of the piles already stacked on the side table. He motioned Chance to the chair.

"Thank you, sir," Chance said, taking his seat.

Grenville Dodge had a reputation for being a tough, hard tack taskmaster. A former Indian fighter, he had the air of a man confident about his purposes. In person he was a wiry, bandy rooster of a man, with an unruly mop of shoulder-length, graying hair that fell over his forehead. His lean, lined features framed lively blue eyes behind wire-rimmed glasses. Drooping mustaches were every bit as unkempt as his hair.

"Where would you like to begin, Marshal?"

"As you know, the President is concerned about the cost overruns on the project. He believes the project is the victim of shoddy management at the least, or outright fraud at the worst. I'm here to get to the bottom of the matter."

Chance had intended the "shoddy management" comment to put Dodge on the defensive. If it were true, he must personally shoulder a good share of the blame. The suggestion of fraud let Dodge know that he hadn't ruled out criminal responsibility. The chief engineer took both comments in stride, as if he'd expected them.

"Let's take it from the beginning, Colonel. What can you tell me about the problems that have driven your costs so far beyond the original estimates?"

Dodge took a moment to frame his assessment. "A project of the scope we have undertaken in hostile territory is ripe for all manner of hardships, Marshal. Our experience has been no exception. The biggest problem has been keeping contractors preparing the right of way and laying track at a rate that would hold to the project schedule and budget.

"We've been plagued by unreliable contractors going out of business under the pressures of fulfilling their contracts. When these failures occurred, other contractors had to be brought in to take up the slack for those who failed, often on terms less favorable than those originally quoted. In the last year and a half the number of contractors has dwindled to the point where there are fewer and fewer bidders each time a new contract is let. With fewer bidders the contracts became less competitive, and prices moved higher."

"What made it so hard for so many of these companies to stay in business?" Chance asked, puzzled. "They knew what they were gettin' into when they bid for the work, didn't they?"

"That's a good question, Marshal. I don't mind telling you I've asked myself that one a good many times. Unfortunately, the answers are not always easy. Keeping men on the job was a problem for many, what with renegade Indian bands like Roman Nose's harassing the work crews. Even if you could keep men working, they had to be ready to fight at the drop of a hat, and that slowed progress too."

Dodge took off his glasses and wiped the lenses with a soiled handkerchief. "Then there were the usual misfortunes of business: an owner who died, some financial default befalling a small operator. Others suffered unexpected losses by way of a robbery or fire. Seems like it was a different story each time, until only the biggest companies like Right of Way Development and one or two others had the security, good fortune, and financial resources to keep going. Now those companies bid and build at prices substantially higher than the bids we saw when there were more independent contractors."

"What do you mean by 'good fortune,' Colonel? Hostile territory is hostile territory. What does luck have to do with anything?"

"You wouldn't think that it does," Dodge said, fitting his glasses over his ears. "Apart from a brush with the Indians now and then, the biggest surviving contractors have been able to avoid the accidents and labor problems that killed off their smaller competitors. In some ways it is fortunate for us that they did, or we might not have been able to complete the work in the time and cost that we have up to now."

Chance forced a wry smile. "That all sounds a bit simple for a country boy from Missouri. What you're tellin' me is that the fortunate few profited handsomely at the expense of their smaller competitors."

"I'm afraid that's the case," Dodge said. "It doesn't make sense to me either. But what's to be done about it now?"

"That's what I'm here for. I'd like to go through the list of contractors who fell on hard times. I want to know what happened to them and what became of their contracts when they sold out or went out of business."

Over the next hour Dodge provided a straightforward account of all the Union Pacific contractors, including those that had fallen on hard times. An unmistakable pattern emerged. A company by the name of Right of Way Development had bought out or picked up the contracts of one failed independent contractor after another. The company now controlled some seventy percent of the Union Pacific contracts. One of the remaining independents, Stage & Rail Construction, held another twenty percent, with the rest scattered among a handful of companies too small to count for much. The pattern was so consistent that Chance had to wonder if Right of Way Development might be targeting the independent contractors. If they were, Stage & Rail Construction sure looked like the next duck on the pond.

By Dodge's estimation, Jonathon Westfield, owner of Stage & Rail Construction, was an honest, hard-working operator. Like most of the small contractors, Stage & Rail lived hand to mouth on the payments from their government contracts. Dodge knew Westfield relied heavily on his Union Pacific payments to keep the company going. He'd been pretty blunt with Dodge in his efforts to obtain prompt payment for his billings. Chance decided he'd best have a visit with Westfield.

THREE

If it weren't the renegade hostiles harassin' his crews, it was that hard tack Dodge, pinchin' the Union Pacific nickel like to make the buffalo shit.

Jon Westfield mulled his problems, struggling with the thought that maybe he should take Taggert's offer and just sell out like the others. The Right of Way Development offer would do little more than buy a small farm to support him and his daughter, Victoria, at least until she up and married.

The notion of farming just didn't sit well with him. Construction was his whole life. The idea of taking up farming this late in life didn't make any sense to him. The railroad would bring a steady stream of profitable new contracts. Taggert and his backers back east knew that too. They knew those contracts would be even more profitable if companies like Stage & Rail weren't in the bidding. That's why they'd bought out or run off so many of the others. Jonathon Westfield didn't feel right about selling out to an outfit like that.

Westfield turned back to the bleak picture painted by the ledgers piled high on his small desk. The office he maintained adjoined the clapboard shed where he stored the equipment and supplies used in his business. The living quarters he shared with his only daughter were in the back. He wished it were a proper house for Victoria's sake, but they made do with a simple two-bedroom addition to the business front. The residence had a small kitchen and parlor with a woodburning stove. A comfortable porch ran along the side entrance to the living quarters, with a small fenced yard where Victoria tended a flower garden in the warm summer months. He thought his daughter deserved better, but the hard life on the frontier afforded them nothing more.

The door to the office swung open with a clang of the bell that announced visitors. Westfield didn't need to look up to see his caller, for a whispered scent of lavender announced that Victoria was back from Gorham's Emporium with a few days' supply of victuals.

"That was pretty quick, honey," he mumbled over his shoulder, wishing he could make more out of his bank balance than the figures actually allowed.

"Hard to spend much time out in that cold wind, Daddy." Victoria shivered, pulling a blue gingham sunbonnet back from a rich fall of auburn curls. At twenty she was a stunning woman. She had large green eyes and full bowed lips that picked up the natural tones in her hair. The gingham dress she wore might be plain, but the way she filled it cut a fine figure, from the swell of her breasts to a waist so small a big man might circle it with two hands. The long skirt covered trim hips and shapely legs that every eligible man in the territory could only imagine. The fact that she wasn't married certainly wasn't for lack of suitors. They just didn't interest Miss Victoria Westfield. She wanted more than a Union Pacific rail buster, which was about all Cheyenne had to offer. She couldn't say exactly what she was looking for, but she knew she'd recognize him when he came along.

These days she worried more over her daddy than she did about the shortage of men she considered eligible. She worried when he went out on the line with the crews. The dangers of hostile Indian attack were ever present out there. When he came off the line, the worries of his ledgers and the strains of making ends meet waited to vex him. She struggled with the frustration that she could do precious little to help him.

"I'll call you when lunch is ready," she said over her shoulder as she crossed the office toward the door to the living quarters.

Chance collected Salute at the hitch rail and led him across Fifteenth Street, past the row of whorehouse hotels west of the depot that catered to the rail crews. After the long train ride he'd give the big sorrel a day to get his legs back before he rode him. He headed north on Hill Street to the commercial center of town on Sixteenth Street.

The prairie wind blew out of the west into Cheyenne, chasing a ball of dried sage up Sixteenth past Brady Cain's Livery Stable and the Stage & Rail Construction office. Cheyenne rambled along the Union Pacific tracks north of the depot. The town consisted of a handful of dirt streets clustered around Sixteenth Street. The streets were lined with a ragtag collection of rough-hewn log buildings, most one- or two-room homes or businesses. Here and there a larger clapboard structure announced the dwelling of some prominent citizen or a rooming house catering to the travelers arriving in Cheyenne daily with the coming of the railroad. Chance turned into the wind and led Salute up the street past the City National Bank. He crossed Fergusen, past Gorham's Emporium to the Stage & Rail Construction office on the corner of Cody and Sixteenth.

Chance looped a rein over the splintered rail in front of the Stage & Rail office to remind Salute to stay put. A dirty storefront window sign announced Stage & Rail Construction in chipped gold letters. His boots clumped on the boardwalk in front of the office, announcing his arrival before the door opened to a bell clang.

Jonathon Westfield looked up from a stack of ledgers piled high on his desk. He looked to be about fifty. Clear gray eyes took in Chance from behind reading glasses that pinched the bridge of his nose.

"Mr. Westfield, J.R. Chance, U.S. Marshal."

"Afternoon, Marshal. What can I do for you?"

"I'm looking into some financial problems the Union Pacific's been having. I'd like to ask you a few questions."

"Financial problems? How can Dodge have financial problems with all that government money he gets? Ask away, Marshal, though I'm not sure there's much I can tell you. The only financial problem the U.P.'s got that I can see is gettin' Dodge to pay me on time."

"I'm interested in the failures of a number of independent contractors. From what I can see, most of those failures benefited your competitor, Right of Way Development. What can you tell me about Right of Way Development?"

Westfield scowled. "Right of Way is a big outfit. I expect they'd just as soon run us all out of business. They've been tryin' to get me to sell out. Their offer's an insult, pennies on the dollar to the worth of my contracts. I told 'em I wasn't interested in sellin.' The man doin' the talkin' for 'em ain't nothin' more'n a hired gun."

"Who would that be?"

"Feller's name is Taggert. Big man, dresses in black. He packs a .44 Colt that looks more like his business than buildin' railroads. He hasn't exactly threatened me, but he makes it clear Right of Way don't take no for an answer."

"Sounds like a threat to me," Chance mused. "Do you have any idea where I might find this Taggert feller?"

"Last time I saw him was day before yesterday. He was drivin' a heavy loaded freight wagon northeast out of town."

"Much obliged, Mr. Westfield."

"Good luck, Marshal. Take my advice and watch out for that one."

"Again, Mr. Westfield, much obliged. You wouldn't have a recommendation on where a feller might find a room in town, would you?"

"The Rawlins House on the east end of Sixteenth Street's the best we got in town."

"Not on my daily government allowance, I'm afraid." Chance smiled.

"The widow Murphy might have a room. You'll find her place south of the Rawlins on the east end of town."

Back out at the rail Chance turned his back to the wind and followed the tumbleweeds down Sixteenth Street. The commercial center of Cheyenne had grown out of the arrival of the railroad and the ongoing construction of the Union Pacific. Commercial interests of the frontier town consisted mostly of rowdy saloons, restaurants and mercantile outfitters. The sheriff's office and jail held the center of town, keeping the saloons and the City National Bank within reach of the long arm of Sheriff Jess Teet's law. The wind blew out of town past Rawlins House at the east end of Sixteenth Street. There it climbed a low rise past a little white church and one-room schoolhouse. Chance led Salute south from the Rawlins on Dodge toward a whitewashed two-story building that had to be the widow Murphy's rooming house.

After meeting Jon Westfield, Chance had to agree with Dodge's opinion of the Stage & Rail owner. The fact that Right of Way Development wanted to buy out the company fit the pattern. The suggestion they might play rough to get what they wanted fit the pattern too. Chance figured he needed to have a talk with Taggert.

FOUR

Chance saddled up early the next morning. He'd traded his city travel suit for a pair of blue britches and a plain spun shirt. The britches, made by a man name of Strauss, were becoming favored by miners and working men across the west for their hard wearing. He wore a double rig of matching five-shot .38 Colts with 5.5-inch round barrels under his duster. He'd had the lightly blued pistols with polished natural wood grips converted to fire metallic rim cartridges. He'd favored the lighter weight models and shorter barrels for speed in close work since his cavalry days. He backed them up with a saddle-mounted .44 caliber, six shot Army revolver with an 8-inch barrel fitted with a shoulder stock for longer range work. He packed a third Colt pistol, this one with a 3.5-inch barrel and a Sunday-go-to-meetin' shoulder rig, in his saddlebag. The shoulder rig came in handy when polite society frowned on the wearing of sidearms. He pulled on a new gray felt hat and set it at a jaunty angle over his right eye. He gathered Salute's rein and stepped into his saddle.

He picked up Taggert's trail northeast of town. The deep tracks of a heavily loaded freight wagon trailing a saddle horse behind were easy enough to follow. Taggert had forded the North Platte at Torrington Crossing and headed deeper into Indian Territory to the north. The trail led across a vast expanse of rolling gray-green spring sage dotted here and there with white patches of snow that marked winter's hard-fought battle to stave off the onset of spring. The sky ran leaden with gray clouds. A chill wind swept out of the northwest, cutting across his trail. Late on the fourth day the wagon ruts led into a shallow, grassy valley not far south of the Black Hills. Here a large party of riders joined the wagon.

Chance dismounted and walked the area, reading the sign. There were as many as thirty or forty horses, none of them shod. Indian ponies. Usually that spelled trouble. The pony sign appeared fresh, not more than a day or two old. He saw no sign of a struggle. The wagon and the Indian band had moved off together toward the black smudges of mountain to the north. What business did the company man have with a band of thirty or forty Indians? Chance's gut told him the business amounted to no good.

He mounted up and followed the trail. He kept a sharp eye alert to the possibility of hostiles as he moved through the vast expanse of rolling dun green hills broken by jagged ridges and rock formations. He made cold camp that night to avoid making a fire sign. A cloudy night sky and sharp wind blowing out of the mountains to the north made the camp even colder.

The next day dawned clear and bright. He took up the trail again, thankful the sign of such a large party allowed him to follow it while using the terrain to conceal as much of his movement as possible. This way he could avoid breaking the skyline where the trail traveled higher ground.

At midday the trail ended in an abandoned campsite where a fair-sized village of perhaps thirty or forty lodges had stood. Fresh pony sign and the warm embers of cook fires told him the Indians had broken camp and headed west that morning.

The wagon track turned back to the southwest, making shallow tracks. Taggert had unloaded whatever he'd carried. He looked to be headed back to Cheyenne.

Chance mounted up. "C'mon Salute, let's catch us a company man," he chucked to the horse.

A couple of hours later Chance crested a ridge overlooking a grassy valley. He could make out a wagon in the distance maybe a

mile off. The team stood beside the wagon, where the driver prepared to abandon what looked like a breakdown.

Chance kicked up a lope down to the valley floor, closing the
gap. A big man in a black coat saw him coming and mounted his
trail horse. Chance watched him abandon the team and gallop away.
Why would one white man run from another on the trail in hostile
territory? Something to hide? He got his answer when he drew rein
beside the wagon. Empty crates in the freighter bore the stamp
"Winchester Fire Arms Co."

Taggert had a big head start on a good horse. Chance pushed
Salute hard, but he could not close the distance between them before Taggert left the valley at the south end. He lost sight of him in
the jagged ridges and rock formations of the basin beyond. The
chase continued over the next hour. Chance had to study the small
signs left in the rough ground to stay on the trail. Tracking this way
made for slow going. Chance figured he was losing ground, but he
held to the trail, hoping the company man might go to ground somewhere or stop to camp for the night…

Taggert squinted over the sights of the Winchester. His pursuer picked his way down the rocky floor of the dry gulch below,
intent on his trail. *Let him come*, Taggert thought. The rider passed
below Taggert's hiding place in the rock wall above. He'd guessed
right. The tin shield on the man's shirt meant U.S. marshal. Taggert took careful aim at the man's back. It set up for an easy shot at
close range with no wind in the shelter of the gulch. He let out an
easy breath with a light squeeze. The Winchester bucked hard into
his shoulder. The rider pitched forward onto the hard scrabble
floor of the gulch. His horse shied at the rifle report and bolted up
the trail.

Taggert put up the muzzle of the rifle. A wisp of blue smoke
drifted off on the breeze. He'd got him good. The man didn't move.

The lawman was either dead or soon would be. Taggert had been lucky. The man tracking him had to know about the wagonload of rifles he'd delivered to Roman Nose. But why a U.S. marshal? What else did he know?

The old fool sheriff in Cheyenne had no idea how Taggert did his business. He'd made certain of that. Something or somebody else had called a U.S. marshal down on his trail. This one had gotten way too close. He needed to finish the Westfield business and soon. If he did, White would understand the need to lay low for a spell. He'd need to keep a sharp eye out until then. Attract the attention of one federal lawman and there could always be more.

Taggert stood and stretched his lanky, raw-boned frame. He looked over the rim of the gulch at the body below with the cold eye of a killer. The man lay stone still. Satisfied, the hired gun climbed down through the rocks to his horse. He booted his rifle and stepped into the saddle of the big black gelding. Turning the horse southwest, he squeezed up a lope toward Cheyenne and some unfinished business with Jon Westfield.

FIVE

Mourning Dove heard the rifle shot off in the distance and drew rein to listen. She'd ridden out of her father's village that morning searching for choke cherries. She wore knee-length moccasins and a simple buckskin dress, cinched at the waist by a beaded belt for her sheath knife. Her long black hair fluttered on the afternoon breeze where it gathered in simple rawhide bands at each shoulder. A single shot with no answering fire. It could be a hunter, even one of her tribe. So few braves carried guns she doubted it. A gunshot this close to the village could mean many things, most of them bad. Instinct told her to go back to the village. Something she could not dismiss told her that someone needed her help. Sister Eagle circled high in the broken clouds off to the northwest as if she marked the place Dove must go. She turned her paint mare toward Sister Eagle and the direction of the gunshot.

Chance fought his way back from some deep dark place toward a shimmering red light. The cold hit him. A sharp wind forged winter's grip on the struggle for spring. *Use the cold to clear your head*, he told himself. It didn't improve his situation. He was shot pretty good, judging from the burn in his left shoulder and the metallic blood smell pooling against his cheek.

Think, he ordered himself. *What do I do now?* Taggert might still be out there waiting to finish the job at the first sign of movement. Then again, if he didn't get his shoulder bound he'd bleed to death for sure. *Best take my chances on stoppin' the bleeding.* If he could just get himself to his knees, he could get a grip on the wound. He started the struggle to rise. *No gunshot.* He used his last reserves to pick himself up off a world spinning his head. The dark pool of blood swam before his eyes. *This shoulder burns like the devil hisself was pokin' it with his fork. Not a comforting thought for a man lyin' half kilt in Injun country.* He collapsed again. The cold faded to black.

Picking her way cautiously through the rocks and washes, Mourning Dove took care to avoid the skyline until she knew who was out there. A thin cloud of dust rising on the breeze off to the west caught her eye. She pulled her pony to a stop and slipped from her back. She pulled up the hem of her dress and scrambled up the rock formation forming the wall of the wash that concealed her presence. From the topmost rocks she could make out the distant figure of a white man riding southwest. Whatever the shooting meant, it would be somewhere behind him.

She climbed down from the rocks and swung up on her pony. She wheeled the little paint back to the mouth of the wash. She rode west until she crossed the white man's trail. Turning north, she backtracked until she found a place where a horse had been tied. Leaving her pony, she climbed the rocks with the silent skill of one born to rugged terrain. Near the top of the rocks, sunlight flashed on a brass cartridge casing. The acrid smell of burnt powder told her that she had come to the right place. Keeping low, she looked between the rocks to the floor of the gulch below.

A white man lay sprawled in a pool of blood. He did not move. Again her instincts told her to return to the village for help. But if he were alive, he would die before she could return. Looking up, she saw Sister Eagle and knew her purpose. She must help this man. *If he is dead he is no danger. If he is alive he needs help.* She gathered her pony and rode in for a closer look.

He came to again. The bone-chilling cold ached, but that might be loss of blood. Bright sunlight intruded on the comfort of darkness. Pain stabbed his shoulder, white-hot, searing pain. Some-where above him a shadow moved, coming and going nearby. He tried to rise. A shadowy force he could not resist pushed him back down. The shoulder burned like hell fire even to the cool touch of disembodied hands that worked to bind it. He fought desperately to focus his vision. He could not organize light and darkness into shape and shadow. He could feel gentle hands tending his wound. *Strong hands*, he thought, passing back to black.

He has lost much blood. Only the Great One Above can say if he will live. Still, the bullet had gone through clean. If the bleeding was stopped and she got him back to the village, he might live. She used his bandanna to bind the wound. A stick twisted it tight enough to staunch the flow. He showed fight when he opened unseeing clear blue eyes. He would need it, she thought, as she pressed him to lay still. He fell back unconscious again.

A nearby grove of cottonwood trees provided the poles she needed. Riding the short distance to gather them, she found his horse cropping prairie grass near a small stream. A fine sturdy ani-mal, the horse followed her willingly when she led him back to his fallen master. She used the man's blanket to fashion a travois.

She studied him as she removed his gun belt. He looked some summers older than she, but still young. She saw a boyish good-ness in his face. *Strange to think such things of a white man.* She rolled him onto the travois. This would hurt him if he were to awaken. He did not. She lifted the crossed poles over the withers of the man's horse. The horse stood quietly and accepted the burden, sensing his master's need. She tied the poles to the saddle. *The next day or two will tell much.* She mounted her pony and led him away.

Blue sky filtered through a red fog somewhere near consciousness. The shoulder burned like a bed of embers banked against a cold that would not heat. *Damn the cold! Would it never warm?* He bumped along over rough ground tied to the horse-drawn travois, a mean way to travel for a man in his condition. The shoulder felt tight, like it'd been dressed to stop the bleeding. A blanket that refused to warm the cold covered him. The travois probably meant Indians. He still had his hair. He must not be in hostile hands. He passed back to black.

Dim light touched the shadows taking shape before his eyes. He smelled wood smoke and the pungent tang of cured buffalo hide. A shadowy figure knelt beside him as his eyes fought for focus. The shoulder pain burned low, a dull reminder of the fiery rage he remembered while riding the travois. The quiet crackle of a lodge fire and the buffalo robes that covered him finally gave him some warmth.

"Where am I?" His voice sounded a dry croak he didn't recognize.

"Talks with Buffalo village."

Cheyenne. Safe enough, most likely. The voice sounded soft and mellow, like the soulful, low-timbered tones of an Indian flute.

"How long have I been here?"

No answer, only a hand gently lifting his head to a spoon made of buffalo horn. The gamey broth went down warm. It felt good in his belly. Shadows shrouded her face except for luminous dark eyes, large and soft like those of a doe. A couple more swallows of soup and he was all but played out.

"You rest now."

She laid his head back in the robes, where he drifted off, feeling weak as a kitten but warm, warm for the first time in oh so long.

SIX

Taggert turned his sweat-slicked black gelding into the stable yard behind Rawlins House. He stepped down from the saddle and handed the reins to the portly stable hand. "Cool him down good and water him, Morty. See he gets a good ration of grain with his hay too. Ole Black's put up a hard ride the past couple a days." He tossed the stable hand two bits and headed for the saloon.

He found his favorite table, facing the double swinging doors coming in from the lobby. It put his back to the wall, an old habit but a good one, even in a genteel place like the Rawlins. He stretched his legs under the table and put his boots up on the opposite chair.

"The usual, Mr. Taggert?" The bartender placed a glass and the bottle of cut-above bourbon on the table.

"Much obliged, Smitty," Taggert nodded as the bartender poured three fingers stiff.

Taggert took a pull on the whiskey. He bit the tip off an easy drawing cheroot and lit up. He'd made some progress the past couple of days, he thought, taking a draw on his cigar. The renegade they called Roman Nose after his most distinguishing feature had his new repeaters. They could do some real damage the next time he needed to call them out on a stubborn operator's crew. He'd also cleared that lawman off his trail. He blew a cloud of blue smoke and wondered again how he'd come in for the attention of a U.S. marshal. It didn't make sense. He hadn't done anything that would attract federal law. Well, he had now. A dead U.S. marshal would come in for plenty of attention. He needed to finish his business with Jon Westfield to get White off his ass and lay low for a spell. Taggert tossed off his drink.

Westfield would sell his Union Pacific contracts. The only question was how rough he'd have to play to get it done. But that's what they paid him to do, eliminate the competition. He'd been doing it just over two years now, following the orders of the mysterious Mr. White. He got paid good steady money for it too. Not many men in his line of work could afford to live in the style of the Rawlins House.

Sometimes the operator made it easy. Maybe a fire or a little Indian trouble would convince a contractor to default on his contracts or sell out to Right of Way Development. Sometimes an owner would get stubborn. Then Taggert would have to play rough. He didn't mind playing rough. It came easy. In fact, he enjoyed it.

Westfield showed signs of being stubborn. He'd refused Right of Way Development's last offer to buy out his contracts. In Taggert's experience, Right of Way wasn't much given to taking no for an answer. He expected the next time he heard from White, the game would start to get rough.

Taggert poured himself another three fingers. He liked the way the smooth bourbon mellowed the cigar smoke. Life had gotten good the day he went to work for the company two years ago. He remembered it like yesterday. That city dude from back east had strolled into the Silver Dollar Saloon in Denver dressed like a funeral looking for someplace to happen. Burnswick, he called himself, the one and only time Taggert ever laid eyes on him. The gent walked right over and introduced himself. He said he had a job for him. The job paid two hundred a month steady. That got Taggert's attention all right. Taggert didn't know Burnswick but Burnswick knew him, by reputation at least. He also knew one more thing that amazed Taggert. He knew he could read. Not many men in his line of work did. Not many men in his line of work had had a schoolmarm for a mother. Reading became important when it came to his orders.

He'd signed on then and there. For two hundred a month steady, a man didn't need to think twice. His duties were to look after the competition in matters as directed by a Mr. White. Taggert only knew White as the name that signed his orders. Burnswick told him that was all he needed to know. When he asked about the company's business, Burnswick said "Railroad construction."

The money came every month after that, deposited by draft to his account over at the City National Bank of Cheyenne, Cheyenne being the logical place to work from with all the railroad construction going on out this way. He got his instructions by telegraph wire from White. The telegrams were nothing but a bunch of numbers signed "White" with no real meaning unless you knew what to do with them. That's where the book Burnswick had given him came in. The paired numbers referred to a page and a word on that page out of Mr. Webster's dictionary. Actual numbers were written out in words. He used the book to send telegrams to White at a rooming house in St. Louis. That part still seemed odd. All of White's telegrams came from New York.

Food and rest were the enforced order of the days that followed. Slowly but surely Chance gained strength. He bridled at the confinement, angered that Taggert had gotten away. The frustration of being too weak to do anything about it ate at him. Bryson and the general would be righteously pissed. He didn't even want to think about filing that report.

True to Chance's nickname, the bullet had shot through clean without breaking any bones. The Indian who'd saved him had dressed the wound proper when they got back to the village. Someone cauterized the bleeding with a hot knife and knit him up with a couple of stitches to help the healing. He'd been out over most of that. The wound would heal right enough. Rest would bring his strength back in time. Time meant waiting, and waiting meant that Taggert's trail grew colder.

When it came to rest, he got plenty of attention to that. He hadn't had a dose of tender care like this since he took sick with a fever as a farm boy back in Missouri. The quiet young woman who took care of him behind those great dark eyes couldn't be more kind or gentle. She fed him like a baby, which would have irked him if he'd had the strength. He knew she dressed his wound regularly too, though he found it hard to stay awake very long. He slept most of the time. When he did wake up, she tended him with more of the hot broth or a sip of cool water from a ladle hollowed out of a gourd. He wondered if she ever slept.

In a few days he had the strength to stay awake for brief periods. "What's your name?" He hardly recognized the dry rasp that came out for his voice.

"Mourning Dove."

The sound of her voice might have come from the coo of that gentle bird. "That's a pretty name." *Pretty as the gal who owns it too.* The thought surprised him. He hadn't had much experience with women. He'd left the farm to join the army of the Missouri in '62. The war hadn't left any time for women. This was about as much time as he'd ever spent with one other than his mother.

"What your name?" She asked it with an expectant tilt to her chin.

"J.R. Chance, ma'am, but my friends call me Lucky."

"Lah Kee Shantz." She rolled the unfamiliar sounds carefully around her tongue.

Chance chuckled. It hurt. He patted her hand to let her know he wasn't making fun of her. "Lah Kee will do just fine."

She leaned forward with that serious tilt to her chin again. "Mourning Dove not know this white man's word. What means this name?"

27

It was a natural question. All Indian names were chosen for their meaning. But how did he explain his name? He didn't know if Indians understood the notion of luck.

"It means good fortune."

Dove knit her brows, still unable to connect the meaning of the words.

Chance, too, groped for a way to answer her question. For some reason it seemed important that he give her an answer. As luck would have it, the explanation he chose came with more meaning than the simple question deserved.

"It's like a gift from your spirit guide."

Dove brightened at that. She remembered Sister Eagle circling high over the place where she'd found him. In the beliefs of her people, animal spirit guides gave people wisdom. Spirit guides assisted them along the path of life, in harmony with the natural order of things. Dove's spirit guide had come to her on the riverbank in the season of her first moon cycle. Sister Eagle brought her quiet strength, determination and an independent spirit born of a deep love of her freedom. The gift of a spirit guide was a treasure sacred to the Indian.

"It good name for man who get shot where Mourning Dove find him."

She had no more to say on the subject. Chance didn't realize it, but in her mind he'd been given to her by her spirit guide, and that made for a powerful connection.

As the days wore on he could feel his strength return. In spite of his restless mewling over Taggert, he reckoned things could be a lot worse. For one thing, a man could get used to the kind of care she gave him. *She's doggone easy to look at too,* he caught himself thinking as she went about the daily chores caring for him. She filled the tipi with a quiet strength, like the scent of good earth in the spring. Her long black hair framed high coppery cheekbones and large doe-like eyes so brown they deepened to black. Her eyes had a language all their own. Deep with concern at his first recollection, he learned they could turn soft or merry in ways that warmed him inside. Her pretty lips generally composed a serious set, though her smile could light the dim confines of the tipi when given reason to. Her simple buckskin dress revealed the swell of firm breasts and round hips in the full flower of womanhood. Chance reckoned he must be getting stronger with the notice of such things. He'd be back on Taggert's trail in no time.

In a few days he could sit up and take some solid food. Evening fell quiet on the peaceful camp as the sun drifted into deep purple shadows lengthening on the western hills. Dove brought him a slab of roasted buffalo hump and a corn meal cake. Simple fare to be sure, but it tasted good.

"Dove honey, this is better'n one of my mama's Christmas dinners."

Her cheeks warmed at that, even though she wasn't exactly sure what he meant by a Christmas dinner. He seemed a good man, quiet and thoughtful. He gave no sign of looking down on her or her people like some other whites. She liked this white man. The first one she'd ever known. Maybe her father was right. Maybe there were more whites like this one.

Chance sensed a quiet strength about this woman. He felt it in her hands when she dressed his wound or helped him sit up. He didn't know when she slept, for she tended him whenever he had a conscious moment. He knew he'd never be able to repay her, for surely she'd saved his life.

Drifting off to sleep that night, he realized she gave him a feeling like being at home. Home was long ago and far away. He hadn't thought about it much in quite some time. The old farmhouse turned over in his mind's eye with the one-room school two miles down the road. He saw the creek where he had played with his brothers and one sister. As the oldest, he had a hand in looking after the younger ones after school when he wasn't helping his father around the farm.

He remembered his father, a soft-spoken man of few words. He worked hard to support his family on their small farm. His mother saw to the needs of her husband and children with a sunny smile to offer even when things were a little tight, which they were most of the time. Thinking back, he wondered how she did it.

It'd been a hard separation when he'd gone off to enlist. His father took it without much encouragement. Chance suspected that for him it meant one less mouth to feed at the expense of one able-bodied farm hand. According to the letter he got from his sister Mary, it'd been even harder when his brother Tom went off to war. Mary wrote when they lost Tom at Chickamauga. He'd written his mother after hearing about Tom, but he hadn't gone home after the war.

The war and Army life had changed him. The death and destruction he'd seen left him unable to turn his sword into plowshares when the war was over. His younger brother Seth would provide the help his parents needed to maintain the farm. It suited him. At least that's how Chance had satisfied himself with his decision to join the Marshals Service.

SEVEN

Morning sun poured through the tipi opening. This day would show some sign of spring warmth. Dove came in with a bowl of buffalo jerky and a warm corn cake. She knelt beside the robes and held the bowl out to him. Chance broke the corn cake and shared it with her. She accepted it with the shadow of a question beneath the surface of her eyes. Chance guessed that a gesture of kindness coming from a white man might be a strange experience for her.

He knew the conflict between the white man and the Indian from white accounts of Indian hostilities. White men came west seeking land and gold. The land and the buffalo herds sustained the plains Indians. They fought to protect their way of life. The railroad made a powerful symbol of that conflict. It divided the land and disrupted the herds. It threatened to change the old ways forever. For this the Indian had little kindness for the white man.

Dove studied him as she ate corn cake. "My father says we must find ways to live in peace with the whites. Can this be?"

He liked the way she tilted her chin when she asked him questions. She had a genuine curiosity he'd grown to respect. He considered the question. It deserved an honest answer. "I think in time our people can learn to live together, though it will be hard. Many things separate our two people. We can find ways to live in peace, but as we have already seen, it is not easy. Is Talks with Buffalo your father?"

She nodded.

That explained the way she spoke English and her interest in the prospects for peace with the whites. As chief of the Southern Cheyenne, Talks with Buffalo was a strong voice for peace. He had made treaties for his people when white settlers and miners flooded Cheyenne lands in western Kansas and eastern Colorado. He held firm to his belief in the possibility of peace in spite of an endless succession of broken promises and violence inflicted on his people.

"Cheyenne people make treaty," she continued. "Move to reservation. White man come take more land. Build iron horse trail. Iron horse divide the people's land. Bring even more white men. Cheyenne people move out of white man's way. It never far enough."

Chance did not have an answer for her. She said much in that. He nodded that he understood and handed her the bowl. She took it and left. He'd never questioned the westward expansion of the nation. He'd never considered what it might mean to the Indian. He doubted many white men ever had. These things were basic to the Indian way of life. He could understand why some of them would fight.

That evening she brought their meal to the tipi. They ate most of their meals quietly together. Chance felt a sense of comfort in her presence. He guessed she must feel it too, or she would spend this time with her family and not some wounded stranger.

Spending as much time together as they did, he became conscious of being undressed down to his union suit. "Mourning Dove, what happened to my clothes and guns?"

She considered the question. He must feel better. He was thinking about the day he would leave.

She got up and crossed the tipi and knelt beside a buffalo robe in the shadows. He vaguely remembered that she'd slept there those first few nights when no one knew if he would live. She returned with a neatly folded bundle of his clothes with his pistol rig laid on top. She set it down beside him and continued eating.

They were finishing their meal when he heard the rider gallop into the village. It raised a noisy ruckus with the howling camp dogs. He could see over Dove's shoulder through the tipi opening. A lone brave pulled a flashy Appaloosa to a stop in front of the lodge. He leaped down from the big war pony and pulled a buffalo robe from the saddle. He folded it in his arms over his chest. Chance recognized the custom. *This brave come a-courtin.'*

He stood before the tipi with the proud bearing of a warrior, tall and strong, built in the wiry muscled way of his people. Three eagle feathers hung in his long black braids, fluttering on the gentle evening breeze. His eyes were bright black pits that glittered in the dim light of early evening below a prominent brow and hooked nose. He wore a bone breastplate over a broad chest with buckskin leggings and a simple breach clout.

His voice rang clear and commanding when he broke into a speech Chance didn't understand. He did pick up Dove's given Cheyenne name in what he guessed was some flowery greeting. Finished, the brave stood there stony-like, waiting.

According to custom, the maiden would come out of her lodge to meet her suitor. They would cover their heads with the buffalo robe, declaring their feelings for one another in private while standing in full view of the village and posing no risk to the maiden's virtue. At least that's how the custom went. In this case Dove made no move to greet her visitor. She straightened her back and sat still. Chance could feel the color rise in her cheeks.

Time passed, the warrior's invitation answered by a silence that grew awkward. The longer he waited, the more embarrassing things became for the proud-eyed suitor. The indignity wasn't helped any by a mangy, rust-colored camp dog curiously sniffing at his heels. Chance waited for him to favor the dog with a swift kick, but he maintained his bearing, seeming to take no notice of the dog. Dove maintained her bearing too, holding her ground and setting her jaw in a determined sort of way. *It's a test of wills, all right.* Without knowing the brave, Chance placed his bet on Dove.

It wasn't long before the hot-blooded brave ran out of patience. He made another little speech—not quite so flowery this time, Chance judged—and threw the buffalo robe back on his pony. He swung up behind it and in one fluid motion he drew what looked like a new '66 model Winchester rifle from the saddle boot. His last look didn't need an interpreter to read the man's insult. He charged the rifle into the air with a whoop as he spun the big App and lit out the way he'd come like the devil himself was hot on his tail.

Pretty fancy shootin' iron for an Indian, Chance noted and thought back to Taggert's trail and the broken down wagon.

When the dogs were satisfied they'd run off the intruder, the camp fell quiet again. It matched the silence in the tipi.

'Course, it ain't rightly none of my business. Then again, being an investigator sort of made curiosity his profession. For some reason he couldn't help having his curiosity aroused by a matter involving the heart of the woman who'd nursed him back from death's door. "Who is he?"

"Him Spotted Hawk."

A woman of few words for a fact, Chance noted. A rare and desirable trait by his limited experience with women, though that wasn't making this interrogation go any easier.

"What'd he want?" *Sometimes playin' dumb is just good investigatin'.*

"Him want Mourning Dove share blanket for squaw."

"Well now, that don't sound so bad." Shameless, the way he coaxed the innocent.

"Him Roman Nose Dog Soldier. Make trouble for my people with the white eyes."

Chance knew some about Roman Nose. He led the renegade Cheyenne warrior society known as Dog Soldiers. Colonel Dodge had told the general about him while trying to explain the financial woes of the Union Pacific. Roman Nose surely played a part in the troubles that plagued the railroad. It sure looked like Taggert had a direct connection to the renegades. The empty crates in his wagon made pretty damaging evidence. Spotted Hawk's Winchester only confirmed his suspicion. This case might have started with financial troubles, but it sure looked like it might run to Indian trouble too.

"Wild ones cause much trouble fighting with whites. White men blame all the people for what Dog Soldiers do. Pony soldiers kill peaceful people at Sand Creek for Dog Soldier raids. Spotted Hawk believes Dog Soldiers can stop iron horse coming. Dog Soldiers believe they can drive white men from Indian lands. Dog Soldiers believe that bring buffalo back. Bring back the old ways. Mourning Dove see trouble for her people in this."

She spoke quietly with a steel edge in her voice, with words that came from her heart. Chance could hear the conviction. She would not bend in this. This test of wills ran deeper than courtship.

"Him say he come back with bride price. Many ponies. Talks with Buffalo not refuse."

"Why, a man like that'd make most young gals pretty happy." He went on prying without the slightest shred of guilt. What made him so interested?

Dove looked up at him for a long moment with those big brown eyes that could make him melt. She stuck out her chin with a determined look. "Spotted Hawk not make Mourning Dove heart sing."

No more need be said. Why did that please him?

EIGHT

A few days later Chance could feel his strength beginning to return. Dove came to the tipi early one morning carrying a large iron kettle filled with heated water. She set the kettle beside the buffalo robes where he lay and looked him up and down with an appraising eye.

"Good day to walk village. Make you stronger. First you wash. Make Lah Kee smell better. Give Mourning Dove clothes. Mourning Dove wash. Make smell better too."

It was an order, not a request. Now when it came to clothes, she meant his union suit. He guessed he probably did need a bath, but considering his humble circumstances, he wasn't about to strip down naked in front of her. She seemed to sense his mind and giggled. "Mourning Dove wait outside. Lah Kee hand Mourning Dove clothes. Then wash."

Chance had to give her the point about his needing a bath. He peeled the rank underwear off his body and handed it through the hide flap covering the lodge opening. Washing with one arm took time. Lying on his back for so many days had left him stiff and weak. The shoulder still ached some. Thanks to her dressing the wound, it was the only part of him that passed for some kind of clean. The warm water turned gray with the washing. His beard had grown pretty scruffy by the feel of it. He could use a shave, but that would have to wait until he got back to Cheyenne. By the time he finished rinsing himself, he needed a rest. Still, he felt better for cleaning the worst of the grime off his hide.

Autumn Snow joined Dove for the walk to the river with their washing. Dove and Snow were so close they could have been sisters. They'd been inseparable from the day they'd toddled between their family lodges. They'd grown up together from childhood to womanhood. They came into their moon cycles the same day, leading some of the old women to say that if one were cut the other would bleed.

They were kindred spirits. They had shared their hopes and dreams, feelings and fears for so many summers that each knew the other's thoughts without speaking them. Walking side by side to the river bank, both knew they had much to discuss.

Autumn Snow carried her Cheyenne beauty quiet and still, like drifted snow. Her wide-set dark eyes pooled deep and thoughtful, like a mountain lake. She wore her black hair in traditional braids framing the smooth copper planes of her face. A simple buckskin dress covered her tall, willowy frame. She would make a fine wife one day to the brave fortunate enough to win her, though the man of her dreams wore his heart for another.

They dropped to their knees at the river bank. Each chose a flat rock for her washing. They began the ritual in silence, listening to the gurgle of the river, the slosh of the wash and the buzz of summer insects finally rousing from a long winter's sleep. A gentle breeze played on the warmth of a pleasant morning.

The question that burned closest to Snow's heart found its voice. "Why does Mourning Dove not hear the words of Spotted Hawk's heart?"

Dove looked at her friend. Snow continued her washing as though her question were no more than idle women's talk. Dove knew her sister and she knew her question had deeper, more personal meaning. She knew it even if Spotted Hawk did not.

"Spotted Hawk's heart is with Roman Nose and the Dog Soldiers. He wants a woman to fill his belly and keep his lodge while he makes war on the white man."

Snow put down her washing. "Spotted Hawk is a great warrior. He would bring much honor to the lodge of any woman he chooses."

"Spotted Hawk is a fool like Roman Nose. They live for the old ways. They think they can drive the whites from our land. They do not see that more white men come with every summer. Now they come with their iron horse. Soon they will ride the iron horse from the great sea of the rising sun to the great sea of the setting sun. They will come as many as grasshoppers in summer. My father says we must find ways to live in peace with the white man. Counting coup and taking scalps are the old ways of men. These ways make trouble for our people. They bring blue coat pony soldiers come with their long knives and guns. Our people die the death of Sand Creek."

Snow heard her sister's words. They spoke powerful truth, though it seemed not to answer the question of a woman's heart and the giving of it to a man. She knew her friend. Dove believed these words. In her heart Snow wondered if there might be more to Dove's feelings.

"You do the white man's washing." It amused Snow to point out that her friend cared for the white eyes in the things she dismissed for Spotted Hawk's desires.

Dove caught the teasing tone in Snow's words, cocking her eye in a sidelong glance before she answered. Snow pretended great interest in her washing. "He grows stronger slowly. He lost much blood before Mourning Dove found him."

Mourning Dove did not speak her heart, Snow knew. "White ways are strange. They look down on our people. This one you saved from death. Does it make him respect our people?"

"This one is different. He is kind. His eyes smile. I think he is a good man."

Snow heard the hint of warmth in her sister's words. It sounded as hers might when speaking of Spotted Hawk. A girlish sense of mischief amused her. "Will you go with him when he leaves?"

Dove dropped Chance's union suit and stared at her sister in surprise. She saw the twinkle in Snow's eye. Her words poked at feelings Dove had yet to admit might be growing for Lah Kee. "He would never have me," she said, dismissing the idea.

Snow smiled within. Her sister's heart did not say no.

NINE

Later that morning, Dove came back with Chance's union suit freshly washed and sun dried. She also had his pants and shirt all cleaned up with the bullet hole mended. Not much you could do for the blood stains. If she had his saddlebags somewhere, he had a spare shirt in there.

She waited outside while he dressed. Once more he moved slowly and painfully, but he managed it. When he stepped out of the tipi she held out his hat and boots. Pulling on his boots took more effort than washing or dressing, but he managed that too. At that he stood in front of the lodge as upright and presentable as he'd been in some time. *She'll make my ole self outta me yet.*

"Come walk," Dove said. "Make Lah Kee strong." She led him toward the next tipi.

The village consisted of forty or fifty lodges meandering along the banks of the North Platte. The women folk tended the quiet rhythms of their domestic chores, cooking, sewing, washing and gathering wood for the cook fires. Most took no note of his slow, tentative steps, though a few looked up from their work in curiosity. Children ran here and there or knotted in groups, laughing at play in the noisy company of the camp dogs. Braves came and went one by one or in groups, busy about hunting or fishing. All in all it made for a pretty good place for a man to heal a wound.

He didn't make it very far that first day. No more than a few lodges before the effects of the day's exertions began to tucker him

40

out. He did make it far enough for Dove to introduce him to her father.

Talks with Buffalo studied Chance with an intensity that could penetrate to the core of a man. His clear-eyed gaze seemed touched by sad expectation at what he so often found there. A burly man, his broad face etched in deep lines told the story of a life filled with trials.

"Lah Kee Shance welcome in Talks with Buffalo village."

Chance nodded. "I can't thank you enough for all you and Mourning Dove done for me. I'd have died sure if she hadn't come along and helped me the way she done."

"How you get shot?"

"The man I'm after must have doubled back on his trail."

Talks with Buffalo arched an eyebrow. "You white man's law?"

"U.S. Marshal." Chance nodded.

"What bad man do?"

"We think he makes trouble for the railroad. President Grant sent me out here to get to the bottom of it."

"You work for Great Father in Washington?" Talks with Buffalo looked impressed.

"I do."

"We talk more of Great Father before you leave."

Chance nodded. "Mourning Dove says I need to walk to get my strength back. Would you let her walk with me?"

Talks with Buffalo flashed him that look again. Whatever he saw, he nodded.

They walked every day after that. At first around the village, and then, as he grew stronger, they wandered the wooded hills along the river bottom. In time their walks favored a warm grassy spot on the banks of the Platte upstream from the village. Here they would sit and talk or quietly search their thoughts together.

Sitting beside the woman who'd saved his life, Chance knew death had given him a pretty close shave this time. He'd seen a lot of death in the war. He'd lost friends. He'd lost his brother. He'd been lucky. The fighting had been less personal after the general appointed him to his staff. Still, death had surrounded them in battle after battle until their final victory.

He wondered how much longer he could go on dodging bullets in the U.S. Marshals Service before his luck ran out. He needed to finish the Taggert business. The President was counting on him. He owed the general a lot. He would do his duty. After that, though, he meant to think about settling down to something less dangerous.

Dove enjoyed the walks, the talk and the quiet times. At first their talks were simple exchanges over the meaning of a Cheyenne word or symbol or the explanation of some unfamiliar custom of the white man.

In time they spoke from their hearts. Chance told Dove stories of his childhood in Missouri. She knew this land, for it touched the eastern range of the Cheyenne lands she'd known as a child. She felt a connection to these lands. In another small way it connected her to him. They came from different peoples, yet many small things made them alike.

"My father moved our people from the lands of the Missouri to make treaty with the whites. He said Cheyenne must find ways to live in peace with the white man. Hunting on reservation lands did not feed the people. The white man's treaty promised Cheyenne cattle. Few cattle came."

Broken promises. Chance knew there were many in his people's dealing with the Indians. Mostly he knew these things from sterile newspaper accounts told from the white man's point of view. In his talks with Dove he learned things as the Indians saw them.

Another time Dove asked Chance about the great war. She knew fighting among Indian tribes. She wondered why white men would fight among themselves.

"We fought to abolish slavery," Chance told her, choosing his words carefully so she would understand. "White men in the south made slaves of black people. People in the north said slavery is wrong. The southern states tried to break away from our nation to keep their slaves. The North fought to free the slaves and preserve the nation."

"Lah Kee fight to free slaves?" she asked with that serious tilt to her chin.

"I did. I fought with the great father ."

She studied his eyes. Chance guessed she must like what she saw. She nodded. "Good."

During another of these talks she told him the story of Sand Creek. The Southern Cheyenne had agreed to move to the Sand Creek reservation in southeastern Colorado following the discovery of gold at Pikes Peak. The Treaty of 1861 opened the way for the flood of miners and settlers that descended on Cheyenne lands.

Chance knew the newspaper accounts of the "heroic" battle at Sand Creek as reported back east. The provocation story came out later. Dove told her very personal account in a tight, choked voice with tears trailing down her cheeks.

"Pony soldier come Sand Creek at sun up. We wake to rifle fire. Soldiers ride through village. Shoot any peoples that move. Talks with Buffalo take Mourning Dove and my mother from our lodge. We run to get out of village. Pony soldier shoot Sweet Medicine. We keep running with other peoples. My father hide Mourning Dove in sand hills not far from village. Then he go back to creek to look for my mother.

"Mourning Dove hide in hills, frightened for her father and mother. She hear people scream the songs of dying the death of the long knives. My father find my mother back in creek. She wounded. He bring her to safety in the sand hills. Some others escape too, though many died." Her eyes filled with pain.

"Why pony soldiers come kill my peoples? Cheyenne make treaty. Go to reservation. Live in peace. Why make war on peaceful people? It only anger hot bloods like Roman Nose and Spotted Hawk for more killing."

These were more words than he'd heard from the girl in any one stretch. It hurt to see so much pain in such a kind and gentle heart. He put his good arm around her and held her sobs to his chest. He held her even after her sobs quieted. A feeling of comfort and caring came over him at that moment. Something he wanted to hold. Something he did not want to let go.

Resting her head on his chest, Dove did not know why she had told this white man the story of Sand Creek. She carried this painful memory in her heart with the things she kept to herself. They were not signs to be painted on the side of a tipi or songs to be sung in the circle of the people. Why did she feel the need for this white man to know and understand?

Because she knew in her heart he would understand. She had no way to know this. She had only a strong feeling there was good in his heart. She could feel it in the strength of the arm that held her.

This white man seemed not like the others she had known. He spoke soft words to her. He did not look down on her as other whites so often did. He spoke with a twinkle in his eye. She saw it when he told her the meaning of his name. It pleased him that she understood. Except for her father, no man in her knowing, red or white, would care for such a thing. She saw it too when he asked about Spotted Hawk in the prying way that looked into her heart. What did he hope to find there? Could it be that it beat a little faster when he asked?

The white man's account of the massacre had come in two versions. The first held that the Colorado Militia fought a heroic battle to subdue a band of hostile Indians terrorizing the citizens of the Colorado Territory. The second account came out later.

The massacre occurred during the war of secession. Colorado militiamen were regularly called away to serve in the Union ranks, much to the chagrin of Colonel John M. Chivington, commander of the Third Colorado Volunteer Militia. Chivington put great store by the prestige and influence of his position as it might serve to advance his political ambitions. The post accounted for the most prestigious command in the former preacher's otherwise undistinguished military career.

In Chivington's mind it just didn't do to have one's command ordered away to fight some eastern war when they were commissioned to protect the citizens of Colorado from hostile Indians. The conscriptions demeaned the stature of his command, and he vowed to show Washington and the War Department the error of their ways.

The Bureau of Indian Affairs, which administered the reservations and treaties, served the Southern Cheyenne at Sand Creek about as well as it did everywhere else. Indian agents routinely lined their pockets with federal money intended to provide for Indian needs as agreed by the more generous terms of the treaties. Terms that most times never quite found their way to the benefit of the tribes.

For the Southern Cheyenne at Sand Creek, this meant beef cattle to supplement what they could take from the meager hunting grounds ceded to the tribe on the reservation. The cattle seldom reached the people in sufficient supply to feed the tribe. Faced with starvation, an Indian hunting party might run off a cow or two from a white settler. Just such an incident gave Chivington the cause of action he sought.

In the dawning hour of November 29, 1864, Chivington led his Colorado militia in a surprise assault on the villages of Black Kettle and White Antelope at Sand Creek. White Antelope woke to the call of the bugle and stepped out of his tipi. He looked to the Great One above. He searched for understanding as he walked slowly toward the charging cavalry line. He raised his arms as a sign of peace and filled his throat with the mournful tones of his death song before a hail of bullets tore it from his chest.

It took the militia two hours to do its grisly work. More than two hundred Indians were cut down, their bodies mutilated for trophies. Most were women and children. Later investigation reported that many of the courageous fighters under Chivington's command were drunk.

Hearing the bloody account as seen through the eyes of a child turned Chance's gut to bile. He felt a deep sense of shame for his people. He had already seen too much war and too much senseless killing in his life. The idea of soldiers killing and mutilating women and children disgraced the uniform he'd once worn with pride.

TEN

Chance could feel strength return to his grip. The shoulder remained stiff and tender, but he could move it some. He gained more use of it every day as he measured it in the managing of his boots. No time like the present to test it, he figured one morning. He pulled on his pants, light blue spare shirt and boots. He stepped out of the tipi as Mourning Dove came across the camp toward him in the bright morning sun. She carried a warm corn cake for his breakfast. He admired the easy way she moved. *A man could get used to this kind of treatment.*

She handed him the warm cake. They sat in front of the tipi. Chance broke off a piece of the cake for her. He guessed she might be shorting her own portions to make sure there was enough for him. They ate as they often did, without saying much. He knew he would miss her when he left. Today would tell some about how soon that would be.

"What say we take a ride today?"

She held his eyes with hers for a moment as if she understood the underlying meaning of the request. She gave a resigned nod and continued to munch the corn cake.

"Maybe we can find a place to take a little target practice too," Chance continued. His mind moved on to the business of Taggert.

Dove finished her cake and headed off in the direction of the picket line where the horses were tethered. She came back a few minutes later, leading Salute and a sturdy black and white tobiano mare she called Sage. She'd tacked up Salute with a loose cinch.

Salute greeted him with a nuzzle and a flicker of recognition in one big brown eye at the sight of him. *Man couldn't ask for a better horse than him.*

"Well now, if you don't just look all fat and happy. Dove been takin' real good care of you all lazy like, I bet."

Chance strapped on his rig. He spun the light blued cylinders, checking the loads. The feel of the polished natural wood handles reminded him that he had a score to settle with Taggert. He tightened the cinch and stepped into the well-worn seat of his tooled leather saddle.

Dove made an effortless swing to the back of the little mustang. She wheeled the pony and picked up her trot toward the river. She looked as good on her horse as she did on the ground, Chance decided, maybe even better for the fine shape of calf showing out the hem of her buckskins. *I surely must be feelin' better with the notice of such things.*

They rode along the river bank at a slow lope through scrub oak and gray-green sage rolling across the basin toward the dark smudges of distant mountains that ridged the north and southeastern horizons. The sun rode high overhead in a cloudless sky with no sign of life for miles, save an occasional hawk soaring on the warm early spring breeze, searching the prairie below for some unsuspecting critter.

Flooding from the spring melt had receded back to the river's normal banks, leaving the flood plain flat, firm and dry. It made a good place to test the shoulder with a faster pace and get Salute some badly needed exercise. The horse had had plenty of rest during the idle time of Chance's recovery and didn't look to be suffering from a lack of fodder either. Chance figured they could both use a little airing out.

"Race you to the big rock yonder," Chance called. Before he could ask Salute for his burst, he found himself looking at the flying heels of the little mustang, with Dove bent over her neck at a full-out run.

Salute wasn't about to play second fiddle to the little mustang. He gathered his hindquarters and exploded into a stretched-out gallop. He stretched the powerful drive of his chest, eating up the gap behind the little paint.

The wind whipped Chance's face with a warm wash as they pounded down the dry river bed toward the big sentinel rock. It felt good to be free of the long days of his confinement. The thrill of the race pounded in his chest with the beat of the horse's hooves. Salute pulled even with the little mustang as they neared the finish. Dove looked back over her shoulder at Chance. She flashed a hint of a smile, and with a determined look in her eye she put her heels to the pony for a burst to the finish that beat him to the rock by a nose.

They pulled up laughing, pawing and prancing, riders and horses all.

"You got my horse fat and lazy while you been fixin' me up," Chance laughed.

Dove split into a broad beaming smile that warmed him with the joy of her spirit. She truly gave beauty to the day.

"Sage good pony," she said, her voice filled with the joy of the moment.

Salute had his wind and was ready for more. He tossed his head and pranced in tight circles. Chance, on the other hand, felt more like basking in the merry light shining in Dove's eyes. Looking further up the river bank past the sentinel rock, he spotted a cottonwood thicket where a small stream tumbled out of the rolling prairie to join the river. It looked like a good place to water the horses and rest.

He led them out at an easy trot to the stream and the shade of the thicket. Chance ground tied the horses while Dove spread her saddle blanket and produced dried buffalo jerky from a pouch tied to her saddle.

With only the babble of the stream along the river bank and the buzzing of an occasional insect to disturb the serenity, Chance reckoned he'd found about as perfect a picnic spot as a feller could want, and in right pleasant company too.

Sitting in her quiet company chewing the jerky, Chance thought about all Dove had done for him since she'd found him on the trail. Surely she had saved his life. How could he ever repay the kindness of this gentle young woman? He knew the time had come for him to go back to work. That thought came with the gnawing realization that he would miss her.

"Mourning Dove, I cain't thank you enough for all you done for me. I'd have died for sure if you hadn't come along and taken care a me the way you done."

Dove averted her eyes, a light flush deepening the color in her cheek.

"Where Lah Kee go now?" she asked, deflecting the conversation away from herself.

"Pretty soon I gotta get after the man who shot me. He's a bad man, and the Great Father Grant wants him brought to justice."

It only confirmed what she already knew in her heart. He would go back to his people without seeing the gift of a spirit guide for more than his healing. Perhaps she could yet find a way to make him stay longer, but in her heart she knew the ways of men in hunting and war. Those ways left little room for the wants of a woman. Still, she had the days that remained before he left.

When they finished the jerky Chance looked around, picking out likely targets for some shooting practice. He settled on a stand of prickly pear cactus fighting for existence in the dry scrub beyond the shade of the cottonwoods.

"Well, let's see if I can still hit anything."

Chance walked out of the thicket and squared up to the cactus some twenty paces off. Dove followed along to watch. Chance reached down and picked up a pebble and handed it to her.

"Stand behind me and toss the stone whenever ye're ready. When it lands, that cactus over yonder's gonna lose its top three ears."

Dove waited a few seconds before tossing the pebble in a high arc that landed with a clatter on the rocky river bank. In that split second Chance drew his right hand Colt and cracked three quick shots that exploded the top sections of the cactus, one, two and three.

He knew he wouldn't be doing any fast draws on the left side for some time. Still he drew and fired at another cactus, hitting his mark all right, though the recoil sent a sharp pain through his damaged shoulder.

He winced. "Looks like I'll be right handed for a spell."

"Lah Kee let Mourning Dove try?"

Well now, what do we have here? A woman who rides like the wind wants to learn to shoot besides? Well, if she wanted to learn to shoot he'd be happy to teach her. He figured he couldn't refuse any request she might make of him with what he owed her. Well, almost any request, he'd come to find out.

"Sure you can try. Hold on a minute."

He ambled over to where Salute cropped grass by the river bank. Rummaging in the saddlebag, he pulled out the Colt pocket pistol with its shoulder holster. The smaller piece was blued and handled to match his sidearms. It was lighter weight and he reckoned it'd be a sight easier for her to handle. He loaded all five chambers, walking back to where Dove stood waiting.

He showed her how to work the single action firing mechanism and set her up facing a cactus target at about ten feet. He stepped behind her and extended her right arm, aiming the pistol over her shoulder as they stood cheek to cheek.

The pistol charge jolted Dove back into his arms. The shot missed high and right. Dove threw her head back with a low throaty laugh that tinkled like a music box. She didn't pull away and Chance didn't mind that she didn't.

"Mourning Dove try again?"

She got no argument from Chance. He reset her aim and held her as she squeezed off one round and the next until all five rounds were spent. The last two shots blew holes in the cactus.

She turned to him with those luminous dark eyes shining with delight. He thought he should say something nice about her shooting, but he never gave a conscious thought to what happened next. He just wrapped her up in his arms and gave her the sweetest take-your-breath-away kiss he could imagine. It surprised him as much as it must have surprised her. Time stood still for no counting how long as he held her, all soft and round and warm like. The kiss sure enough put a charge in his chamber.

Dove must have felt it too, for she caught herself and pulled back with a flush on her cheek.

"Lah Kee teach Mourning Dove shoot good." Her whisper caught heavy with her breath.

Her whisper scarcely rose above the gurgling of the creek, or was it the blood rushing in his ears? Chance couldn't be sure. *Where'd that come from?* he wondered. He guessed she probably wondered that too, though for him somehow it just seemed right.

"Come, we go back village now," she said, handing him the Colt.

"No, Mourning Dove, you keep it. I don't shoot it half as good as you," he said, handing her the holster.

She looked up at him, her eyes clouded in some confusion as she nodded slowly and went off to collect Sage, leaving Chance wondering if he'd offended her with his impulsive behavior.

ELEVEN

Jake Gelb savored the soft mellow draw of his finely aged Cuban cigar. He limited his vices to fine cigars and hundred-year-old French cognacs. Jake Gelb could afford the best. He watched the rain splash the cobbles on Wall Street below from the window of his fifth floor penthouse office suite. From this lofty perch he directed the shadowy network of his empire.

He dressed impeccably as always in his gray flannel frock coat, black satin vest, matching tie and white shirt starched crisp with his favorite pointed collar. He'd gone bald at an early age. The barber shaved his head, which gave prominence to cool gray eyes that pierced the façades of the lesser men with whom he dealt. He waxed his black moustache to a gleam over a square jaw set in the hint of a perpetual scowl.

The world below unfolded at his feet. Small men and their beasts of burden trod paths of mediocrity punctuated by the occasional pile of excrement. Gelb stood above that world. His world brought him a far-flung empire of financial power, political influence and of course, profit. Not bad for a man who'd not yet reached his thirty-fifth year.

Jake Gelb knew how to make money. He'd seen the building of the transcontinental railroad for a tremendous profit opportunity early on. How could it be anything else, with the government pouring money into the project as fast as he and his empire could gobble it up? It had been a simple matter to put the syndicate together. Politicians, railroad high rollers and government bureaucrats made eager conspirators when the money was easy and there was lots of it. Credit Mobilier would control most of the contracts for building the historic line. That amounted to tens of millions of dollars. Not a bad payday, but only the beginning. The contracts came with land grants along the right of way. Developing those grants would produce a river of profits as far into the future as the eye could see.

Tens of millions of dollars poured out of the federal treasury into the shadowy network of corporations and trusts owned and controlled by Credit Mobilier. Of course, you'd never find Jake Gelb among the officers, directors or shareholders of any of these holdings. No, the corporate labyrinth Jake Gelb controlled ended in a blind trust held by a Swiss bank in Zurich. Queensland Bank of Zurich held his majority interest in Credit Mobilier, which in turn controlled a network of companies like of Right of Way Development and the cutout operatives who did his anonymous bidding.

A quiet knock at the massive double door to the suite called him back from the reverie of his shrouded power. As expected, it announced the arrival of Mr. Burnswick. A solidly built six feet, Burnswick cut an imposing figure. He dressed in a black frock coat and suit that matched his oiled curls, mustache and sideburns. Ladies found him handsome if they overlooked the cold, cruel glint lighting his eyes. Some found the red scar that lined his left cheek exciting, without knowing it for the memento of a knife-wielding bowery tough who'd found out the hard way that Burnswick could handle a .38 and had no scruples when it came to using it. Gelb employed him at Right of Way Development, where he acted on behalf of the alias Mr. White.

"Any word from our man in Cheyenne on the Westfield offer?" Gelb wasted no time on civility or small talk.

"Yes sir. I'm afraid the news is not good. Mr. Westfield will need some encouragement." Burnswick chose the word carefully.

Gelb scowled. "What have you got in mind?"

"Our man over at Pinkerton tells me the regular Union Pacific gold shipment is due out of the Kansas City mint on the 315 train on the twenty-fifth. Westfield needs his invoices paid to pay his crew at the end of the month. Our banker friend in Cheyenne tells me his credit is played out. If he can't make payroll, he'll have no choice but to accept our offer."

Gelb considered Burnswick's analysis, blowing a cloud of blue smoke. If that shipment failed, Westfield would be forced out of the competition. His were among the last of the Union Pacific contracts Gelb didn't control. With completion of the line approaching, he meant to control development rights to as much of the right of way as he could. This land grab promised wealth beyond anyone's wildest imagination. "Get word to our man in Cheyenne and let's have done with it."

Burnswick nodded and left the way he'd come without another word.

He paid the cabby and hurried across the rain-splattered cobbles into the shelter of a shabby doorway. The dirty window sign proclaimed the Bowery Saloon. Burnswick stepped inside and allowed his eyes to adjust to the dim light. The smoke-filled air smelled of sweat, sawdust, tobacco and beer. A sordid handful of patrons sat at a table engaged in a game of poker. A streetworn prostitute sat at another table taking a drink with a longshoreman who looked like a hard case it might be best to avoid.

Burnswick spotted his man at the bar, a small time hoodlum named Shorty who'd do small jobs for a few dollars and the price of a drink. His rumpled, threadbare appearance suited the dump where he drank. An unremarkable face in the crowd of unremarkable faces Burnswick hired to do White's bidding.

Burnswick stepped up to the bar at the little man's elbow. "Evening, Shorty."

"Evenin', Mr. White. Got somethin' for me?"

"What'll it be?" The bartender's stained apron hadn't seen the inside of a washtub anytime in recent memory. Burnswick knew he kept a baseball bat and a sawed-off shotgun behind the bar. They provided all the law and order the Bowery needed.

"Whiskey, Tubby, and make it the good stuff," Burnswick said without looking up.

The bartender set down a glass, poured three fingers of bourbon and moved off with his sweat smell. Burnswick slid the envelope and a twenty-dollar gold piece across the bar to Shorty.

"Telegram for our man in Cheyenne. There'll be another drink waiting when you come back with the receipt."

Shorty scooped up the envelope along with the gold piece and left the Bowery.

Things got quiet late on a rainy afternoon in the Western Union office on East 14th Street. Most folks did the important business of the day early, so by this time if it wasn't real important it didn't make sense to go out in the rain. O'Keefe finished the *Times* and started to think about a pint at O'Tool's come five o'clock. The store front door opened with a clang, announcing the arrival of a customer.

O'Keefe studied the little man in the dingy coat standing at the counter. "What can I do for you?"

"Gotta telegram to send." He pushed an envelope across the counter to O'Keefe.

O'Keefe opened the envelope and wrinkled up his nose as he squinted at the page. He tugged on his once-fiery-red moustache now muted in shades of gray. He'd seen messages like this before. Nothing but a bunch of numbers addressed to somebody named Taggert care of the Rawlins House in Cheyenne. He'd never understand why anyone would spend good money to send such gibberish all the way to Wyoming Territory. *Well, it isn't my money*, he thought as he sat down to his key. The staccato rattle of dots and dashes chattered their way down the wire. The little man in the dirty coat waited patiently for the receipt, dripping rainwater on the floor in front of the counter.

Taggert stretched his lanky frame under the table and propped his boots on the chair across from where he sat in his favorite corner of the Rawlins House Saloon. He smoothed the red droop of his moustaches to the point of his chin as he looked around the bar. He liked the feel of the room's rich appointments. Dark polished woods, heavy red draperies and red leather cushioned chairs complete with antique brass studs, all freighted up from Denver or brought in by rail from back east. They gave the room the cut above look Taggert had come to appreciate. The Rawlins afforded its guests the appointments of the finest hostellery in the Wyoming Territory. A quiet, genteel retreat, it set its guests apart from the rough, bawdy atmosphere of a frontier town.

Taggert favored the Rawlins for the quiet elegance of the accommodations and the cut above sour mash they served, which he judged to be a damn sight better'n the mule piss served over at the Paladium. Then too, you didn't have to worry much about the risk of getting shot in some dispute over a card game gone wrong. This day there were only two other patrons in the bar, a shabbily dressed pair probably from back east somewhere. They looked to be a couple of drummers having a quiet conversation over a beer at a table across the room. They probably weren't even armed, but then a man could never be too careful.

He'd come to appreciate the good life since coming to work for the company. He could afford the expense at his salary, not to mention the little bonuses that came along from time to time courtesy of the competition. Smitty the barkeep kept an eye on his glass, so a man with an easy drawing cheroot lived about as well off as a king in these parts.

" 'Nother round, Mr. Taggert?" Smitty stood by the bottle, ready to pour.

Taggert nodded as the swinging doors from the lobby opened and the young man who ran telegrams for Western Union came in. He spied Taggert at his corner table and came straight over, very businesslike, in keeping with the importance of delivering the telegram he laid on the table. Taggert tossed the lad two bits as he picked up the thick envelope and tucked it in the inside pocket of his coat. No point opening it here. He wondered what White had in mind for Jon Westfield and Stage & Rail Construction this time. He tossed off his drink and left the bar. He had an appointment in his room with Mr. Webster.

TWELVE

Sweet Medicine roasted the prairie hen to perfection. Chance had bagged it with a quick shot on their ride back to the village. He'd given it to Dove for Talks with Buffalo's cook fire in the hope that she might forgive him for his unseemly behavior back at the river. In return, Talks with Buffalo invited him to share the bird at his lodge fire with Sweet Medicine and Mourning Dove. The four of them shared the meal and a pleasant evening around the lodge fire. Chance wasn't sure the invitation made Dove any too happy. She ate quietly with her eyes cast down, listening to her father and Chance talk.

"Um, good." Talks with Buffalo nodded to Sweet Medicine, chewing on a mouthful of hen. "It take good shot to bring little bird down with pistol," he said, turning to Chance.

"There might have been a little luck to the shot," Chance said, deferring the compliment. "You should have seen Mourning Dove shoot today. She handled my backup pistol better than I do. I made a present of it to her. I hope you don't mind."

"Not many daughters learn to shoot," Talks with Buffalo said with pride.

Mourning Dove remained silent with her eyes cast down, though Chance sensed she might have colored at the mention of her shooting. She didn't seem real pleased to have him here. The concern that he might have offended her with the kiss tugged at his heart. He'd had no intention to do that.

"Shoulder must be better for Lah Kee to ride and shoot," Talks with Buffalo observed.

"The shoulder is much better. Mourning Dove is a fine medicine woman. I cain't thank you enough for all she's done for me." Chance hoped the compliment would draw her into the conversation. It did not. She'd been quiet even by her standards on the ride back to the village. Her mood seemed clearly downcast. Chance chided himself for his impetuous behavior. The kiss obviously had offended her. He didn't want to leave things that way with her, but it looked like that's how things were going to turn out.

"Soon you go back to work for Great Father?" Talks with Buffalo asked, dropping the last of his thigh bones into his bowl.

"After today I'm strong enough to ride. I got some unfinished business with the man who shot me." There, he'd said it. The time to leave had come.

"We smoke. Then talk of Great Father."

The women quietly rose and cleared away the remains of the meal. They disappeared into the lodge. Talks with Buffalo slowly filled his long-stemmed pipe with the sacred tobacco.

Chance had met the old chief on the occasion of his first walk in the village, but they hadn't spent much time together until tonight. Talks with Buffalo lit the pipe on the ember of a small twig he improvised to a match in the fire. He puffed the sweet smoke and passed the pipe to Chance.

Chance accepted the pipe, listening to the soothing sounds of the crackling fire and muted night sounds of a peaceful camp as he took his draw. He passed the pipe back to the chief in the companionship of the ritual. Talks with Buffalo honored Chance with the passing of the pipe and the hospitality of his lodge. Chance acknowledged the honor with respect and appreciation for these gentle people and all they had done to return him to health.

"You go back to work for Great Father Grant?"

"Yes."

Talks with Buffalo shook his head sadly. "Iron horse make much trouble for all peoples. White men kill buffalo to make way for iron horse trail. Anger hot bloods like Roman Nose. Dog Soldiers make white man trouble for my people."

"I think the man who shot me may have something to do with that. Do you know how Spotted Hawk come by that repeatin' rifle he packs?"

Talks with Buffalo let these words sink in. He tamped the pipe and puffed a new cloud of sweet smoke into the night breeze. Somewhere in the dark, beyond the circle of firelight, the soulful notes of a flute took up a trilling melody. The sound floated on the night breeze, as if carrying the smoke away to the higher purpose of prayer it symbolized to the people. The old chief narrowed his gaze with a quiet nod.

"Spotted Hawk brag to Swift Pony all Roman Nose Dog Soldiers get new guns. White man give to Roman Nose. White man tell Roman Nose where to make trouble for iron horse trail. Roman Nose think white man funny. Give Roman Nose guns to make war on his people."

Chance suspected as much. Running guns to the Indians gave him reason enough to bring Taggert in, and for more than just questioning.

As the pipe passed for the last time, Talks with Buffalo looked past the crackling sparks of the fire to the star-covered blanket of night sky beyond.

"You tell Great Father Grant, stop Roman Nose before he make more trouble between our peoples."

Dove knelt in the shadows beside Talks with Buffalo's lodge, watching her father and Lah Kee talk as they passed the sacred pipe. She thought of the joy she'd felt when he taught her to shoot. It brought a song to her heart. She blushed inwardly with the thought that she would know more of this touching of lips for the unfamiliar yearnings it stirred in her. The vision of him holding her shone bright beside the dark feeling of loss she would know when he left. She passed this thought to another vision of this white man and her father smoking as they talked. This talk would be of another coming together. If only it were true.

They were of different peoples, white and red. Their peoples struggled to find ways to live together in peace. The whites had a limitless greed for the land that had sustained her people for as long as their grandmother's grandmothers could remember. They pushed the buffalo away, denying her people the river of life. There seemed little to bring them together in peace as her father hoped.

Still, this white man seemed different. She could feel a quiet goodness about him. She felt at peace with him. Something of him spoke to her spirit. She could see his eyes soften when they met hers, and she knew her eyes were soft for him too. She wished he would not go, yet she knew he would. When she opened her heart she knew she would go with him if he would take her. She knew that some white men took Indian women. Her heart told her she could come together with this white man. Would he ever see a coming together with her? Could they find a path to do what their people could not?

She appeared out of the shadows at the side of his lodge, stopping him in the tracks of his return from the smoke with Talks with Buffalo. They stood in silence, her face shrouded in shadow.

"Mourning Dove, I'm sorry if I offended you today. I didn't mean no harm."

She hushed him, putting two fingers to his lips and holding his gaze in hers as she touched her fingers back to her lips.

Chance guessed the kiss hadn't offended her after all. They stood silent, unmoving for several minutes, lost in the night sounds of crickets and the occasional bark of a dog. Dove lowered her eyes.

"Chance go away soon."

It was a statement, not a question. He'd heard it. He nodded.

"I got a job to do." It sounded lame in the saying of it. The silence that followed hung heavy between them, unlike the comfortable silence they so often shared. This awkward silence groped for the right thing to say.

"Lah Kee take Mourning Dove with him?"

Another statement took the form of a question. He lifted her chin, risking a look into those glistening pools he knew he might drown in.

"The places I go and the things I do, like gettin' shot at, ain't no place for a nice gal, let alone one pretty as you."

"Lah Kee teach Mourning Dove shoot back."

She could be downright determined when she set her mind to it.

"Now, now, you know I care for you. Truth is, I care too much to take you ridin' a dangerous trail like mine. Tell you what, I'll come back for a visit soon as this business with Taggert is done."

Damn, he hated it when he saw pain in those eyes, and the well of her tears like to broke his heart. When she ran off like she did, the pain in his heart hurt worse than the shoulder ever had.

The next morning he found a leather pouch filled with pemmican, corn meal and dried berries left at the flap of his lodge. He took it for one last act of caring.

Chance saddled Salute in the early morning sun as the village began stirring to life. He led him by Talks with Buffalo's lodge, hoping to see her and say a proper good-bye. Only Talks with Buffalo came out to see him off.

He clasped Talks with Buffalo's forearm in his. "Thank you again for all you've done. Tell Mourning Dove I'll come back for a visit as soon as I'm done with the business of the bad man."

Talks with Buffalo nodded. "You tell Great Father Grant Cheyenne live in peace with the white man. Roman Nose Dog Soldiers make trouble for Cheyenne when they make trouble for iron horse."

"I will bring the words of the great chief, Talks with Buffalo, to the Great Father Grant."

With his respects paid and good-byes said, he mounted up with a heavy heart. Why hadn't she come out to see him off? He hoped she might be inside the lodge to hear his promise to return, but he saw no sign of her.

"C'mon, Salute, let's go to Cheyenne." As long as Jon Westfield hadn't sold out, Stage & Rail Construction would remain unfinished business for Taggert. If that were the case, then one way or another Taggert had or would show up there again.

Dove watched him go from the dim confines of her father's tipi. She did not understand the white man or his ways, but in this she understood him only for a man. They would do what they saw they must in matters of hunting or war. They did not take time to listen to the higher calling of the spirits or the songs in their heart. This she must teach him if ever he returned. The pain of this last she counted as loss, putting it away in the private place in her heart where she carried such things.

THIRTEEN

A long ride alone gave a man a lot of time to think. He'd learned much in his time with Mourning Dove and her people. Things he'd thought he'd known he now realized were things he had learned from his white man's world. Through the eyes of Dove and her people, he now saw another side to many of the differences that separated the white man and the Indian. He could understand the anger of the hot bloods, though they fought a fight they could not win.

He knew the President believed the Indians had been treated unjustly. The general had said that reforming Indian policy would be an important part of his presidency. Chance would deliver Talks with Buffalo's message to him. It would reinforce the President's own beliefs and maybe lead to improved treatment for Dove and her people.

Dove had given him a second chance. Taggert's bullet had him assigned to meet his maker. How much longer would his luck hold out? He didn't want to think about that. He wanted to get a collar on Taggert, find out who was behind the Union Pacific's troubles, and then think about the direction of his life.

He'd grown up with a strong sense of right and wrong. For him the war meant righting the injustice of slavery. The Army had taught him to ride and shoot. He discovered a natural gift for command. He could solve problems and deal with conflict. After his Army life was over, the Marshals Service seemed a fitting occupation for the man he'd become. He could apply his skills to righting wrongs by bringing criminals to justice.

He'd never questioned the life he'd chosen for himself before Taggert's bullet took him down. He'd seen plenty of death before, but this time it looked real personal. He wondered if there might be another life for him away from the lethal business of gunplay.

Chance would ride back to Talks with Buffalo's village and make things right with Dove as soon as this business with Taggert was over. He'd found plenty of time to think while he was with her. It would be a good place to figure things out.

As the late afternoon sun turned the hilltops crimson in the west, he spotted a fast-running creek twisting a path out of the north. It disappeared into a sheltered wash. It looked like a good place to camp for the night. It didn't take any time at all to un-saddle Salute and gather wood for a fire. Purple shadows spilled over the foothills of the Laramie Mountains as darkness gathered around the rise of the evening star. Chance settled himself beside the creek in the shelter of the wash. The warmth of a small fire held off the evening chill. He munched a mouthful of pemmican and listened to muted night sounds interrupted by the occasional bark of a coyote.

His mind drifted back to Mourning Dove and the familiar times he'd found with her, quiet peaceful times like this. He felt a connection to her in the light of the evening star, and he wondered if she were watching it now. The decision not to take her with him was the right thing to do. Why didn't he feel good about it? She didn't want any part of being married off to Spotted Hawk, but that didn't make it right for her to go tagging along with a U.S. marshal on the trail of an hombre who'd shoot a man in the back. She'd saved his life for a fact. He owed her for that, but it didn't make any sense to expose her to that kind of danger. When he had the right of it, he had the right of it. No doubt about it.

Still, as he rolled up in his blanket, he had a strong sense he'd left something of himself back in Talks with Buffalo's village, something important. The feeling that haunted his dreams that night came to him soft and warm and round.

Chance stepped down from the saddle in front of the Stage & Rail Construction office and brushed off as much trail dust as he could. He looped a rein over the hitch rail just to let Salute know to stay put.

Jonathon Westfield looked up from his ledgers at the sound of boots scraping the boardwalk even before the clang of the visitor bell. He pushed his spectacles up the bridge of his nose and smoothed a wild fringe of gray hair.

"Marshal Chance, good to see you again." Westfield rose to shake hands. "Did you ever catch up with Taggert?"

"I reckon I did, after a fashion. I been more'n a month recoverin' from my introduction to that sidewinder, though I cain't rightly prove it was him bushwhacked me."

Chance briefly told Westfield the story of tracking Taggert to the broken-down wagon and the chase that had ended in ambush. He kept to himself his suspicions about Taggert supplying repeating rifles to Roman Nose.

"So after all that, I got even more interest in talkin' to him. He been around since I left?"

"Come by a couple o' weeks back pressin' me to take the Right of Way Development offer and sell out. I told him no again, though truth is I'm hangin' by a thread to make payroll the end of the month from my next U.P. payment. Some days it's enough to make a man wonder if it's all worth it."

Chance nodded sympathetically.

She came through the back door of the office that led to the living quarters. Like to take a man's breath away with all that red hair, a complexion like his mother's fine-made porcelain tea cups, smoky green eyes and a gingham dress. *That dress couldn't a been filled out no better*, Chance thought.

"Marshal Chance, my daughter Victoria," Westfield offered by way of introduction.

"Pleased to meet you, ma'am," Chance offered, tipping his hat.

"That's Miss, Marshal Chance. Pleased to make your acquaintance." She favored him with a smile that lit the dusty corners of the run-down construction office.

That smile like to put sunshine to shame, Chance thought as he caught himself staring.

"I was just coming to tell you that lunch is ready, Daddy. Will the marshal be joining us?"

"I'm afraid I can't stay, Miss Westfield, but thanks for the offer."

"I'm sorry to hear that," she said, appraising him beneath long, half-lidded lashes. "Perhaps another time then."

"I'd enjoy that, I'm sure, Miss. One more question before I go. Mr. Westfield, any idea where I might find Taggert now?"

"He stays at the Rawlins House when he's in town. Hangs out in the bar some. You might try lookin' for him there."

"Much obliged. Last time you told me to watch out for him. Now I'm returnin' the warning. He's up to no good, and he don't think twice about usin' a gun when it suits his purpose. I'll let you know if I find out anything, but until then my advice is to stay clear of him and don't sell out."

"Thanks, Marshal. I truly don't intend to sell, but I appreciate the advice."

"Good day, Miss." Chance tipped his hat, preparing to leave.

"Good day, Marshal. You will have to come back when you can stay a little longer."

"I'd like that, Miss Westfield."

Now this is no Union Pacific rail buster, Victoria Westfield thought, watching him through the dusty office window as he made an easy swing into the saddle of the big sorrel and wheeled him down Sixteenth Street toward Rawlins House.

John Quincy Adams Rawlins' Rawlins House anchored Sixteenth Street at the east end of town. Chance and Salute covered the distance at a comfortable trot in a few minutes. The bustling frontier town of Cheyenne had grown up on the railhead a day's ride north of the Colorado gold fields and a little more than three days to the up-and-coming city of Denver. Denver aspired to be the Union Pacific railhead, but Grenville Dodge had selected the northern route for the relative ease of the mountain passage. Cheyenne owed its existence to the routing of the transcontinental rail line.

The Rawlins House offered the finest accommodations in town. It catered to the upper crust of visitors from back east. Rates at the Rawlins were way beyond what Chance could afford on his federal daily allotment. He'd taken a room at the widow Murphy's boarding house over on Dodge Street when he arrived in Cheyenne. At six bits a day with two meals included, the widow kept a clean and comfortable place, if lacking in the amenities of the Rawlins.

Chance dropped a rein at the Rawlins hitch rail and clumped up the boardwalk. He sauntered into the dark-wood-muted glow of the lobby, dimmed red by heavy drapes framing the windows. He nodded to the sleepy desk clerk and made his way through the batwing doors to the saloon. He found the place deserted this early in the afternoon. The bartender dozed on a stool at the far end of the bar.

"What'll it be, stranger?" the wiry little man asked, coming alert to serve his new customer.

"I'll have a beer." By some standards it might be early in the day for a beer, but it had been a long dusty trail coming down from the north and even longer since he'd had any kind of a drink during the weeks of his recovery. A beer would taste mighty good about now.

The bartender filled a sudsy stein from a bucket iced in a box at the back of the bar, needlessly wiping the bar before setting it down. Chance lifted the cold beer in toast and took a long cool pull on the nutty mellow brew.

"I'm lookin' for a friend stays here sometimes. Feller by the name of Taggert, know him?"

"Mr. Taggert? You bet. Comes in pretty regular when he's in town."

"Is he here now?"

"Nah. Left a couple of days ago. Headed for Denver on business, he said."

"Sorry I missed him. What sort of business is he in these days?"

"I don't rightly know, Marshal," the bartender said, taking note of his badge. "Somethin' to do with railroad construction," seemed like enough of an answer. "He don't talk about it much and I don't ask questions."

Denver. Better have another beer. I got another long dry trail ahead.

FOURTEEN

Denver bustled with the gold boom on the front range of the Rockies, two days' ride south of the gold fields around Central City and Clear Creek Canyon, and a day's ride north of the foothills around Pike's Peak and Manitou Springs. The town teemed with gold seekers, those who'd struck it rich and those more than happy to help them spend it. Gold was king here. Money flowed freely through the commercial interests of a city that made its business out of catering to the needs of miners who'd struck it rich, and the greater numbers of those hoping to.

Taggert found the Betcher brothers in their usual haunt, the Silver Dollar Saloon, the day he arrived in Denver. The Silver Dollar owed its prosperous condition to a brisk business in whiskey, gambling and ladies for hire. Day or night it made for a raucous mixture of tobacco smoke, stale beer, laughter, shouting, and tin pan piano when they could keep the player sober. The local sheriff, Ben Prentice, kept the peace most of the time, but places like the Silver Dollar could turn violent at the drop of a hat—or more likely, the turn of a card. The place attracted the rough crowd who frequented the muddy ruts that passed for Denver's streets.

Rank and Matt Betcher were a couple of the meanest hard cases you could find in the rough crowd hanging around the Denver mining boom. The elder brother, Rank, had ridden with Mosby's Raiders in the hills of northern Virginia during the war. No one knew how he'd come by the name Rank, but it surely suited his mean streak and the cutthroat doings that had made Mosby's reputation.

The younger Betcher, Matt, looked to be about eighteen, though the lack of record keeping in the West Virginia hills where he was born left his exact age in doubt. It didn't matter. He'd grown up hardscrabble, with ready fists, a fast gun and a short fuse.

Taggert used the brothers from time to time. They were reliable men when the situation called for it, and taking down a train definitely called for it.

"Afternoon, boys." Taggert sidled up to the table where they sat counting up the money they had to stake them to a poker game. Times looked to be a little strained.

"Taggert." Rank spoke for the brothers.

"Got time for a drink?" Taggert asked.

"Hell, we always got time for that when you're buyin'," Rank said. He pushed back an empty chair with his boot.

Taggert signaled the bartender for a bottle and glasses and sat down. The bartender delivered the bottle and poured.

Taggert waited until the bartender was well out of hearing. "I gotta job you boys can help me with."

"What you got in mind?" Rank asked, lifting his drink.

"Takin' down a train," Taggert said, as though announcing that he had to take a piss.

Rank caught his glass in mid-swallow. "Just the three of us?"

"That's right. 'Course, we'll have a little inside help." Taggert tossed back his drink and poured another.

"What's the take?" Rank asked, holding out his glass for a refill.

"Gold shipment out of the Kansas City Mint," Taggert said, fixing the killer with a look that said he knew the brothers could use the money.

This sounded almost too good to be true to Rank. "How do you know which train it'll be on?"

"Like I said, we'll have a little inside help."

"How much?" Rank asked, warming to the idea.

"Twenty thousand." Taggert picked at the dirt under a finger-nail.

A slow smile twisted Rank Betcher's scowl. Even Matt Betcher's dull-witted gaze brightened as they lifted their glasses and knocked back another round of drinks.

Taggert took a room upstairs at the Silver Dollar for the anonymity it afforded. He'd have been more comfortable over at the Brown Palace, but at the Silver Dollar his comings and goings would be no matter of note. The sparse, dirty room made up for its lack of amenities by being expensive, the rate being set by the money that might be brought in by the use of the whores.

Taggert spent the evening studying the route map for the 315 train. The likeliest spot looked to be a watering stop at Drainsville Station, a sleepy little crossroads in Nebraska just east of the Wyoming border. They'd need to ride out there and plan the details of hitting the train, but for now Taggert had enough to report to White.

First thing the next morning Taggert coded up a message describing the time and the place where he and the Betchers would meet the 315 train. The telegrapher, with the Western Union key set up as a side business in his general store, took the message with a puzzled look, keyed it up and pocketed the fee without much thought beyond that. The message rattled its way down the wires to St. Louis.

In New York City Burnswick met his Pinkerton man at a back corner table in O'Malley's over on 3rd Avenue. O'Malley's made a pretense of respectability, though it catered to the rougher elements of the eastside crowd.

73

The Pinkerton man went by the name of Able, though Burnswick knew it for nothing more than an alias. A dumpy, middle-sized man with a paunch, his shiny round face was made all the more so by a ruddy complexion and a bald pate. A well-worn derby was cocked over one eye. The warm spring day stained his heavy suit with sweat. He wiped his brow nervously with a handkerchief gone wet with the task.

They ordered whiskey without any pleasantries or conversation. Both men knew why they were there. They didn't have anything to say and there were too many ears around to hear if they did. Burnswick slid a folded slip of paper across the table as the drinks arrived. He fingered the scar on his cheek absently as he picked up his drink.

The Pinkerton man opened the slip of paper and read, 3:15 Drainsville Station April 28. He slipped the note in his vest pocket.

Burnswick withdrew a fat manila envelope from his coat pocket and slid it across the table. The Pinkerton man stuffed it into his inside coat pocket, tossed off his drink and left with no more than a nod.

Chance made it to Denver by the 27th in good time. He pushed Salute at a slow lope the Morgan could hold over a long haul. He rode into town on Colorado Street. Miners, mules, freight wagons, horse-drawn carriages and horsemen clogged the muddy ruts Denver counted for its main street. He pulled Salute down to a jog, weaving in and out of the congestion as he made his way to the Brown Palace. He figured Taggert's tastes ran to the better-class establishments. The Brown Palace fit the pattern. It was the best Denver had to offer. Chance stepped down at the hitch rack and looped a rein over the well-worn rail. He stretched out the kinks after a long hard ride and climbed the step to the boardwalk.

The Brown Palace opened to a spacious, elegant lobby with dark-wood-paneled walls, dark green velvet drapes and rich leather-upholstered chairs and a settee. A sandy-haired young man waited at the registration counter.

"Good afternoon, Marshal," he said, noticing the badge. "What can I do for you?"

"I'm lookin' for a man named Taggert. Big feller, dresses in black. He's got a bushy red moustache."

The clerk scanned the registration. "Nobody here by that name," he commented absently.

"Have you seen anybody to match his description?"

"No, Marshal, I cain't say that I have. Sorry I cain't be more help."

"Thanks anyway. Where can I find the sheriff's office?"

"Two blocks that way." The young man jerked his thumb east.

"Much obliged."

Sheriff Ben Prentice had come to Denver from Kansas like so many others hoping to strike it rich. He soon discovered that the best claims had already been struck. The claims that were left afforded slim pickings for those too infected with gold fever or too foolish to know when to quit. A capable young man, Prentice skull busted a pair of wild ones about to shoot up the town and likely some of Denver's citizenry in the bargain. The city fathers rewarded him by handing him the sheriff's star. It wasn't going to make a man rich, but it would keep a roof over his head and a meal in his belly. Then Molly Malone had come along and Denver took on a charm of its own.

Chance caught up with the sheriff in his office. "Afternoon, Sheriff."

"Afternoon, Marshal. What can I do for you?"

"I'm lookin' for a man name of Taggert. Big fella, dresses in black. Wears a red moustache goin' gray."

"Don't recall seeing anyone that fits that description recently, leastwise nobody that got in trouble with me. We might check over at the Silver Dollar. If he's on the edge of the law, that'd be the place you might find him."

The bartender at the Silver Dollar confirmed that a man resembling Taggert's description had been there a couple days back, but he hadn't seen him recently and couldn't offer any help on where the company man might have gone. That left Chance puzzled and at an apparent dead end, though that wouldn't last long.

FIFTEEN

Taggert and the Betcher brothers rode into Drainsville just after sunset on the 27th. Drainsville amounted to little more than a wide spot on the Union Pacific right of way. Calling it a town somewhat overstated the case. It consisted of a small, rough-cut log depot across two dusty sets of wagon ruts from a log-built one-room general store and open air blacksmith shop. The other building in town was a one-spittoon saloon with a bartender a man had to wake up for service.

The watering station where the engine would park stood on the west end of town up the line from the depot. No telling where the mail car would be. That would depend on the length of the train. The depot staff consisted of a stationmaster and a telegraph operator during the day, with only one of them on duty at night.

It didn't take long to size up the place. On the surface it looked like easy pickin's as train robberies go.

Taggert and the Betchers rode up to the shadowed east side of the depot at ten forty-five the night of the 28th. The 315 train was due in at eleven o'clock. Taggert and Rank Betcher grabbed two sets of saddlebags. After making sure no one was watching the depot, they edged their way around the building to the front door. Matt stayed in the shadows with the horses, well out of sight of the privy in back of the west side of the depot.

The stationmaster nearly peed his pants when Rank Betcher and Taggert busted through the depot door, masked up with bandannas and guns drawn. Rank put him to sleep with the butt of a

Colt. He had him tied and gagged before the first faint sound of a train whistle drifted in over the night breeze.

Hollis Doyle roused himself from a light doze and pulled a well-worn pocket watch out of his vest pocket. He popped the cover open with practiced precision. Ten fifty; the 315 would make Drainsville by eleven on schedule. *On schedule*, comforting words to a conductor who lived by train time.

Carrying a gold shipment from the Kansas City Mint bound for Cheyenne made this something more than a routine run. The Pinkerton man on board guarded the mail car forward of the caboose where Doyle maintained his post. Road agents generally found overland stage shipments easier targets than trying to take down a train. Doyle didn't expect any trouble, but he still kept a sawed-off shotgun handy in the caboose just in case. He'd feel better with the gold safely delivered to the City National Bank vault.

Drainsville would be a short stop to take on water, just about enough time for Hollis to drink a cup of coffee in hopes of staying awake for the run to Cheyenne.

The 315 rumbled into the Drainsville station and ground to a halt in a shower of sparks, belching great clouds of steam. Her one shining headlamp lit up the watering station where she parked. Taggert waited, watching the mail car across the station platform one car forward of the caboose. Two freight cars made up the rest of the train along with the wood tender and locomotive.

The mail car door slid open as the train came to a halt. The Pinkerton man stepped down to the platform. He paused to check the time on the face of his shiny new gold watch. He snapped the engraved cover back in place with a self-satisfied nod and ambled off in the direction of the privy. Taggert nodded to Rank. "Let's move."

They crossed the depot platform to the open mail car as the Pinkerton man disappeared around the far corner of the depot. Taggert found the key to the strongbox padlock hanging on a peg by the door. They might as well have given him an engraved invitation. He opened the strongbox and both men hastily stuffed the saddlebags with four canvas bags bearing the distinctive blue wax seal of the Kansas City Mint. The seals confirmed that each bag contained two hundred and fifty twenty-dollar gold pieces.

Back out on the platform Matt led the horses out of the shadows to the east side of the depot platform as Taggert and Rank emerged from the mail car. They hurried across the platform past the caboose, their boots clumping the platform planks. They threw the heavily loaded saddlebags up on their horses, preparing to mount.

The commotion of running boots on the platform and the sound of the horses roused Hollis Doyle's attention. He looked out the window of the caboose and saw two masked men throwing heavily loaded saddlebags on horses waiting at the end of the platform. It looked like a robbery, but with no sign of a struggle. *What the hell happened to the Pinkerton man?* Doyle grabbed his scatter gun and threw open the door of the caboose. He stepped out on the platform at the back of the car and leveled the shotgun at the bandits.

The flash and report of Matt Betcher's .44 roared out of the dark. The heavy slug slammed the conductor hard in the chest. Doyle pitched back over the rail at the back of the caboose. His shotgun thundered its discharge harmlessly into the air as he toppled face down on the tracks.

Damn, thought Taggert, stepping into the saddle from the platform. He spurred his horse around the fallen conductor and led them out east along the right of way toward a line of trees. They turned south into the tree line, letting the night swallow them up. *Nothin' gets a posse more riled up than a dead man.*

Sheriff Ben Prentice got word of the Drainsville train robbery by telegram the morning of the 29th. Drainsville didn't have its own sheriff, making Prentice the closest lawman to the scene of the robbery. He organized a posse and headed up to Drainsville to see if he could pick up the trail of the bandits. Chance took it for an empty gesture, with about as much chance of finding the outlaws as finding the needle in that haystack folks always talked about.

The fact that the bandits had gotten away with a gold shipment bound for the Union Pacific in Cheyenne gave Chance a powerful hunch that this had to be some of Taggert's work. That gave him a pretty good idea of where to pick up his trail, though it meant turning around for the long ride back to Cheyenne. First, though, he had to find a way to keep Stage & Rail Construction out of the long greedy arms of Right of Way Development. He headed for the general store. He'd need supplies for the ride back to Cheyenne. He also had a wire to send.

Spotted Hawk lay hidden in tall prairie grass on a knoll overlooking a shallow valley below. His broad shoulders and back reflected a light sheen in the soft twilight. His eagle feathers fluttered on the evening breeze. He wore a bone breastplate, breach clout and leggings. A wisp of gray smoke rose from the chimney of a small ranch house to the blue haze descending on the valley from the painted buttes off to the west. He studied the remuda milling around in the corral behind the house. The small herd numbered ten or twelve sturdy ponies, the leader a flashy white stallion. Get a loop on the stallion and the herd would follow.

Young Bull and She Bear waited with the ponies at the base of the knoll. Spotted Hawk drew back from the crest and rejoined his brothers.

"Spotted Hawk circle there," he said, pointing south around the base of the knoll. "Young Bull and She Bear circle there." He pointed north. "Cover white man's lodge. Spotted Hawk run ponies off there." He pointed south again. "If white man fight, kill them from behind."

Young Bull and She Bear nodded. They mounted their ponies. She Bear took Spotted Hawk's pony on his lead. They rode north along the grassy bottom out of sight of the ranch house. Spotted Hawk took his rope and turned south at a jog. When the ranch house came into view around the south slope of the knoll, he dropped to his belly and melted into the prairie.

He worked his way patiently toward the corral. It took most of an hour to reach the bottom rail of the corral undetected. He took care to make his approach downwind of the remuda. His move must be quiet and sure. Stir up the herd and the white men would come with guns. He must get his loop on the stallion first.

The herd stood quietly in the north end of the corral between Spotted Hawk and the ranch house. He would use this to his advantage. The moon scudded in and out of a low-running cloud cover. He waited for its pale light to darken before crawling under the rail into the corral. He did not attempt to conceal himself. He squatted on his knees near the center of the corral and held his position fast and still.

The white sensed him at once. He pricked up his ears with a low snort. When the low shadow held still, the stallion fixed his attention on the intruder. He did not see the eyes of a predator. It gave him no sense of alarm. Slowly his curiosity roused. He lowered his head and pawed the corral dust. It did not move. He tossed his head, flaring his nostrils to the night breeze. He smelled no tang of danger. Still the shadow did not move. The stallion took his first cautious step toward the newcomer.

Spotted Hawk watched the stallion through the veil of his braids. He muted his breathing, giving no scent of excitement. The herd was quiet. They accepted his presence. The greatest risk of ruining the raid had passed without incident. He need only wait as the stallion took another cautious step toward him.

Cutting a small cattle ranch out of the no-man's land between Cheyenne and the Oklahoma Indian territory north of the Washita River was a solitary and risky business. Luther Hatch knew that. He also knew that the coming of the railroad meant he could get his cattle to market without the risks and costs of a long trail drive. Hatch and his partner Cody Tull had held their own for two years now. They had a small market selling beeves to the Union Pacific crews. That brought in what little cash money they needed. The herd was growing nicely on the lush prairie grass. On a quiet night like tonight, after a hard day's work and a decent meal, a man could take some satisfaction in what he'd accomplished.

Both men dozed by the small fireplace, not yet ready to turn in, but not fully awake either. A horse whinnied out in the corral. Hatch snapped awake and listened for only a moment. The horses were moving.

"Cody, wake up! We got trouble," Hatch said urgently, grabbing his Winchester from the rack at the door to the rough-hewn log ranch house. He dashed out the front door and ran down the front porch toward the corral. The moon flashed free of the clouds, lighting the cloud of dust rising behind the remuda. He could see his white stallion high tailing it through the corral gate, the black shadow of a lone rider hunched over his back. The herd followed the stallion south. *Injuns*, Hatch thought, throwing up the Winchester and loosing a charge at the dark rider.

He heard Cody's boots clomp to the front porch framed in the lighted doorway. It was a fatal mistake. Whoops sounded out of the night, galloping out of the north past the ranch house to the east. Muzzles flashed and rifles roared as the warriors galloped in on them. Cody grunted and slowly dropped to his knees following the clatter of his Winchester hitting the porch. Hatch spun to his left and dropped to his knee, lighting up the raiders racing by in the dim light. Return fire bit a chunk out of a log off his right shoulder. A second round thumped the porch to his left.

The shooting fell silent almost as fast as it had begun. Luther Hatch stood alone, fuming to the dull beat of fading horses.

SIXTEEN

Chief U.S. Marshal Bryson had learned to respect J.R. Chance as an effective field officer. When the telegram Chance had sent from Denver reached Washington, he headed straight for the attorney general's office. Chance might be a Missouri farm boy, but he didn't think like one. Bryson couldn't fill this request on his own authority. *Who would even have thought of asking for this kind of help? J.R. Chance, that's who,* Bryson thought, answering his own question.

Attorney General Ebenezer Rockwood Hoar scanned the yellow foolscap the chief marshal had handed him. The sartorial Massachusetts lawyer had a reputation for being a competent judge. A cultivated, sociable man, his usual good humor became subdued by the urgency of the matter at hand.

"We'd best head over to the White House, Bryson. We'll need Treasury help on this one, and the President best authorize that."

Thirty minutes later Hoar and Bryson were pacing impatiently in the reception to the Oval Office.

"The President will see you now, Mr. Secretary."

Hoar turned on his heel with a slight nod of acknowledgement to Horace Porter and headed straight for the Oval Office, disdaining the formality of being shown in. Bryson followed along on his boss's heels.

"Rockwood, what have you got for me that's so all-fired urgent?" Grant asked, looking up from the report he was reading with an acknowledging nod to Bryson. He fished in his vest for a match to relight the cigar gone cold in the crystal ashtray.

"A report from Marshal Chance, Mr. President. It came in by wire an hour ago." Grant lit his cigar while the attorney general continued.

"A train carrying a Union Pacific gold shipment out of the Kansas City Mint was robbed last night on its way to Cheyenne. Chance believes it was stolen to cause the failure of another independent construction company under contract to the railroad. If the Union Pacific doesn't make the payment due Stage & Rail Construction in Cheyenne by day after tomorrow, the company won't make payroll and will be forced to sell out to Right of Way Development.

"Marshal Chance can't prove it yet," Bryson added, "but he thinks this Right of Way Development outfit is somehow mixed up in the troubles of the transcontinental railroad project. It seems every time something goes wrong with a Union Pacific contract, Right of Way Development is there to take advantage of it one way or another. Right of Way Development is after Stage & Rail Construction. Marshal Chance says that keeping Stage & Rail going is the bait he needs to keep the Right of Way operative he's after out in the open. He thinks it's his best chance of finding out who's responsible for all the trouble."

"So what does Lucky suggest we do?" Grant asked, looking to Hoar for the answer.

"He says we need to wire twenty thousand dollars to the City National Bank of Cheyenne and then send instructions to Grenville Dodge to make the Stage & Rail payment by tomorrow."

Grant nodded, blowing a cloud of blue smoke. Times like these you had to support the men in the field.

"Horace," Grant called. "Send an orderly for Secretary Boutwell over at Treasury and then come in here and take a wire for Grenville Dodge."

Blanton Collier knew most everyone in Cheyenne. He knew their businesses too because he made that his business as president and cashier of the City National Bank of Cheyenne. People liked the heavyset, jovial man in his early fifties. More important, they trusted the man in the conservative dark suit with their money.

He sat sipping coffee as he did every morning at the large wooden desk prominently positioned next to the vault in the back corner of the bank lobby across from the teller line. He studied the reconciliation of the bank's accounts from the previous day, as he did in the quiet morning hours before the lobby grew busy with customers. He patted a light sheen of perspiration on his pudgy round face and shiny bald pate with a crisp linen handkerchief. He glanced up when the lobby door opened.

The Fisher boy who ran telegrams for Western Union came in and headed straight for his desk.

"Telegram for the cashier," he announced, handing the small sealed yellow envelope to Collier.

Collier tossed the boy a quarter with a perfunctory smile and adjusted the spectacles pinched on the bridge of his nose. He tore open the envelope and scanned the telegram, his jowls dropping in disbelief.

United States Treasury Department
Washington, D.C.
29 April 1869

Cashier
City National Bank of Cheyenne
Cheyenne, Wyoming

Please accept this letter of credit in the amount of twenty thousand dollars for credit to the deposit account of the Union Pacific Railroad held in your bank. Please credit the full amount in good funds for the immediate availability of the accountholder.

George S. Boutwell
Secretary of the Treasury

It wasn't every day a small territorial bank president got a telegram from the Secretary of the Treasury in Washington. Somebody important must be paying close attention to the loss of that Union Pacific gold shipment for it to be replaced this fast and in such extraordinary fashion. It made a man wonder what was so all fired important that it couldn't wait a few days for another shipment.

Later that afternoon, Collier got part of the answer to his question when Jon Westfield came in to deposit a Union Pacific draft in the amount of forty-five hundred dollars, eighteen hundred of which he withdrew to cover the pay due his work crews. If Collier had known the order Grenville Dodge received to pay Stage & Rail came straight from the White House, he would have been even more amazed. Even without knowing that, Collier knew these transactions were sure to interest Right of Way Development considering their commercial interest in the Stage & Rail Construction business.

Collier closed the bank promptly at three o'clock and headed over to the Western Union office at the depot. It took him out of his way of going home, but City National enjoyed substantial account relationships with Right of Way Development, and Mr. White always appreciated this sort of information. Collier prided himself and City National on the sort of service that went beyond the customer's expectation.

Jon Westfield heard boots on the boardwalk even before the doorbell clanged announcing the arrival of his caller.

"Afternoon Taggert, thought you'd be by before long."

"Afternoon, Westfield, just thought I'd drop by to see if you'd reconsider our offer after I heard about the unfortunate loss of that Union Pacific gold shipment."

"Well, no need of your concern about that. Colonel Dodge paid me on time and I've no plan to sell, even if you'd made a fair offer."

Taggert stared. "That so? I'm surprised Dodge had that kind of cash left on hand."

"He didn't. Dodge told me the money come from Washington by wire on the say so of the President."

"The President, you say? Well, if that don't beat all. Someone important must be payin' real close attention to the U. P.'s payment obligations," Taggert mused. *That might also explain where that U.S. marshal came from.* He shifted his hand to the butt of the .44 on his hip.

"Now listen here, Westfield, and listen good," Taggert said. "If you know what's good for you, you'll think real hard about the offer we've made. This is a risky business. It can get downright dangerous if you're not careful. What we're offerin's gonna look real good compared to nothin', if you take my meanin'."

His meaning hung silent in the stuffy air of the small office. The buzz of a fly broke the silence. Westfield fought to maintain a calm veneer over the surge churning his gut. No point going for the gun in his desk drawer. He'd be a dead man before he could cock the hammer. No, this standoff had to be done with words and will. He met the gunslinger's stare, hoping there was more conviction in his eyes than he felt.

"Don't threaten me, Taggert. I been takin' care of myself a long time now, and I've seen way worse than the likes a you. Now get the hell out of my office before I call Sheriff Teet over yonder to do it for me."

Taggert glanced over his shoulder in the direction Westfield indicated just as Sheriff Jess Teet rode by headed for Brady Cain's livery next door. It seemed Westfield had no end to his luck.

"We'll see, Westfield. We'll just see," Taggert said, adjusting the set of his pistol as he left the office.

"It can't miss, Jake. We'll make a fortune in no more than a few days and be out of the market before Treasury can stabilize the situation."

Gelb wiped at the oiled sheen on his shaved head with a linen handkerchief as he studied his guest. Diamond Jim Trask had some new tricks up his sleeve. Gelb had done business with Trask for years. Mostly railroad speculations where the politics or the financing stacked the deck in favor of the speculators. Trask's new idea involved a play in the gold market. Sentiment had been overwhelmingly bearish since the end of the war. All the smart money had gone short. Trask had a bold plan to turn that imbalance into trading advantage.

A knock at the door interrupted the quiet conversation. The disturbance annoyed Gelb. "Yeah?"

"Sorry to interrupt, Mr. Gelb, but I have news from Cheyenne I thought you should hear."

"Come in, Burnswick. Mr. Trask and I were just finishing. I don't know, Jim. That market is a risky place to be these days. Come back and see me when you know more."

Burnswick waited for Trask to leave. "I'm afraid the news from Cheyenne is not what we expected. Our banker friend tells us the Union Pacific paid Stage & Rail on time in spite of their recent financial inconvenience."

"I'm surprised Dodge had that kind of money on hand."

"He didn't. He got a letter of credit by wire from the Secretary of the Treasury, no less."

"Secretary of the Treasury?" Gelb could hardly believe his ears. "What in thunder has he got to do with a lousy little gold shipment?"

"There's more. Our man Taggert reports that Westfield still says he won't sell. He says that the order Dodge received to pay him came from the President."

Gelb's jaw dropped. His eyebrows knit in furrows of concentration. "It looks like people in some very high places are taking a big interest in the Union Pacific finances and Stage & Rail Construction in particular, but why?"

"You think maybe we should back off on Stage & Rail, Jake?"

Gelb thought about it. For whatever reason, federal authorities had suddenly taken an interest in the railroad construction business, and at a very high level. Still, the stakes amounted to a bloody fortune. They couldn't touch him. That was why he'd built the organization the way he had. It couldn't amount to anything more than fishing. "Hell no, Burnswick. We're not about to back down. What have you got to bring the Westfield matter to an end?"

"Dodge is riding the crews pretty hard now to complete the line this spring. He's laid down some deadlines and threatened to cancel the contracts of any company that doesn't keep up the pace. Perhaps our Indian friends can impress the Stage & Rail work crews with something the loss of a payroll could not. Westfield can't deliver his commitments if his crew runs off."

"Let's hope so. See to it. Speaking of Dodge, have you made any progress with him yet?"

"I'm afraid not. He's a tough old bird. Not one we can turn to our advantage easily."

"He has his price. You just haven't found it yet. Having him assist us in our bidding would be easier than dealing with five and dime operators like Westfield. Ten thousand shares should turn his head. Take care of that item too, Mr. Brunswick."

"Yes sir."

"And one more thing." Gelb's eyes turned hard. "See if one of our Washington friends can find out why in hell the President is interested in railroad construction."

SEVENTEEN

Chance and Salute made the long ride back to Cheyenne in good time. He'd covered a lot of ground in the last week, but it hadn't gotten him any closer to Taggert. He jogged Salute up Sixteenth Street to the Stage & Rail office. He found Jon Westfield in the equipment shed adjoining the office, working on replacing a broken wagon tongue.

"Afternoon, Marshal. Good to see you again."

"Afternoon, Mr. Westfield."

"Please, call me Jon. I expect you're responsible for the President wiring that money and orderin' Dodge to pay me after the train robbery. I'm mighty obliged."

Chance nodded, pushing his hat back on his head and wiping his brow with the back of his hand. "I'm glad the money got here in time."

"Were you able to catch up with Taggert and have that talk with him?"

"Nah. It seems I'm always one step behind that back shooter. Did he show up here after the robbery?"

"Couple of days ago. Weren't none too happy when I told him I wouldn't sell, either. He made it pretty plain that Right of Way don't take no for an answer and that I better reconsider for my own good. I threw him out of the office, but if Sheriff Teet hadn't come by Brady Cain's when he did, I'm not so sure I could have called him off."

"That's about what I figured," Chance mused. That left him with nothing more than a strong hunch about what Taggert's next move might be. Then again, sometimes a good hunch worked out better than a hard lead.

"You need to watch out for Taggert, Jon. I cain't prove he bushwhacked me or that he had anything to do with the Drainsville train robbery yet, but I sure got a strong feelin' about both."

Westfield reached under the seat of the wagon and drew out a .44 Colt. "I'm keeping this little feller a lot closer now than I did the last time he came for a visit."

"That's good, Jon, but be careful. Taggert's a professional. If you think you're gonna need that thing, make sure you use it before he has a chance to make his play."

"I understand, Marshal. Much obliged."

She appeared in the sunlit doorframe of the dimly lit shed. Westfield hastily returned the pistol to its place under the wagon seat. Victoria Westfield brightened the place with a halo of sunshine lighting her auburn curls. A light scent of lavender followed her, floating sweetness over the shed smells of axle grease, straw and sweat.

"Why, hello, Marshal Chance, I thought that might be your horse. I'm sorry to interrupt, but I just wanted to stop by and thank you for all you've done for Daddy."

"Haven't done all that much, Miss Westfield." Chance smiled, tipping his hat.

"You're far too modest, Marshal. And please, call me Victoria."

"Then you'll have to call me Lucky."

"The least we can do to repay you is to treat you to a home-cooked meal. Will you join us for dinner this evening?"

Chance's hunch told him he needed to head Taggert off before his next move. Still, he had one more possibility to check out before leaving Cheyenne. By then it would be too late in the day to get very far. A night in town in a civilized bed would feel pretty good after the long ride back from Denver. Besides, what red-blooded man could resist an invitation to a home-cooked meal offered by a woman as beautiful as Victoria Westfield?

"Why, that'd be right nice, Victoria. I'd be pleased to come to dinner."

"Splendid. Shall we say seven then?"

"I'll be by then."

She flashed him a smile that lit up the dusty confines of the shed as she sashayed off on a flounce of gingham and petticoats.

Chance trotted Salute up Sixteenth Street, weaving in and out of teamsters driving freight wagons and mountain men leading pack animals. The bustle of traffic clogged the dusty dirt ruts seething and bawling with plodding commerce. Chance drew rein in front of the Rawlins House and stepped down from the saddle, looping a rein over the hitching post.

He threw his saddlebags over his shoulder and crossed the busy boardwalk. The quiet elegance of the Rawlins lobby made stark contrast to the bustle of the street outside. Late afternoon sun bathed the polished woods and rich upholsteries in a warm glow filtered through the heavy draperies. The desk clerk was a thin, balding little man in a clean white shirt with wire-rimmed eye-glasses perched on a hawk-like beak nose.

"Afternoon, Marshal. What can we do for you?"

"I need a room for the night."

"Pleased to oblige," the clerk said, turning the guest registry for Chance to sign.

He scanned the register while the clerk selected a room key from the pegboard on the wall behind the registration desk. Taggert, room 210, checked out.

"That'll be two dollars," the clerk said, passing Chance the key to room 205.

Chance exchanged two silver dollars for the room key, thinking Bryson would be none too pleased about that item on his expense voucher, and headed for the stairs.

He paused on the second floor landing, making sure the hallway was clear before strolling down to room 210. Chance drew a Colt with his good right hand and stepped outside of the doorframe as a precaution. He knocked softly on the door. No answer and no sound of movement within. He holstered his pistol and got out his pocketknife. He opened the smaller second blade that had been ground down to a fine pick. A few deft strokes picked the lock, and the door to room 210 swung open.

The small room had been freshly made up. The furnishings were simple: a bed, washstand, chair and a small dresser opposite the bed. Chance opened the dresser drawers and found them all empty.

As he turned to leave he spotted something blue behind one foot of the washstand. He bent down and picked up a small piece of blue wax. The broken disk looked to be part of a seal stamped "U.S." The next character was broken, though it looked like it might be an "M." Chance bent down and felt around under the washstand to see if he could find more pieces of the seal. Finding nothing there, he turned to the dresser. He pulled it away from the wall. Another fragment lay on the floor. He picked it up and turned it over. This piece was stamped "K.C."

"U.S.M.K.C." United States Mint, Kansas City.

EIGHTEEN

Chance arrived at the Westfield residence at seven o'clock, bathed, barbered and armed with a fresh-picked bouquet of wild spring columbine. Victoria made a great fuss over the flowers, arranging them in a blue flowered vase. She wore a green dress that matched her eyes and accented a figure that spoke for itself. It brought out the auburn in her hair. She looked so good Chance found himself captivated watching her do those simple domestic things women did in preparing a meal. Things he hadn't watched with such interest since seeing his mother care for her family.

"Care for a drink, Marshal?" Westfield offered.

Chance tore himself away from watching her. "That sounds mighty good about now, Jon. Where can I hang these?" he asked, unbuckling his gun belt.

"There's a peg by the door," Westfield called over his shoulder as he produced a bottle from the sideboard and poured two glasses of bourbon.

Chance lifted his glass in salute and took a pull on the mellow, cut above whiskey. It went down real nice.

"Where's your crew workin' now, Jon?"

"They're finishin' the roadbed out at red rock cut. Why do you ask?"

"I'm buildin' a pretty good case against Taggert. I've found some evidence tying him to the Drainsville train robbery. I suspect he intended it to drive you out of business. What I don't know is how he knew about the gold shipment, or that you needed the

cash as bad as you did. He came back to Cheyenne after the robbery and checked into the Rawlins House. He stayed long enough
to find out you wasn't gonna sell.

"He checked out again this mornin'," Chance continued. "I
got some evidence he's been runnin' guns to Roman Nose and his
renegades. You might want to send word to your crew to be on
the lookout for Injun trouble. I got a hunch that'll be his next
move. I'm headin' out that way in the mornin'. I'll see if I can pick
up his trail or some sign of Roman Nose and his band."

"I'm much obliged, Lucky. I'll send word first thing in the
mornin'. My foreman out there is Joe Clark. Joe's a competent man.
He fought Injuns under Dodge before Dodge took up railroadin'.
Joe will know what to do."

"What do you know about Dodge, Jon?" Chance asked.

"He's a hard ass skinflint, that one. He pushes the hell out of
his contractors, at least the small ones like me. I don't know if he
can push the big ones like Right of Way around. I'd be surprised if
he could, though I'm damn sure he'd try."

"Do you think Dodge could be mixed up with Right of Way
Development?"

Westfield thought a moment. "I can cuss Colonel Dodge with
the best of 'em, but far as I know the man is honest. If he does
have an interest in Right of Way's business, I never seen any sign
of it."

"Taggert ever mention him?"

Westfield shook his head. "He never said anything to me about
Dodge."

"Dinner is served, gentlemen," Victoria announced, breaking
up the shop talk and summoning them to the table.

They sat down to a fried chicken dinner with all the fixin's.
The biscuits fairly floated off the plate, and the gravy that went
with them poured smooth and rich. Even the green beans were
good for green beans.

"Where is your family, Lucky?" Victoria asked.

"They're farmers back in Missouri. Dad and my youngest brother Seth work the farm. Mom looks after them. My sister's married. Her husband has a farm in the next county."

Home. It seemed a long way off. A place full of warm pleasant memories back before the war and all the killing. He recalled it again now in Victoria's question. Funny, he hadn't thought about home in a long time, and now here he was, thinking about it for the second time in a little more than a month, first with Dove and now with Victoria.

By the time she served pie and coffee, Victoria had turned her questions to Washington and the social excitement of the nation's capital.

"Washington must be very exciting." Victoria's eyes glittered with interest.

"Have you been to the White House, Lucky?"

"I have, a time or two. Mrs. Grant likes to entertain, so she's always havin' a dinner party or cotillion when the occasion arises. Society wise, I probably wouldn't make the guest list for such things except I've been with the general a long time and I think Julia, er, Mrs. Grant kind of likes me."

"Oh, you must tell me all about it. I can hardly imagine it, a cotillion ball at the White House! All the ladies must be dressed in the most elegant gowns and the gentlemen dressed in suits, too. Why, it must look finer than a funeral. Do you dance, Lucky?"

"Well, I've been known to, Victoria, though I cain't claim any special talent for it."

"Oh, I'm sure you do just fine. Is there anyone special you escort to those parties?"

Now there was a loaded question. Chance hadn't thought about Amanda Belleveau much since he'd come west on this assignment, so he guessed that meant she wasn't special. He could see her now, blonde curls, blue eyes and a figure to fill out those fine party dresses she wore. She came from a wealthy Maryland family that raised thoroughbred horses northeast of Washington. Not a lot of bullets whining around those white fenced pastures with all those beautiful horses.

Julia had introduced them not long after he'd gone to work for the Marshals Service. He'd taken her to a social function or a picnic from time to tim,e including the President's inaugural ball. She might have become special, Chance supposed, if he hadn't been sent west. He guessed Julia would have liked that.

"No, Victoria, no one special."

She seemed to like that answer. She favored him with the warmest of smiles. Nope, no one special back east, he was pretty sure. *Back on the banks of the North Platte, that might be another question,* he reflected.

"Victoria, I haven't had a dinner like that since the last one my mama made before I went off to enlist," Chance said, changing the subject to something a little less personal.

She blushed at the compliment. He liked the color of it on her. A man living on the edge couldn't help but think about a life that ended its days in pleasant home-cooked meals like this one.

They cleared away the dinner dishes and moved out to the porch. A pleasant, quiet evening breeze accompanied the occasional hum of a night insect. Jon Westfield filled his pipe and the three of them continued their conversation.

"How much longer until the Union and Central link up?" Chance asked.

"No more than a few weeks, I reckon," Westfield said, lighting his pipe. "It'd be tomorrow if Dodge could get it done out of pure ornery."

"It'll sure change the way the country does business. A man will be able to travel from New York to San Francisco in ten days," Chance marveled. "It's hard to imagine all that might mean."

"Why, Lucky, it means a person can visit places like San Francisco or New York or even Washington," Victoria gushed. "Oh, I would so dearly love to see places like that. Places with paved streets and genteel society. After Washington, Lucky, how can you ever bear Cheyenne?"

"Cheyenne's not so bad. Why, some of the company's right pleasant." He knew he shouldn't lead her on like that, but she looked real pretty when she blushed.

"Time for the ole man to turn in," Westfield announced, tamping out his pipe. "I got a long day tomorrow. You're more'n welcome to stay and visit with Victoria a spell, Lucky."

"Why, thanks, Jon, and thanks for dinner."

"Least we could do. Good night now."

"Good night."

Jon Westfield smiled to himself, closing the door. His daughter obviously enjoyed this pleasant young man. Something about him had gotten past the defenses she put up when most any other young man showed the slightest interest in her. Westfield liked this Lucky Chance, and if Victoria did too, well, so much the better.

The stars spread a glittering blanket across the black throw of night sky. The moon rose in the east, rounding toward full. Silence settled around them, broken only by the chirp of crickets. Victoria gazed up at the sky, her features muted in shadow. Soft lamplight spilled out of the window behind the porch swing where she sat. *She surely is pretty*, Chance thought, feeling the peace and quiet of the porch after a pleasant evening meal.

"I heard you tell Daddy that you're leaving in the morning, Lucky. Where do you think you are going to find Taggert?"

"Injun country's my hunch, likely hooked up with Roman Nose."

"Oh my, that sounds dangerous. You will be careful, won't you? I couldn't bear the thought of you being shot again."

"I'll do my best to avoid that. I'm none too fond of the thought myself."

"How long will you be gone? I mean, you will come back this way again, won't you?"

"Why, Victoria, you feed a feller a meal like that, you can be sure he'll figure some excuse to come back."

"I hope fried chicken wouldn't be the only reason you'd need to come back."

He couldn't see the look she gave him from the veiled shadows that covered her eyes, but even a country boy from Missouri could take her meaning from that.

"Well, that apple pie was mighty fine too," Chance offered with a twinkle in his eye. They both chuckled. Victoria flushed again, though the shadows kept it her secret.

"Thank you for a right pleasant evening, Victoria, but it's gittin' late and I've got a lot of ground to cover tomorrow." Chance got to his feet.

Victoria got up from the porch swing and stepped up to the toes of his boots, near enough for the lavender scent of her to color the night breeze. She looked up at him with starlight catching the gleam in her green eyes.

"Do take care of yourself, Lucky, and hurry back when you can."

Her voice whispered like a soft gentle breeze warming his heart. "I'll do my best," he said, giving her hand a squeeze. He tore himself away from the pull of her upturned lips. He could taste the sweetness he knew he would find there. He had one strong vote for taking that kiss. For some reason he felt the need for some distance. Kiss her and he knew he'd find himself in a circumstance more tangled than he could sort his way through.

Salute waited at the hitching rail out front. The clean air out there breathed easier than the close constrictions he'd felt back there on the porch. He made a show of checking his cinch to give himself a little time to ease his step into the saddle. He turned Salute with a wave to the shadowed figure on the porch watching him go.

NINETEEN

With the joining of the rail lines little more than days away, Grenville Dodge could see the end in sight. It had been a long, arduous undertaking. The achievement would come at great cost when measured in lives lost and resources expended. Still, it would be an achievement in which he could take great personal satisfaction. But that would have to wait until they finished. At the moment he didn't have time for anything but the countless details that needed to come together before the momentous day when they would drive that ceremonial spike. His crews were laying track at a good pace to assure they would best the Central Pacific in the miles they covered. But all that depended on Jon Westfield's crew finishing the roadbed and laying the track at the red rock cut in time for the westbound train that would join the lines.

They'd blasted the cut out of a red rock butte. Creating the cut saved miles of track it would have taken to go around it. In one of his shrewder moves, Dodge sent the main body of track laying work crews around the red rock to continue laying track west toward Utah without waiting for the cut to be finished. Now they needed that section of track to connect the line in time to join the Union and Central Pacific. It had been a smart call, but now it all depended on Jon Westfield.

Weighed down by his preoccupations, Dodge had little patience for the interruption when Westfield came calling.

"Colonel Dodge."

"Afternoon, Westfield. What can I do for you?"

"I want to make sure that my latest billing will be paid on time."

"You'll get your money when the roadbed at the red rock cut is finished. We've only got a couple of weeks before I need to put a train through there for the joining of the lines."

"You know my boys are doin' the best they can. I got to pay 'em to keep 'em goin.'

"That's your problem, Westfield. I got a railroad to build."

"Well, it won't get built without workin' crews. All I'm askin' is for you to do what's fair and do it on time."

Dodge grimaced. "You finish the cut, Jon. I'll see what I can do. Now good day to you, sir."

Westfield stalked off, having taken little comfort from his exchange with the crusty chief engineer.

Westfield wanted more assurance than that, but Dodge wasn't about to bend over until he finished that cut. He couldn't help the fact that Westfield was stretched so thin. If the man couldn't take the heat, maybe he should get out of the kitchen. He'd heard that Right of Way Development wanted to buy him out. While he shared the President's concern over the concentration of the Union Pacific contracts in so few hands, he still had a railroad to build. If Right of Way Development could fulfill its contracts better than Jon Westfield, well, that's just the way things were.

Right of Way would profit handsomely from its U.P. contracts and the follow-on development opportunities that would attend them. The contracts all came with land grants along the railroad right of way. The commerce certain to follow the rails would make these land grants worth a fortune, not to mention the lucrative construction contracts that would be available to develop the land. Whole towns would spring up along the railroad line, boom towns that would make their owners and investors wealthy men.

Someone named White had offered him stock in the company. "A friend of the family," the letter called it. "Friend of the family" he knew meant favoring the company in winning additional contracts. The company would surely earn windfall profits once they completed the line. That made it tempting.

Still, Dodge had resisted the offer to avoid any appearance of conflict of interest. Then the share certificates made out to him showed up in a plain brown envelope. Ten thousand shares of Right of Way Development dropped in his lap. These shares were sure to be worth a fortune someday. Now what was he supposed to do?

He'd think about that later. For now he had a railroad to finish, and that wouldn't wait.

Mourning Dove missed him, most of all in the evenings. This evening she went to the picket line as she often did. Sage greeted her with an affectionate nuzzle. She found comfort in the gentle companionship of the little horse, soothing comfort for a heavy heart.

This night the little mustang seemed restless. She stamped and snorted as Dove stroked her neck. She tossed her head, wide eyed, flaring her nostrils in the breeze. She lifted a throaty whicker at the glimmer of the evening star.

Once before Sage had been the bearer of a spirit message. It had forged a bond that led Dove to listen to the mustang with her heart. It seemed the little mare might be trying to reach her with another message this night. Dove put her arms around the horse's neck. She rested her forehead against the rippling muscles and opened her spirit. The vision took shape slowly as the gathering of a storm cloud. There in the sky, circling high overhead, searching for prey, a spread of spotted tail feathers caught the sun.

Alone in her lodge, Mourning Dove rolled her buckskin dress and medicine bag in her blanket. She dressed in the bloodstained shirt she'd mended for him, breach clout and soft moccasins laced to the knee. She holstered the short barrel pistol butt forward on her left hip, her knife sheathed on the right.

Dressed as a man, she would be a lone rider to the horizon, not a maiden traveling alone. She thought it an important deception for the journey ahead. She filled a drawstring hide sack with corn meal, pemmican and dried berries. Her preparations complete, she left the lodge.

She stepped into a cool pre-dawn breeze and paused to listen to the quiet sounds of the sleeping village. She would miss the familiar warmth of the circle of the people and the comfort of her family. Still, she knew she must leave. She would not wait for Spotted Hawk and his bride price to forge the path of her life.

She hurried toward the picket line at the back of the village. She was so intent on her purpose she nearly ran into her mother when Sweet Medicine stepped between the lodges. The obvious question went unspoken. Dove lowered her eyes in respect, speaking the simple words of her Cheyenne tongue.

"Spotted Hawk is coming with his bride price. Mourning Dove saw it in a vision from my spirit messenger. Spotted Hawk makes trouble for the people. Mourning Dove must go away. She will not be Spotted Hawk's woman."

Sweet Medicine listened without judgment. "Does my daughter go to follow the white eyes who makes her heart sing?"

Dove made no reply. She knew her heart. She did not know her path.

Sweet Medicine nodded knowingly. "Then follow your heart in the wisdom of your spirit."

TWENTY

Senator Thurman Carswell, Colonel CSA (ret.), paced the marbled floor of the reception area outside the Secretary's office, steeped in thought. Boutwell was the logical choice, of course. He'd signed the Union Pacific letter of credit. He was also one of Grant's closest advisors. If anyone knew what the son of a bitch was up to in regard to the railroad, Boutwell would. The question was, how could he plausibly draw him out on the subject without drawing attention to his interest?

Tall and patrician, Carswell appeared the quintessential southern gentleman, with carefully groomed, prematurely gray hair and moustache. He'd won his way to the Senate as a Dixie Democrat on the promise of wresting southern states' rights from the control of Republican Yankee carpetbaggers. That promise made him an arch political adversary of Grant and his whole damnable administration. Seeking the favor of information from one of Grant's trusted inner circle made for an unnatural political act. That likely accounted for the fact that the good Secretary kept a sitting U.S. Senator cooling his heels in his reception area. At least he could use the time to figure out how to get the information Burnswick wanted.

He'd taken the shares in the railroad construction company. The war had left him in need of rebuilding the family fortune. He'd been only too pleased when the influential power brokers behind Right of Way Holdings had offered him shares in the company. Right of Way Holdings owned some of the largest and most successful construction companies under contract to build the Union Pacific railroad. It was perfectly understandable why they would want a member of the Senate committee charged with overseeing the project to have Right of Way's interests at heart. It made sense. The dividends and stock price appreciation compensated him nicely for keeping the company apprised of the Senate perspective on the progress of the project. This latest request from Right of Way's representative, Mr. Burnswick, didn't make sense.

According to Burnswick, the administration had taken action recently to the benefit of another Union Pacific contractor. Stage & Rail Construction of Cheyenne competed with certain Right of Way companies. Burnswick wanted to know about the administration's interest in Stage & Rail. How the hell was he supposed to find that out without coming right out and asking? It begged the obvious question as to the source of his interest. Carswell saw no merit in raising that question, let alone answering it.

"The Secretary will see you now, Senator."

Ah, necessity, the mother of all invention. The germ of an idea sprouted in Carswell as the appointments secretary showed him in.

"Good afternoon, Mr. Secretary." Carswell turned on his soft-spoken South Carolina charm. "Good of you to see me."

"Senator Carswell, this is something of a surprise," Boutwell offered in bland understatement. Secretary of the Treasury George S. Boutwell was a former Massachusetts governor, congressman and Harvard overseer. The President had appointed him to lead his reconstruction policy at Treasury. A competent man in matters of money and markets, Boutwell quickly earned Grant's deepest respect. Gawky and angular of appearance, he looked a bit like Lincoln, though shorter of stature. Graying at his temples and beard, Boutwell's eyes burned with an alert, earnest intensity, as if perpetually calculating the import of the subject at hand. "Please have a seat." He indicated a small circle of brocade wing chairs drawn up around a low table and polished silver coffee service. "Would you care for a cup of coffee?"

"Yes, thank you, a little cream if you please."

The appointments secretary, a severely prim older woman who appeared comfortable with the chore, poured two servings in fine china cups and withdrew.

"Now, Senator, what can I do for you?"

"More to the point, I thought there might be something I can do for you. As you know, I'm a ranking member on the Senate Oversight Committee on the Union Pacific railroad project. I thought you might have some questions I could help you with, given the size and complexity of the undertaking and the fact that you are new to this office."

"How very thoughtful of you, Senator." Boutwell smiled to cover his sense of disbelief at what he'd just heard. "I wouldn't have expected a man in your position to find the time for so generous a gesture. As a matter of fact, I'm becoming quite versed on the state of the project, as are my colleagues over at Justice. The President is concerned at the magnitude of the cost overruns. He's directed Secretary Hoar and me to look into the project."

Carswell lifted his cup and sipped the steaming coffee. "Candidly, Mr. Secretary, I'm pleased to hear that. I have had some of the same concerns myself. I'm pleased to see that the President has given the project a priority it deserves and placed it in such capable hands. How are your investigations progressing?"

"My auditors are just getting started, Senator, so it's a bit premature for me to comment. I know Rockwood is making some progress over at Justice. He's got a Special Services Agent over at the Marshals Service doing some work in the field. I've been asked to act on some of his findings recently by the President himself."

"That's welcome news, Mr. Secretary. It makes my offer ever more timely then. If there is anything I can do, please don't hesitate to call on me."

TWENTY-ONE

Spotted Hawk rode into Talks with Buffalo's village at midday, leading a string of five ponies, the lead a flashy white stallion. The villagers stopped the affairs of the day, recognizing the arrival of a suitor with a handsome bride price. A curious crowd gathered to follow him to the lodge of the favored maiden. Everyone knew Mourning Dove had refused Spotted Hawk's courtship. Speculation among the villagers was divided over whether the proud Dog Soldier would try to take Mourning Dove over her objection or choose another maiden. All could agree on one thing. It would be hard for any father to refuse such a dowry.

Autumn Snow saw him enter the village and hurried to her father's lodge. Her heart pounded with hope. Mourning Dove had rejected him. She'd left the village to make her decision final. Surely Spotted Hawk must see the feeling Snow held in her heart for him. He would bring his bride price to her father.

Spotted Hawk rode through the village slowly, aware of the crowd gathering behind him. He would make his offer of marriage before all the people. Talks with Buffalo could not refuse such a dowry. All the people would know the father's will for an obedient daughter. She could not refuse him. If she resisted, all the people would know she deserved the beating he would give her. Either way, she would be his.

Talks with Buffalo came out to greet his visitor. Spotted Hawk sat his great war pony, looking down at Talks with Buffalo with a stony gaze. He held the lead of the ponies on his string. He let Talks with Buffalo study the quality of the horses, including the stallion who would give him many more fine horses.

"Spotted Hawk brings the great chief Talks with Buffalo these ponies as bride price for his daughter."

Talks with Buffalo listened to Spotted Hawk's proposal. This fine string of ponies would bring honor to the lodge of any maiden and her father, but he could not accept them. Mourning Dove had left the village to avoid this mating. He would spare the proud warrior the details of her rejection.

"Mourning Dove has left our village. Talks with Buffalo does not know where she has gone. Talks with Buffalo cannot accept bride price for such a daughter."

Spotted Hawk took the news impassively. His eyes narrowed, smoldering as he weighed the chief's words.

"Talks with Buffalo hold pony string," Spotted Hawk said, handing him the stallion's lead. "Spotted Hawk will bring Mourning Dove back to respect her father's wishes."

Spotted Hawk wheeled his big App to the south. The assembled crowd parted as he kicked up a trot, leaving the village and the noisy camp dogs behind.

Snow watched him go. A tear trickled down her cheek. Insult and anger blinded him. He could not see the path she would make for him. She offered a prayer to the Great One Above. Spotted Hawk must not find Mourning Dove, for Dove's sake and for her own.

He rode at a gallop, letting the wind whip his face. It could not cool his anger. Mourning Dove's disrespect and disobedience had insulted him. He'd lost face among the people for it. She must be brought to heel. He would search for her trail to the south and the west. She would go in search of the white eyes. The white man had caused Mourning Dove to turn her heart cold to him. If he found her with him, he would kill the white eyes. He would have his bride. He would have his way with her. The people would respect Spotted Hawk as they should.

Chance rode out of Cheyenne at dawn the next morning. Clear blue sky flared pink at the first flame of daybreak. The thing about running an investigation on the back of a hunch was, it didn't take much of a plan. Since the train robbery hadn't forced Jon Westfield to sell, Chance reasoned Taggert's next move would likely be to stir up Roman Nose and his renegades to run off the Stage & Rail work crew. If that were the case, Taggert would likely be out here somewhere. The best bet would be to look for some sign of Roman Nose and his band making a move toward the red rock cut. The Union Pacific tracks ran west out of Cheyenne. He could follow them out there easily enough, but Roman Nose, and Taggert if he was with the band, would come down from the north. He rode west-northwest into Indian country.

He puzzled over the questions he'd posed to Jon Westfield the night before. How did Taggert know about the Union Pacific gold shipment? More importantly, how did he know Jon Westfield needed payment as bad as he did? The answers to both questions seemed to lead to the same place: Grenville Dodge.

Dodge surely knew about the gold shipment. He'd told Chance that Westfield survived "hand to mouth." In fact, Dodge's position fit the larger pattern of the investigation too. Dodge controlled the Union Pacific construction project. He had the perfect opportunity to line the pockets of operators like Right of Way Development, and his own in the bargain, if he were of a mind to. Even his treatment of Westfield fit the pattern. "Squeezin' the Union Pacific nickel like to make the buffalo shit," was how Westfield put it. Was that taking care of the railroad's interests, or was it just another way of putting pressure on Westfield? A couple of things were certain.

He needed to have a talk with Dodge, and he needed to be on the lookout for a connection between Taggert and Dodge.

The sun rode high, warming his back. Spiny rock-faced ridges rose here and there, turning the prairie to valleys of rolling hills. Deep gullies, ravines and washes cut the valley floors. Gray-green patches of sage dotted the oceans of gold-tinged prairie grass flowing across the floor of one valley after another. Cottonwood and scrub oak gathered in small clumps along the banks of the occasional creek, or in low places that collected precious rainwater.

Puffy white clouds so low a man could almost reach out and touch them ran east traveling a river of blue sky. They reminded Chance of the cotton puffs that lined the roadways of Tennessee and Virginia. Fields of pastoral serenity caught in stark contrast to the bloody conflict that swirled around them and trampled them underfoot. Thankfully that conflict had passed. The memory drifted off with the clouds.

His thoughts drifted too to more pleasant prospects, like Victoria Westfield. She'd made no secret of her interest in seeing more of him. What man wouldn't be attracted to the attentions of a woman as pretty as that? He could sure get used to dinners like the one she'd served him last night. Right comfortable company too, he thought, reflecting on the conversation and pleasant evening that followed.

Jon Westfield would probably get plenty of encouragement to take him on at Stage & Rail if he decided to settle down after he finished this case. He figured he'd do that someday. *That someday better come 'fore a sidewinder like Taggert puts a hole in me that don't heal so good.* The thought haunted him. He didn't like the notion. He didn't need the distraction. Not when he had to face down a professional killer like Taggert.

He'd thought about settling down during the long days of his recovery. He'd come pretty close to cashing it in this time. He would have if Dove hadn't come along and done what she did for him. He'd faced death before, many times during the war, and heaven knows he'd seen more than enough of it. But this time it'd struck home real personal with Taggert's bullet. Then along comes Victoria Westfield and the possibility of a settled down life that likely wouldn't attract near so many bullets. He surely owed it some thought.

Another quiet presence invaded his thoughts again, as it had every so often in the weeks since he'd left. The shoulder was about healed now thanks to her, but the mark she'd left on him went deeper than the new pink scar covering the wound.

Something about her and the way she cared for him had touched him deeply. It made for a connection he couldn't explain. He wondered what had become of her. Had Spotted Hawk come back to take her for the bride price Talks with Buffalo could not refuse? He remembered the warm, comfortable feel of her in his arms and the taste of her kiss, like sweet new spring grass. He needed to go back to the village on the North Platte as soon as he finished this Taggert business. He needed to sit beside the river with her before he had any more thoughts about settling down in some construction business with a woman like Victoria Westfield. Dove felt like unfinished business to him. He couldn't rightly put his finger on why, but he knew he needed to come to the root of those feelings before he could have any clear cut feelings for Victoria.

Further north, rock ridge faces turned terracotta red, layered with pink and gray. Stands of dark green pine meandered along the hillsides, fighting for footing in the rocky places. Salute picked his way along a ridge line as the sun climbed to mid-afternoon. Chance kept him well below the crest of the ridge, out of the skyline. This far into Indian country a man had to be careful not to set himself up to be spotted at a distance. He surveyed his surroundings carefully, alert to any movement on the horizon or any sign of riders passing this way that might suggest he wasn't alone.

Suddenly Salute pricked up his ears and tossed his head toward the crest of the ridge. He flared his nostrils, testing the breeze with a low whicker. Salute had an acute sense of his surroundings he'd learned as a war horse. He definitely sensed something. Chance had learned to trust the horse's instincts over the years. He gave him his head, letting him climb to the crest of the ridge. It wasn't the smartest thing to do in hostile country, but something he couldn't see had gotten the horse's attention, and Salute wanted to have a look.

At the top of the ridge the terrain fell away. A grassy-bottomed valley some two miles long ran from north to south. Here and there rock formations and patches of dusty green sage dotted the valley floor. Chance drew Salute up. The big horse pawed and pranced. He tossed his head and turned in tight circles, chortling with excitement. Something sure had him charged up.

"Easy, big fella," Chance gentled him, stroking his neck. Then he saw what Salute had already sensed. A lone rider burst from the rocks a mile or so off at the north end of the valley. The horse stretched out flat at a dead run. Within seconds a second rider stormed into view, giving chase about a quarter mile behind. At about half a mile Chance made out the distinctive black and white markings of a tobiano paint that registered instant recognition. The little horse sure looked like Sage, though the rider looked like a brave. Whatever the reason, the rider on the paint looked hell bent on getting away from the brave stretching out a big App in hot pursuit. That rider sure could be Spotted Hawk. That meant the first rider might be Dove. That possibility made it his business.

He rocked back in his saddle and set his stirrups, giving the big Morgan the only cue he needed to start picking his way down the rocky slope to the valley floor below. Salute fought for footing, sleighing and sliding down the ridge in a shower of rocks and dust with an urgent sense of the chase ahead. They reached the valley floor as the paint shot past, racing south down the valley some two hundred yards off.

Both riders were so intent on the chase that neither noticed Chance until he put Salute into a gallop, closing on the gap between pursued and pursuer. He pulled his right hand Colt and fired a warning shot into the air over the head of the brave on the Appaloosa. Thinking back on it later, he would guess he should have put the shot to more lethal purpose.

Spotted Hawk checked the big war pony and pulled his Winchester from its saddle boot. He wheeled on Chance with a whoop.

Chance slid Salute to a stop and spun him in a tight circle. They lit out southeast down the valley, drawing Spotted Hawk away from the rider who turned the paint southwest. Chance asked Salute for all he had. The big Morgan stretched out at a dead run. They thundered down the valley toward a rocky box a mile distant.

A bullet buzzed by Chance's left ear like an angry bee, cutting through the rushing wind, chased by the muffled rifle report. Chance filled his left hand with saddle horn and rolled over the left side of Salute's neck, offering Spotted Hawk less target. He thumbed the hammer of his Colt, looking back at his pursuer. Spotted Hawk charged hard on his tail with his rein bit down between his teeth and the Winchester shouldered for another shot.

Chance popped a round in front of the big war pony. The App jumped right, spoiling Spotted Hawk's shot and nearly unseating him in the bargain. Spotted Hawk fought to regain control of his horse. That slowed him long enough for Chance to put more distance between them. Salute surged toward a stand of rocks at the head of the valley. Chance wheeled around the rock formation with the whine of another rifle shot spraying rock splinters behind him. He pulled Salute to a sliding stop and leaped from the saddle. He took cover behind a large boulder and came up slinging hot lead with both hands.

In an instant Spotted Hawk found himself out in the open facing a gunman forted up in rock cover. He wheeled his pony out of the line of fire and angled him west to a shallow ravine, where he dropped into cover. Leaping from his pony, he levered a round into the Winchester and returned fire.

Chance held his position. He exchanged buzzing lead and whining ricochets with the Cheyenne renegade. The terrain didn't offer much opportunity to flank Spotted Hawk's position or gain the advantage of a clean shot at him. Spotted Hawk didn't have much cover to maneuver either. After a time the exchange of gunfire became a pointless waste of ammunition.

The shooting subsided in futility. The standoff lapsed into a waiting game. The afternoon sun rode high and hot. That alone would test the mettle of the adversaries. Neither could move. Neither would offer a target. Time crept by as the afternoon wore on.

Chance's mind raced ahead. The moon would offer more light tonight than it had the night before. Still, darkness would create the opportunity for both of them to move to some decisive advantage. Which of them would put it to best advantage? The answer to that question would likely sign the death warrant of the other. Chance couldn't help thinking how far this moonlit night would be from the moonlit porch with Victoria Westfield. Far enough to have him dodging bullets again.

The late afternoon sun had drifted toward the purple and pink buttes that formed the west wall of the valley when a calm, cool voice broke over the hot, stifling stillness. Dove's Cheyenne words for Spotted Hawk were spoken with a quiet determination. Chance could feel the steel edge in her voice even though he didn't understand what she said. He didn't know if she could put an end to the standoff, but the sound of her voice confirmed his hunch. At least he'd put himself in this position for good reason.

Dove fell silent after a time, apparently having said her piece. Chance wondered if whatever she'd said would be enough to make

Spotted Hawk reconsider his position. Chance risked a look around the side of the boulder as Spotted Hawk shouted his reply. He fired a shot at Chance to emphasize his side of the argument. Chance fired back to no good effect. It didn't look like woman's words would be good enough for this warrior.

Woman's words might not be the answer, but when Dove opened fire from her position behind Spotted Hawk, things changed. They had him caught in a crossfire. The advantage turned to Chance and Dove. Sundown would put Spotted Hawk in mortal danger. That realization was likely what brought the standoff to an end. The renegade swung up on the back of his pony with a whoop. He snapped off one final shot and lit out up the valley to the north.

Chance holstered his pistols and came out from behind the rocks. He watched Spotted Hawk ride off. He could have given chase and maybe put an end to him, but at the moment he was more concerned with Dove's safety. Hindsight might judge that one another poor choice.

Dove stepped out of the rocks west of Spotted Hawk's position, leading Sage. Salute tossed his head and nickered his welcome to the little mustang mare. Sage returned the greeting with a whinny. *Well, the horses are happy to be together again.*

Dove walked up to him and stood there looking up at him without saying a word. Her eyes seemed filled with the questions that haunted him. Her eyes were the first thing he'd noticed about her. He guessed they'd be enough to take any man prisoner. Even the unfamiliar costume of her man dress and his old bloodstained shirt couldn't hide the figure he remembered. He didn't know what to say. It seemed they were starting up right where they'd left off, in awkward silence.

It might have been relief that the shooting had stopped, or the fact that he felt more awkward than Dove, but the next thing he knew he had her in his arms, holding her close, all round and soft and warm like. A strange sense of home flooded him in that moment, and his heart warmed in a way he couldn't explain.

"What are you doin' way out here?" He whispered the question into her hair.

The story poured out of her into his chest, from the vision Sage had given her to her decision to run away. Spotted Hawk, as it turned out, wasn't a buck to take no for an answer. He'd tracked her until he caught up with her no more than a long run from the entrance to the valley where they stood.

"And just where did you think you was runnin' off to?"

Dove lifted her chin and captured him in the liquid depths of her eyes. "Here," she said simply, returning her head to his chest as if there were no point to his question.

What could he do now? Taggert's trail lay along the way of following Spotted Hawk back to Roman Nose, but he couldn't just leave her here. If he took her back to the Platte River village, Spotted Hawk would be gone, and with him the best chance he could figure to find Taggert.

"Chance look for bad man who make trouble with Roman Nose."

She had a way of making statements out of questions as if she could read his mind.

"Mourning Dove help Chance track Spotted Hawk to Roman Nose and bad man."

Now if that don't beat all. Here they were having the same conversation they'd had back in Talks with Buffalo's village. He bit back his first thought to object. They'd had that conversation once before and it had come to this. She was safer out here with him than she'd be if he said something that sent her running off like before. Maybe Spotted Hawk's trail would lead back toward the village, or someplace that offered a way to send her back home safely.

Still it troubled him. It didn't seem right, her riding out on the trail of a bushwhacker like Taggert. He needed to buy some time to figure things out.

"So what did you tell Spotted Hawk to convince him to give up and go away?"

"Mourning Dove tell Spotted Hawk he not make her heart sing. Her heart sing for the gift of her spirit guide. Mourning Dove tell Spotted Hawk take his ponies and go. Spotted Hawk no fight spirit guide."

This last she said with the confident finality of one putting an end to the matter.

"So who's this gift of your spirit guide?" Why did he feel the need to pry these things out of her? He might have guessed her answer, but would never have guessed the reply he got.

Dove looked up into his eyes and lifted her face to the full light of the fading sun. Chance followed her gaze to the cloudless blue sky above, where it caught the shadow of a lone eagle circling the spot where they stood.

"Sister Eagle give Lah Kee to Mourning Dove this day like before."

When she came into his arms again, Chance knew what Spotted Hawk should have known. *A man can't argue with a spirit guide, much less a woman with a gun.*

TWENTY-TWO

Dove took the lead following Spotted Hawk's trail as it drifted northeast. Her tracking skills held to the trail over difficult ground where a less skilled tracker might have easily lost his way. Chance had to admit he would have lost the trail if he hadn't had her with him.

Late in the day the sun drifted slowly toward the horizon, painting the distant cloud-capped peaks deep purple and vivid orange burning to red. Soon it would be dark and time to make camp or risk losing the trail. Chance spotted an inviting grove of trees nearby where the slanting rays of the setting sun filtered through the leaves. They soon reached the small stand of cotton-woods grown up in the willow breaks along the banks of a slow-moving creek. Stepping down from his saddle, Chance sensed a quiet tranquility about the place. It felt like more than a good place to camp.

They unsaddled the horses and picketed them together on the bank of the stream, where they had prairie grass to crop and plenty of fresh water to drink. They made a cold camp, not wanting to risk a fire without knowing how close Roman Nose and his band might be.

They shared their provisions, munching pemmican and hard tack biscuits with a few dried currants. The meal brought Chance back to the quiet comfort they'd shared together in the long days of his recovery.

Dove felt the warmth of a homecoming in the cool evening breeze of a fireless camp. She knew she had found the path her heart had longed for when she'd left her village. Sister Eagle had returned Lah Kee to her in a time of need. She prayed such strong medicine as this would carry him to her with the same feelings she held for him.

As evening settled into darkness, the sky lit up a blanket of stars so bright it looked as though a man could reach up and pluck one down. Chance reflected on a porch and a campsite and the unique feelings of home each spoke to him. He sat beneath the same blanket of stars standing watch over the change in his circumstance from last night and now.

Chance mulled the situation. Riding the trail together presented a new problem. Bedding down for the night could be the cause of awkward feelings. He reckoned Dove might be frightened by that, owing to his impulsive behavior down on the river bank a few weeks back. He had no intention of taking advantage of the woman who'd nursed him back from death's door. He felt an honest need to keep his distance until he sorted out his jumbled feelings for the two women who'd come into his life. He decided to put her at ease by taking to his own blanket first.

He stood, stretched and unbuckled his gun belt. He rolled out his blanket at the base of a cottonwood, pulled off his boots and settled himself. He positioned his pistols within reach under his saddle out of habit before laying his head on the seat of that hard leather pillow. With his hat pulled down and his eyes closed, he never saw it coming.

Dove dropped her blanket next to his and rolled up beside him, her head coming to rest on his chest. Without thinking, he wrapped a protective arm around her. That's when his conflicted condition hit him. It seemed Dove had her mind made up on how she wanted this partnership to work.

Still, he hadn't sorted out the question of Victoria Westfield and the idea of settling down after he finished the Taggert business. Until he settled that, he wasn't about to do anything unfair to this caring young woman who also had feelings for him. He had feelings for her too. He just hadn't come to an understanding of what they might mean. A lot of culture stood between them, along with the nagging question of where Victoria Westfield fit in. It seemed more than a man could digest at one time.

One thing stood out, though. For a cold camp, this one felt plenty warm, and more like home than he'd felt in a long time.

Spotted Hawk pushed the big Appaloosa toward Roman Nose's camp. The white eyes had stolen his woman. He'd turned her heart against him. Mourning Dove had made bad medicine with the talk of her spirit guide. She'd joined the white eyes in the gunfight against him. She'd forced him to break off his attack. No woman should be allowed to do such a thing to a warrior. He vowed to avenge his honor. He would kill the white eyes and take his bride. If Mourning Dove drew her gun against him again, he would kill her too.

Taggert and Roman Nose sat by a small campfire as early evening darkened into night. Taggert had brought whiskey and ammunition to exchange for the raid he wanted at the red rock cut. The Dog Soldier band scattered around the campsite, filling themselves with firewater or lying dead drunk from what they'd already consumed.

As head of the Cheyenne Dog Soldier warrior society, Roman Nose exercised great influence over the young warriors who followed him, like Spotted Hawk. He cut an imposing figure that might have been hewn out of the red rock common to the area. Crags and crevices lined his chiseled features about the prominent nose that gave Moquinto his white man's name. A jagged scar on his right cheek added to a fearsome countenance. His fiery black eyes blazed with anger over the coming of the white man and the destruction of the old ways of his people.

Roman Nose managed broken English in his dealings with Taggert. He despised the white man as a traitor to his own people, but he used the white man for arms and ammunition in his private war against the iron horse, the great symbol of the white man's coming. The white man brought trade for a new attack on the iron horse white eyes. It spoke of the low character of a people who made war on their own kind.

The beat of a fast horse pounded out of the night beyond the circle of firelight. It announced the arrival of a lone rider. Spotted Hawk galloped into the camp and made straight for Roman Nose's fire. He leaped down from the heaving war pony and launched into an animated report, gesturing to the southwest as he spoke.

Taggert took a pull on his bottle as he watched the two exchange Cheyenne palaver that must have been of some import, because something sure had the brave riled up. When the warrior finished his report, Roman Nose turned to Taggert.

"Spotted Hawk say white man sent by Great Father steal his bride."

Sent by the Great Father. Taggert played the words over in his mind and decided it might be another U.S. marshal.

"How does he know the Great Father sent this white man?"

Roman Nose put Taggert's question to the brave.

"Spotted Hawk say Talks with Buffalo's daughter find wounded white man. Take him to village. Make medicine to heal him. White man tell Talks with Buffalo he sent by Great Father to find bad man who make trouble for iron horse trail."

At least it's the same U.S. marshal. Too bad I didn't finish the son of a bitch the first time. "Ask him where the white man is now."

Roman Nose and Spotted Hawk made more palaver.

"Spotted Hawk say white man half day ride back on the trail. Spotted Hawk say him take warriors, go back and kill him."

"Sounds like a good idea. Send a brave who speaks English and I'll ride along with 'em. Seems like I should take his killin' personal since he's got such an interest in me."

Roman Nose grunted agreement and took his turn at a pull from the bottle.

TWENTY-THREE

The next morning Dove rose with the sun. She rolled her blanket and went off to wash in the creek and tend the horses. It might have been a cold camp on hard ground, but her heart had warmed her the whole night with a sense of peace and a feeling of home.

Chance, on the other hand, hadn't slept much at all. Crosscurrents of feeling roiled his mind through the night, making sleep little more than an occasional doze. He could feel the warmth and simple devotion of this young woman who would follow him in spite of the dangers he faced. Victoria Westfield tugged at his heartstrings with the promise of a settled-down life free from hot lead. He owed Dove much, but she wanted more than gratitude, and for that she deserved honesty. No, he needed to sort all this out before anyone got hurt. He needed to do it pretty fast too, because a man on the trail of a killer like Taggert didn't need this kind of distraction.

They were saddling the horses when Sage tossed her head to the horizon, flared her nostrils, and pawed the ground. Dove spoke gentle Cheyenne words to the little mustang, but there seemed to be no calming the horse. Chance watched as Dove circled her arms around the little mustang's neck and rested her forehead against the bunched muscles there, as if listening to the senses disturbing her.

Chance remembered the story of Spotted Hawk and the vision of his coming with the bride price. This business of spirit guides and visions struck him as strange, but he wasn't about to argue with things he didn't understand. Whatever the reason, she'd been right about Spotted Hawk coming after her. He wondered what the little mustang's agitation this morning might mean.

Sage finally settled and Dove stepped back, gazing off to the north with a faraway look. She knit her brow as if coming to some conclusion.

"Bad men come look for Lah Kee. Mount up and follow Mourning Dove."

She gave the order with a quiet determination that left no room for disagreement. Chance didn't know what had passed between Dove and her horse, but there seemed no point in questioning it now.

Dove swung up on Sage as Chance stepped into his saddle. She led them out of the campsite heading northeast in the general direction of Talks with Buffalo's village. The trail they laid down led to a patch of rocky ground climbing a butte a quarter mile or so from the campsite. When they reached the hard scrabble, Dove drew rein and dropped to the ground. She picked up a branch of dried sage and handed Chance Sage's lead.

"Take Sage. Ride back to creek and wait for Dove there."

Chance grasped her plan and rode back to the creek upstream from the campsite. He stopped the horses in the middle of the stream and waited while Dove swept away the sign of their back trail. When she finished she waded into the stream and mounted up. She led them south in the creek another quarter mile or so below the campsite to a rocky dry wash. They left the creek there and hid the horses in the wash. Dove swept away the tracks leading from the creek to the wash. They hid in the rocks where they could watch over their campsite and the false trail.

Chance checked the loads in both Colts and the shoulder-fired .44. If trouble was headed their way, he planned to be ready. Dove took his lead, checking the loads in the .38 on her hip. She didn't seem the least bit shy of a fight if it came to that. She studied the terrain to the north, convinced Sage had sensed trouble. Looking at the determined set of her jaw Chance guessed she meant to prove her point about riding with him.

He used hunches as an investigator all the time. They came to him easily, and he'd learned to trust them. Visions and messages from animal spirit guides didn't strike him the same way. He felt a little foolish hiding in a dry wash because a horse had gotten a little skittish. He understood Salute's sensing Sage the way he had the day before, but animal spirit messengers? He just didn't have that kind of religious belief. Belief or no, she had him hiding in these rocks watching an abandoned campsite. His doubts aside, he didn't have to wait long to find out they were hidden for good reason.

Within the hour a half dozen horsemen came riding in from the north. As they drew closer Chance could make out Spotted Hawk and four Roman Nose renegades, along with a big man in a black frock coat riding a big black horse. It looked like the same man he'd seen at the broken-down wagon at the start of the chase that had ended in ambush. The list of charges he'd bring Taggert in on just kept getting longer.

They drew rein at the campsite and fanned out in a circle until one of the warriors picked up the trail leading northeast. They would soon lose the trail, but Dove's plan made it look like they were headed for Talks with Buffalo's village. It worked too. When they fanned out to look for some sign of the lost trail, Spotted Hawk called off the search and led them out to the northeast in the direction of the village.

When they were gone Chance turned to Dove and put his arm around her in a gentle hug. It seemed the natural thing to do, though the minute he had her in his arm he knew he shouldn't have done it.

"I don't know how you saw that comin', but you sure saved our bacon this time."

Dove smiled a knowing smile. She wasn't sure what her vision had to do with bacon, but Lah Kee seemed pleased with her, and that warmed her heart.

"Sage tell Dove bad men come. Sage good pony. We go after bad man?"

"He's runnin' with too many friends right now. We'll go back to Cheyenne and wait for him there. He's got some unfinished business there, so it might be best to just let him come to us."

Come to us. He would take her along after all. Sister Eagle could not be denied.

Spotted Hawk led Taggert and his band into Talks with Buffalo's village. Villagers followed the war party, the crowd curious at the presence of a white man with the Dog Soldiers. Spotted Hawk drew to a halt at Talks with Buffalo's lodge and dropped from his pony.

Talks with Buffalo stepped out of his lodge, his eyes squinting in the sun, his heavily lined face solemn and unreadable. He did not recognize the white man on the black horse, but he remembered Lah Kee's words of the bad man who made trouble for the iron horse.

"Has your daughter returned to the village with the white eyes who stole her from me?" Spotted Hawk asked.

Talks with Buffalo looked from Spotted Hawk to the white man and back. He had a strong feeling this white man was the one wanted by the Great Father's law.

"Mourning Dove is not here. Spotted Hawk did not find her?"

"Spotted Hawk found her with the white eyes. We followed her trail back to your village."

Talks with Buffalo shrugged. "Mourning Dove is not here."

Spotted Hawk seethed with rage. He had been fooled. The trail of Mourning Dove and the white eyes had been false. He had believed it because he wanted it to be so. She might even have watched him make a fool of himself at the campsite. The circle of the people standing around watching his silence played him for the fool yet again. Was there no end to the woman's treachery?

TWENTY-FOUR

Joe Clark took Jon Westfield's Indian trouble warning seriously. He didn't know what made the old man think they were in for trouble. Roman Nose didn't go around announcing his plans as a rule, but then Clark had kept his scalp for a lot of years by being careful. The rangy, watery-eyed Virginian had served under Grenville Dodge during his days as an Indian fighter before both men turned to railroading. Clark still had the instincts and savvy of an Indian fighter, which served him well out on the line with his Stage & Rail work crew.

Faced with Westfield's warning, Clark posted lookouts day and night. The crew worked the roadbed with their weapons close at hand. At night they pitched their bedrolls stuffed like scarecrows and took cover in the south butte overlooking the camp. None of the men liked the discomfort and light sleep that came with the precaution, but given the risk of a man having his hair lifted, nobody complained much either.

The way Clark explained it, "If Roman Nose comes down out of the north to hit the camp, they'll have a hot lead reception ready and waitin'."

Roman Nose halted his band of some fifty warriors in a gulch about a mile northeast of the red rock cut. He sent Spotted Hawk to scout the work crew and find the best approach to the camp for their raid.

Spotted Hawk trotted off on foot heading south and west over the rocky terrain. It would be easy to hide the war party in the ravines and rock formations that were home to the Cheyenne warrior. A quarter mile north of the cut he melted into the rocks, working his way forward with painstaking stealth. A sleeping rattlesnake made more commotion than an accomplished Indian scout. Spotted Hawk used his craft to slither within a hundred yards of the work crew under the very noses of the two lookouts posted in the rocks overlooking the camp.

Lying in rock shadows lengthening in the late afternoon sun, below the crest of the north butte at the east end of the cut, Spotted Hawk scouted the work crew. Fourteen men made up the crew, a small number in his reckoning. They'd pitched their camp in the center of the cut on the south side of the track, hemmed in on both sides by the rock walls of the north and south buttes. This meant they must cross the iron horse trail to attack the camp. They would need to take care in this. Many ponies would be frightened by crossing the iron rails. If they made noise, the white eyes would be warned and the advantage of surprise would be lost.

The band could approach the butte from the north and follow it back to the mouth of the cut on the east end. From there they would cross the iron horse trail and attack the camp, killing the white eyes from the path of the monster they fought. This vision sang its song for Spotted Hawk as he slipped out of the rocks and made his way back to the band.

Back at the gulch Spotted Hawk told his story to Roman Nose and the elder warriors. When he finished, Roman Nose grunted approval.

"Spotted Hawk will lead us when we attack at dawn."

Spotted Hawk swelled with pride at the honor. The warrior society recognized his courage and skill. Why could Talks with Buffalo's foolish daughter not see him for an honored warrior? What honor could she bring to her father's lodge with the hated white eyes? She called him the gift of her spirit guide. What spirit guide would give her a white man when she could have an honored warrior? No spirit guide would shelter her white eyes from Spotted Hawk's bullet. He would have his death, and in that Spotted Hawk would yet have Mourning Dove for his bride.

Joe Clark hadn't slept well. The rocks overlooking the camp from the south butte were cold and uncomfortable. Then again, he hadn't slept well any night since they'd started spending the night in defensive positions. This night felt different. Clark claimed he could smell Indians. Well, maybe not smell them, but his instincts were so strong he could feel the threat of an attack. Waiting for the skies to gray into dawn, he checked his Winchester one more time. They were out there, all right. He could feel it.

Spotted Hawk led the band along the base of the north butte, working their way east toward the mouth of the cut in the gray light of predawn. Roman Nose and his Dog Soldier brothers strung out in file behind, a determined procession of warriors preparing their spirits for battle.

The eastern sky fired pink and blue in promise to the return of Brother Sun as the band reached the mouth of the cut. They halted there awaiting the arrival of the sun to bless their attack. With the bright light of the sun at their backs, any white men rising to fight would be blinded to their charge.

When the sun rose half over the horizon it filled the cut with new morning light. Roman Nose looked back at his band, meeting the determined gaze of each warrior with a nod. "Brother sun gives us a good day to kill iron horse white eyes."

He led them into the cut at a walk, cautiously beginning the challenge of crossing the tracks. The unfamiliar footing caused several ponies to shy or jump the track, while others needed to be led across. They blindfolded the most skittish before leading them across the tracks. In the end they completed the crossing without raising any visible sign of alarm in the white eyes' camp. The road-bed stretched before them some three hundred yards down to the camp.

Roman Nose led them forward at a walk, black shadows riding out of a bright ball of sun firing the eastern horizon behind them. They followed the rails into the cut, advancing on the sleeping camp.

Clark saw them coming.

"Iowa," he hissed to Iowa Barnes. "We got company. Pass the word. Hold your fire until I give the signal."

Barnes passed the word down the line. Clark settled in to watch the attackers draw into his trap.

As they neared the camp, all remained eerily silent. Spotted Hawk's instinct for danger roused. The white eyes posted lookouts in the day. Why would they not post lookouts at night? The unspoken question gnawed at him as Roman Nose raised his rifle with a throaty war cry that split the morning stillness.

Dozens of others took up the cry as the band surged forward at a gallop, charging volleys of rifle fire into empty tents and bed-rolls. The charge overran the camp, swirling back among the tents, whooping and firing at a resistance that never appeared.

Suddenly the rocks climbing the south butte erupted in a volley of rifle fire and a hail of bullets. Five warriors and two ponies went down in the first salvo as the repeating rifles stitched their deadly work over the camp, catching the band like fish in a barrel.

Clark leveled his Winchester and pictured his sights as he levered round after round at target after target. The veteran Indian fighter rained death on the renegade band with practiced intensity. Up and down the south wall, rail-splitters-turned-Indian-fighters blazed away too, though mostly without Clark's lethal effect.

Instinctively the Dog Soldiers returned fire on the high ground. They filled the red rock cut with muzzle flashes and the thunder of rifle reports. Ricochets whined through the air. A thickening blanket of gunsmoke spread over the cut, hanging in the still morning air over the cries of the wounded and songs of the dying.

Roman Nose recognized the raid for a loss. Somehow the white eyes had known they were coming. He chided himself for not sensing the trap as he rallied the band to follow his lead. They galloped away to the west, escaping the killing field below the south butte. The band turned north, leaping the tracks a hundred yards up the line on ponies that needed no encouragement to get away from the bullet songs that followed them.

"We sure put a whuppin' on 'em that time," Jack Stubbs gloated as the last of the renegades disappeared around the north butte at the far end of the cut.

"Don't get yourself too puffed up, Jack. We ain't likely seen the last of that bunch," Clark said, watching them go. "Roman Nose won't take this sorta lickin' lyin' down. We'll need to double the lookout on both sides of the cut to cover us. That ain't gonna do much for our rate o' progress takin' two more hands off the line, but that's the way of it. Now let's get some breakfast and get to work."

Back in the gulch Roman Nose assessed his losses. Six warriors dead and five others wounded. His rage burned. They had ridden into a trap. How could the white man have known they were coming? The best they could hope for now was to harass the iron horse men from long range and perhaps kill a few. They would bury their dead and look to the spirits for guidance.

Spotted Hawk too wondered how the iron horse white men had known they were coming. He burned with anger at not giving voice to his fear of a trap. Spotted Hawk had a strong feeling that

135

the Great Father's lawman had warned the iron horse white eyes they were coming. He must have been riding to the red rocks when they had fought over Mourning Dove. It gave him one more reason to kill him.

Taggert had watched the aborted raid on the Stage & Rail crew from a rocky outcropping northeast of the cut. The crew had been waiting for them. Old Joe Clark might be a good Indian fighter, but nobody was that good. Somehow he'd been warned and Westfield had dodged another bullet. White would not be happy. Taggert had a hunch what his next move would be, but the boss would have to make that call. For now he needed to get his report back east.

He had another problem too, probably related to the warning of the red rock crew. He had a U.S. marshal on his trail, which made returning to Cheyenne to finish the Stage & Rail job risky. He'd need to take care of that little problem no matter what White decided to do about finishing up with Westfield.

Taggert swung up on the black and wheeled southeast at a lope. He'd head for the mining town of Central City, south of the Colorado border. Central wasn't much of a city, just a tent top saloon and a few rough log cabins thrown up to keep the rain and snow out. It'd be a good place to lay low for a spell while he sent his wire to White and another one to the Betchers down in Denver. He'd meet them in Cheyenne and take care of the marshal while he waited for White's instructions on what to do about Westfield.

TWENTY-FIVE

Chance and Mourning Dove rode into Cheyenne and walked the horses up Sixteenth Street. Dove had traveled to white settlements and forts many times with her father for treaty talks, but riding this street with Lah Kee, she had a strong sense of being out of place. A Cheyenne woman in the company of a white man among white men made her a conspicuous stranger. Her people were proud and strong. Talks with Buffalo and Sweet Medicine had made her strong. She drew her Cheyenne pride around her as she might a warm blanket against a chill Dakota wind. She would find her place in this white man's world.

Chance headed straight for the Stage & Rail Construction Office at the west end of town. They stepped down at the rail and tied the horses. Chance went in to see Westfield while Dove waited with the horses.

Westfield answered the visitor bell from his cluttered desk. "Afternoon, Marshal." His smile creased the corners of his eyes behind smudged spectacles.

"Afternoon, Jon. Any sign of Taggert hereabouts recently?"

"Not since you left. I take it you didn't find him."

"More like he and his friends found me," Chance said, pulling off his hat.

"What do you mean, 'friends'?"

"Taggert come after me with a handful of renegades, part of Roman Nose's band, I reckon. We lost 'em."

"So he is hooked up with Roman Nose. My men at the red rock cut give that bunch a hot welcome a couple days back, thanks to your warning."

"They did hit your crew then."

"Sure did. Joe Clark's tough and smart. All Roman Nose got to show for his raid was some dead Dog Soldiers."

"That's good, Jon. The warnin' was just a hunch. I'm glad it helped out."

"What do you reckon Taggert's next move'll be?"

"I don't know for sure, Jon, but I got another hunch, and that's why I'm here. You're unfinished business for Taggert and whoever's callin' his shots. I'm afraid you might be the target next time."

Westfield paused for a moment, letting Chance's words sink in. "Been takin' care of myself a long time now, Lucky. I reckon I can take care of Taggert too."

"Taggert's a hired gun, Jon. He's a professional. That's why I'd like to help. I plan to keep a lookout over your place until Taggert shows up. I need to take him alive to find out who's behind all the Union Pacific trouble."

"Well, I don't mind tellin' you it'd make me rest a good sight easier if you was to stick around, Lucky. We ain't got much by way of accommodations, but you're welcome to pitch your blanket here in the office."

"I need a place to watch the whole place."

"Then let's talk to Brady Cain at the livery next door. I bet Brady'd put you up in his loft. You'd have a real good lookout from there."

Victoria Westfield stepped out of Gohram's Emporium and started up the boardwalk for home. She spotted Salute standing at the hitching post in front of the office and paused. *He's back.* She shifted her parcels of flour and bacon to her left arm and pushed her bonnet off the back of her head. She fluffed her rich auburn curls in the dusty store window. Satisfied with the effect, she hurried on her way with a lighthearted spring in her step.

She didn't pay much attention to the second horse tied alongside Salute until she crossed Cody Street and stepped up on the boardwalk fronting the Stage & Rail office. That's where she got her first look at the lone Indian standing there waiting with the horses. Indians weren't that uncommon in Cheyenne, but this she could see was no ordinary Indian. This Indian might dress like a brave, but no brave she'd ever seen filled out a shirt the way this one did. Victoria didn't like the look of this one bit. *Where did she come from? Could she actually be riding with him?* Victoria had her mind set on getting to know the handsome marshal much better. Another woman had no place in her plan, let alone some savage. She'd get to the bottom of this little matter in short order. She swept past Dove with a disdainful glance in her cool green eyes and entered the office.

"Why Lucky, what a pleasant surprise," Victoria beamed, laying her hand on his arm in greeting.

"Victoria, it's nice to see you again." Chance smiled, remembering why he'd gotten so conflicted in deciding what to make of the two women he now had in plain sight of one another.

"It's wonderful to have you back with us. I was hoping you'd come back before long. Who is your friend?" she asked, forcing a lilt of casual curiosity to her words.

"Her name is Mourning Dove. She's Talks with Buffalo's daughter. She's the one who patched me up after Taggert bushwhacked me."

"How fortunate for you." The warmth in her voice barely covered the icy drip.

Chance of course missed the sarcastic undertone in her sentiment. He stumbled on with his story. "I had a chance to return the favor out there on the trail. I helped her get away from the advances of an unwelcome suitor."

"Oh, how very gallant of you," Victoria gushed, smiling up into his quizzical blue eyes. "She must be very grateful for that."

"She's ridin' with me 'til I can figure a way to get her safely back to Talks with Buffalo's village."

"What a most kind and generous thing for you to do, Lucky. Hopefully you can find a way to do that real soon," Victoria said, patting his arm.

"Least I can do after all she done for me."

"Of course it is. Will you be staying for dinner?"

"More'n that, Victoria," Jonathon Westfield broke in by way of reminding her that he was still in the room. "Marshal Chance will be stayin' around for a spell to keep an eye out for Taggert."

"Splendid!" Victoria clapped her hands with a bright twinkle in her eye like a child inspecting the pretty wrappings on a Christmas present.

Out at the hitch rail Dove watched through the dirty, streaked window sign painted with the unfamiliar white man's word pictures. The ways of the whites were strange to her, but the ways of women were understood by women of all peoples. She knew what the pretty woman with fire hair had in her mind for the gift of her spirit guide. The thought blew through her heart like a chill wind.

Chance of course missed it all. If he'd had any sense he'd have climbed on Salute and ridden out of the crossfire before the shooting started. That's what he'd have done if he'd had any sense about women, which he didn't.

TWENTY-SIX

Rank Betcher sat in what had become a familiar spot since returning from the Drainsville train robbery: a high stakes game of poker. This time a shiny, slick gambler from St. Louis ran the game. The others were a couple a local hard cases who in Rank's opinion didn't know no better than to sit in on a game they shouldn't have been playing. In truth Rank shouldn't have been playing the game either. But he had every day since getting back to Denver. The game had already taken a toll on his share of the Drainsville take, but he knew his luck was bound to change soon.

Younger brother Matt had his share of the take in his favorite place too. Upstairs he poured it two dollars at a time into Babe, the prettiest little whore in Denver. Matt had practically bought the golden haired beauty's fidelity since coming into his newfound wealth. She was about Matt's age and still retained something of a youthful freshness that would soon grow threadbare in the tough trade of a rough town. Lovestruck, Matt couldn't see it, even with the reminder of a once-broken nose to taint her beauty.

He and Babe holed up for days at a time, disturbing themselves only for food when they needed it. Matt had lost track of her tally and about had himself convinced she loved him.

Babe hadn't lost track of her tally. She had the perfect mark. The cow-eyed boy loved her. She didn't have to put up with any rough stuff, and he had lots of money. In her business, things just didn't get any better than that.

Matt and Babe wouldn't be bothered by the kid delivering the telegram downstairs. The telegram from Taggert offered a new job and instructed the brothers to meet him at the Rawlins House in Cheyenne. No, that telegram would interrupt Rank at the poker table, right before the shooting started.

Rank didn't read much, but he recognized enough to get "Cheyenne" and "Taggert." That likely meant the Rawlins House and a job. That gave him enough information to tip the kid and turn his attention back to his cards and the turn of a queen to go with the one in his hole.

The bet checked to Rank's queen. Rank figured it was worth five bucks to see if anybody cared to see any more. The two hard cases and the gambler called Rank's five. The gambler turned the ten of spades to Rank. He hit the first hard case with deuce to go with a six. The second hard case drew a nine to go with an eight, possible straight. He turned the king of clubs to himself. The gambler bet five dollars on his king. Rank called. The first hard case folded. The second thought hard and bet five.

The gambler wore a long black frock coat with a silk brocade vest and string tie. His shirt was frilled at the collar and cuffs, though it needed a laundering after spending long hours at the gaming tables. He slick oiled his hair, and the barber kept his moustaches neatly trimmed. It gave him the prosperous look of one in control. He wore an impassive mask over the cold concentration in eyes that gave no notion of what he thought.

The gambler turned the ten of hearts to Rank. That made a pair showing, two pair with his queen in the hole. The hard case with the possible straight took a five, no help. The gambler turned the eight of clubs to himself, no help there either. The bet checked to Rank with his pair of tens showing. Two pair was worth a ten-dollar bet. The hard case folded.

The gambler leaned back in his chair and fixed Rank with a cold, flinty stare. He tossed a ten-dollar gold piece into the pot.

The last card went face down in the hole. He slid Rank the five of diamonds and added his second hole card.

Rank figured his queens and tens looked pretty good. He knew his luck was about to change. He raised ten again to see if the gambler might fold.

The gambler furrowed his expression, thinking hard before he pushed his ten in and then ten again. Rank called the raise over a flicker of doubt. He flipped his hole card showing the two pair and reached for the pot.

The gambler's hand came down on top of Rank's hand and the pot. "Not so fast, friend," he said, flipping a pair of kings in his hole, three of a kind for the hand.

"Where'd them kings come from?" Rank's accusatory question hung in the air dripping with menace. "They come from your coat sleeve or the bottom of the deck?"

"You sayin' I cheated, friend?" The gambler's eyes turned cold.

"I'm sayin' that's my pot, and you best let the rightful winner take it before you get hurt." Rank stood and leaned over the table, pulling the pot out from under the gambler's hand.

A metallic click caused Rank to pause. He looked up and found himself staring down the muzzle of a big-bore derringer the gambler leveled between his eyes. The hard cases scraped their chairs backing away from the table. The raucous din in the Silver Dollar fell quiet.

Rank took his hands off the money and stood up slowly, backing his way to the edge of the table. The gambler held his aim, sliding the silver and gold coins toward his side of the table. It made for an ill-advised distraction.

Rank threw the table up into the gambler's face, discharging the derringer harmlessly into the ceiling and slamming the gambler back into the wall. Rank threw the table aside as the gambler made a move to the shoulder holster inside his coat, but the pocket pistol never cleared leather. Rank's Colt fired twice at close range, blowing gaping red holes in the gambler's shiny silk vest. Bright red stains splattered the wall at his back as the gambler's eyes rolled up and he slid down the wall to the floor.

The shooting brought Matt running out of Babe's room, hastily buttoning his pants. When he realized the gunplay involved his brother, he pulled his own pistol and threw down on the patrons standing around the fracas just in case the gambler had any friends in the crowd.

"Nobody move," Matt barked from the balcony above.

Nobody moved as Rank picked up most of his scattered winnings and headed for the swinging doors to the street. Matt eased down the stairs, covering their exit. Out at the hitch rail they grabbed their horses and mounted up.

"Where we headed?" Matt asked.

"Taggert's got a job for us up to Cheyenne. No point in waitin' 'round here to pass the pleasantries of the evenin' with Sheriff Prentice. Let's ride."

Babe and her tally would just have to wait.

They wheeled the horses and lit out of town at a gallop just ahead of Sheriff Ben Prentice hurrying down the street toward the Silver Dollar to find out what the shooting was all about. He sized up the situation at the Silver Dollar pretty quick. The tinhorn gambler had been accused of cheating. Whether he had or not wasn't near as important as the fact that by the accounts of all the witnesses, he'd thrown down on Rank Betcher first. That made the shooting self-defense. He could organize a posse to round up the Betcher brothers, but in the end Rank would get off on this one. The incident had rid Denver of the two of them, at least for awhile, and that seemed a fair resolution.

TWENTY-SEVEN

They found Brady Cain mending a harness in the livery stable across the alley from the Westfield residence. The rumpled old stable man looked up from his work when Jon Westfield came in followed by a U.S. marshal and an Indian.

"Afternoon, Brady," Westfield greeted.

"Afternoon, Jon. What can I do for you?"

"This here's Marshal Chance."

"Howdy, Marshal," Cain said, holding out a rough, calloused hand.

"Mr. Cain." Chance took his hand. "Pleased to meet you."

"Call me Brady, Marshal. Everybody does."

"Thanks, Brady, folks call me Lucky. This here's Mourning Dove."

"Marshal Chance would like to use your loft for a few days. He's lookin' for a man who's likely to come lookin' for me," Westfield explained. "I'd be much obliged if you'd let him and his partner camp out up there."

"You're my neighbor, Jon, no need to say more. It ain't much, Marshal, but you're welcome to it. Go on up and make yourself at home," Cain said, indicating a wooden ladder leading up to the loft.

Chance and Dove settled saddlebags and blankets into Brady Cain's loft and took up their watch that afternoon. The loft offered a good lookout over the Stage & Rail Office, residence and the street, including the side entrance to the residence with its long porch facing the stable and the alley in back. From that observation point no one could get near the office or the residence without being observed.

The loft suited the purpose of catching the bad man, but Dove thought it too close to the lodge of a certain fire-hair woman with eyes for the gift of her spirit guide. That part of the arrangement made her unhappy from the first, but she had no idea what to do about it here in the white man's village.

Chance didn't give much thought to the fact that the two women in his life at the moment would be camping out next door to one another. He had a job to do, and that's all that mattered. He settled them into the loft, posted Dove on the afternoon watch, and headed down to the Union Pacific office at the depot to find Grenville Dodge.

He found Dodge in his cramped, disheveled office. The chief engineer hunched over a pile of telegraph foolscap and hand-drawn ledgers amid the flurry of activity that attended the joining of the lines. His tie and collar were open, and sweat dampened his linen shirt where the heat of the day left its stain. His coat lay over the arm of a wooden swivel chair. He squinted at engineering plans for a spur line to connect Denver to the main line.

"Afternoon, Colonel Dodge." Chance knocked on the open door frame.

Dodge looked up, annoyed at being called back from his concentration. "Oh, Marshal Chance, good afternoon. How's your investigation progressing?"

"Well, I reckon I'm makin' some progress, though I seem to be about a step slow when it comes to catchin' up with the feller responsible for stealin' your gold shipment a couple a weeks back."

"Then you know who did it?"

"I got a pretty good idea, but I cain't seem to catch up with the feller that's got some serious questions to answer. You know a feller works for Right of Way Development goes by the name of Taggert?"

"Taggert, you say? Union Pacific does a lot a business with Right a Way Development, but I cain't say as I've run across a feller named Taggert. What little dealing I've had with Right of Way personally has been with a feller from St. Louie named Hauser. What's this Taggert gent look like?"

Dodge gave no indication of surprise at the mention of Taggert. He was either an accomplished liar or an honest man with an honest question. For now, the circumstances of opportunity and motive had Chance looking at Dodge with suspicion.

"Big man, dresses in a black frock coat, red moustache goin' gray. Rides a big black horse."

"Sorry, Marshal, no help there. What makes you think he's behind the train robbery?"

"I found a broken seal from the Kansas City Mint in his room at the Rawlins House after the hold-up. It may not be proof, but it's reason enough to ask him a few questions."

"What would Right of Way Development have to do with stealing a Union Pacific gold shipment? They get most of it by contract anyway."

Now there's an interesting question if a man wanted to know how much somebody like Chance knew or had guessed.

"It would've put the squeeze on Jon Westfield over at Stage & Rail Construction. Taggert and Right of Way Development are tryin' to buy him out, you know."

"I didn't know that, though it don't surprise me none. They been buying out just about anybody that amounts to anything."

Again Dodge registered no reaction to Chance's connecting the Drainsville train robbery to the pressure it would have put on Jon Westfield.

"Westfield needed payment from that shipment to make his payroll. I'm thinkin' that somehow, Taggert knew that and figured if Westfield couldn't make payroll, he'd be forced to sell out."

"Jon always pushed me pretty hard for his payments, but I had no idea things were that tight. So you must be the one who got Washington all stirred up to wire funds out here with orders to pay Stage & Rail on time after the robbery. That'd keep Stage & Rail going and keep Taggert pressing Jon Westfield to sell."

Dodge had made those connections pretty quick for a man who didn't know what was going on between Taggert and Westfield.

"Taggert's been up to more than just robbin' trains. I got reason to believe he's been runnin' guns to Roman Nose and his renegades. I think he's stirrin' up the hostiles attackin' your work crews. They hit Jon Westfield's crew out at the red rock cut a few days ago."

"I heard about that. Jon's foreman out there, Joe Clark, rode with me when we spent our time fighting Indians before we started building railroads. Joe's a competent man. I understand he give Roman Nose a good accounting of himself. They say he'd been warned to be on the lookout for an attack. Pretty unusual warning. Roman Nose ain't much given to announcing his plans. That some of your work too, Marshal?"

"Just a hunch."

"Pretty good hunch, I'd say. You think the raid might be part of putting pressure on Jon to sell out?"

"Sure looks like it from here, though I got to tell you, Jon Westfield is a stand-up feller with no thought of givin' in to Right of Way and their hired guns."

Chance didn't want to make a target out of Jon Westfield. But if Dodge and Right of Way Development were connected, Chance figured he might smoke out Taggert if Dodge knew that Jon Westfield wasn't about to sell.

"Well, I'm pleased to hear that. Jon Westfield's a good operator. He meets his obligations on time and at a fair price. I'll do what I can to see he gets paid on time from here out."

"Much obliged for that, Colonel. Keep an eye out for Taggert. If you see anyone that fits his description, let Sheriff Teet know. He'll know where to find me."

Chance didn't want Dodge to know he'd be watching the Stage & Rail Office. The interview hadn't done anything to increase his suspicion of Dodge, but it hadn't done much to reduce it either. Dodge might be a straight shooter or a clever actor in a plot to defraud the government and the railroad. Time would tell which.

TWENTY-EIGHT

All things considered, the one most pleased to see Chance and Dove move into the loft over Brady Cain's livery must have been Jon Westfield's old bay gelding, Ned. By about the second night of their watch, Victoria Westfield had figured out that Chance would make an evening round at the Rawlins House to see if Taggert had checked in. When he returned that evening, it just so happened she'd come over to Brady Cain's with an apple for Ned.

"Why, Lucky, wha t a pleasant surprise." Victoria beamed as Chance stepped down from the saddle.

"Evenin', Victoria, what brings you over here?"

"Why, Daddy's old horse Ned here, he surely does love an apple now and then. Speaking of apples, I've got a fresh baked apple pie over to the house. I can brew up a fresh pot of coffee if you'd like to come over for a piece?"

"That sounds right tempting, Victoria. Let me get Salute un-saddled and turned into his stall, and I'll be right with you."

"I'll just go on over and put the coffee on then. You come along as soon as you can."

She left trailing the light scent of lavender. Chance watched the night breeze ruffle her hair as she crossed the alley. He pulled the saddle off Salute and threw it over the saddle rack. He turned him into his stall next to Sage and pulled the hackamore over his ears. "Rest easy, big fella," he said, giving the big Morgan an affectionate pat.

She watched him cross the alley to the shadows of the porch that ran along the side of the Westfield residence. Victoria came through the lighted doorway carrying two plates. She went back inside and returned moments later with two steaming cups. They sat on the porch swing talking and eating. Dove couldn't hear what they were saying, though she might hear a laugh now and then. This sitting in the shadows and talking reminded her of the courting ritual of the buffalo robe. Her heart ached with a dull pain. What could she do to protect the gift of her spirit guide?

After that Ned came in for the treat of an apple most every evening. Victoria Westfield timed her visits to the stable to coincide with the time Chance would saddle Salute for his evening rounds or when he'd return. These chance encounters were about as transparent as they could be, but Dove didn't know what to do about them. They accomplished the fire-hair woman's purpose, for the meetings ended in quiet conversations or an invitation to stop by the Westfield residence after his rounds for lemonade or homemade cookies and milk. They spent these evening visits lingering on the porch, quietly talking and laughing, under the painful watch of unseen dark eyes in the shadows of the stable loft across the alley.

Chance gave no thought to the possibility that these visits were distressful to Dove. Victoria's attentions charmed him easily, and what man wouldn't enjoy pie or cookies or lemonade? He knew she had romantic interests on her mind, and he thought he might have some of the same feelings. The time he spent with Victoria let him get a feel for what it might be like to settle down, if that's what he decided to do once he took care of Taggert.

Watching the Westfield place was tediously boring. Chance and Dove divided the time watching the Stage & Rail office and residence around the clock. Chance didn't figure Taggert would try anything in broad daylight, but you could never be sure, so they kept a constant vigil. Things were pretty quiet on the west end of Sixteenth

Street at night. Most of the action happened further down the street around the cluster of saloons at the center of town, and even that quieted down for the most part by midnight.

The stifling confines of the white village wore on Dove. She longed for the freedom of open country, where she felt at one with the spirits of her people. There she found peace with herself and confidence in the gift of her spirit guide. Her spirits were lost to her in the white man's village. She felt like a stranger here, with no way to deal with the problem of the green-eyed fire-hair.

The woman had no decency in the eyes she made for Lah Kee. She spun a web of wiles Dove did not know how to match. She could only watch as Lah Kee hung in her web, drawn to her purpose without sensing the trap. Her heart ached with frustration. How could she save the gift of her spirit guide from the clutches of the woman who stalked him? She had no answer for this in her simple ways.

Victoria seemed to enjoy the situation. She could show Chance the comforts of home while his little savage stayed cooped up in a barn. She held the advantage of a perfect battleground for the heart of the marshal from Missouri, and she gave no quarter in pressing her advantage.

The tender tug of the two women wore on Chance. He had feelings for each, then both, and seemingly no way to sort out the one from the other. He wished Taggert would show up and put an end to the waiting. Then he could take Dove back to the North Platte Village and put some fresh air between himself and the crosscurrents of emotion pulling him this way and that.

Jon Westfield came into Brady Cain's stable bright and early one morning a few days after Chance and Dove had set up their watch in the loft. Chance came down from the loft to find Ned in a cross tie with Jon harnessing him for a wagon hitch.

"Mornin', Jon. Where you headed?"

"Mornin', Marshal. Joe Clark and his crew are about done out at the red rock cut. I'm takin' a few things they need to finish up out there. I wanna have a look at the job to make sure it's right before I send Dodge my bill."

"Mind if Dove and I tag along? Just to keep an eye on your back."

"I'd be much obliged for that, Lucky."

Dove's spirit lifted at the prospect. Going back to the land of her people would free her from the confines of the white man's village. They would get away from the fire-hair woman, and the gift of her spirit guide would return.

Chance and Dove saddled Salute and Sage while Westfield led Ned over to the shed and hitched him to the wagonload of supplies for the crew. When the wagon pulled out headed west, Chance and Dove trailed along behind.

Victoria stood on the porch watching them go. She worried about Daddy when he went out to the job sites. She felt better this time with Lucky looking out for him, even if he did take his little Indian with him. She refused to believe that anything the Indian might offer could stand in the way of her feelings for Chance, but Mourning Dove's continued presence gnawed at a shred of doubt in an otherwise perfectly delightful situation. She needed to do something about the Indian, but what? A small smile began to spread at the germ of an idea.

The sun rode high on a warm spring day. Westfield set a slow plodding pace west along the rail bed. The red rock cut would connect the rail bed to the westbound run beyond the cut. Soon that would join the Union and Central Pacific lines and bind the vast expanse of a young nation into one.

Chance and Dove trailed behind, maintaining visual contact with the wagon, alert to any sign of trouble. They rode gentle rolling plains carpeted in sun-soaked gray-green sage, dotted with colorful splashes of pale blue chicory, yellow mustard and clumps of green yucca tipped in pink burned to golden brown. The wagon set an easy pace, allowing them to take in the beauty of the day. They took care to keep a low profile to the horizon as they made their way among the hills and washes. They followed the general direction of the rail line across the vast basin bracketed to the north and east and west by cloud-capped peaks.

Chance knew Westfield would make an easy target out here by himself if Taggert were keeping an eye on his movements. Intent on looking out for Westfield, it never occurred to him that he and Dove might become the hunted.

Free of the stifling confines of the white man's village and the fire-hair woman hovering over Lah Kee, Dove felt the rush of freedom and the return of her spirits. Riding beside Chance, she felt restored in her ability to help him in ways that would be more important to him than the treats of the white woman's kitchen. The spirits of her people gave her strength. This she would use to free him from the web of the white woman's ways.

They made the red rock cut as the sun reddened the peaks in the west. Chance marveled at the sight. A solid wall of red rock towered one hundred feet in the air. Westfield said Dodge had decided to blast his way through it rather than add the miles of track required to go around it. He'd sent the mainline track-laying crews around the butte on their way to Utah. Freighters carried rails, ties and other supplies around the cut to supply the track-laying crews. That would all come to an end with the completion of the cut.

Stage & Rail had gotten the contract to open the cut and lay the roadbed that would join with the mainline beyond. They'd blasted the cut through the butte with dynamite. Slowly they'd opened the notch that would reduce the passage of the roadbed to a gentle rise. Clearing the stone debris from the cut had been back-breaking work. The one bright spot was the fact that the constant use of dynamite in the early stages of the project had kept the hostile Indians away. Roman Nose hadn't dared come raiding until the latter stages of the project as they worked on the roadbed.

Joe Clark and the crew welcomed the boss, though they were surprised to find him being trailed by the protective escort of a U.S. marshal. They were even more surprised and even a little suspect of an armed Indian woman making up part of his escort. These misgivings passed quickly into the anticipation of finishing the job and leaving the dangers of Indian country behind for a few days' rest. It made for a festive mood around their campsite that night.

Spotted Hawk watched the wagon arrive from the rocky face of the north butte. It would have made an easy target had he seen it in open country. The two riders trailing behind the wagon were even more interesting. The wagon delivered supplies to the iron horse white eyes, but more than that, it delivered Mourning Dove and the white eyes who had stolen his bride within reach of his rifle.

TWENTY-NINE

The next morning Westfield made a thorough inspection of the work at the cut. The boys had done a good job on the roadbed. The tracks climbed a gentle grade through the cut. They ran straight and true to the westbound roadbed beyond. The crew would use the occasion of Westfield's visit to lay the final section of track that would join the cut and the eastbound track to the westward run. Westfield supervised the laying of the last section of track. As the late afternoon sun descended toward evening, Joe Clark walked over to where Westfield stood with Chance and Dove.

"The boys would be right proud if you'd drive the last spike in the cut section, boss." He handed Westfield a hammer and spike.

Westfield took the hammer and spike and followed Clark up the track to the place where the crew was gathered. Westfield squinted, looking into the sun. The rails ran west straight and true all the way to Utah and the appointed joining of the lines. This spike didn't represent the historic joining of the lines. That would come later to the honor of other men, but this spike would make that spike possible. That accomplishment gave Westfield a real sense of satisfaction in having played a small part in an achievement of historic importance to the nation.

He placed the spike and tapped it into place with the hammer. He looked around at the men of his crew. They and others like them had paid the price of this important work. They had suffered the heat and cold, rain and snow, along with the ever-present dangers of Indian attack. Some of them had died in the effort. *This spike is for all of them*, he thought as he hefted the hammer. He bent to the driving of the spike and the applause of his men. The clangs of his hammer blows rang a triumphant call that reverberated through the walls of the cut to the horizons beyond.

Dove saw the steel iron horse trail stretch as far as the eye could see. It seemed to reach all the way to the place Brother Sun would sleep at the end of the day. The white man's sign lay like a scar on the lands of her people. It divided the land. The white men who would follow this trail would crush the old ways of her people. Her heart hurt with knowing this, but none could stop it. The people must find new strength to live with this change. She must find the strength and the wisdom to live with the new ways. She would take comfort from the gift of her spirit guide to lead her on the path of these ways. She would take comfort if she could keep her gift, her Lah Kee, safe from the web of the fire-hair woman.

Westfield passed another night with his crew while Chance and Dove forted up in the south butte with a good view of the camp. Joe Clark had his guards posted too, but Chance felt better looking out for himself. He brought their tin plates of biscuits and beans up from the crew camp. They ate quietly as they often did. Chance knew Dove took the driving of the spike for a powerful symbol of the coming of the iron horse. He could see it in her eyes as she watched Westfield drive the spike to the cheers of his men. He could feel her pain without knowing the full measure of her loss. It spoke of the connection between them. A connection he could not fully explain.

Night fell crystal clear, with a half moon lighting a star-studded sky. Silence settled all around them on a gentle breeze out of the north with a touch of chill. Dove knew they would return to the white man's village in the morning. It filled her with a dull resignation. She chased the vision of Victoria Westfield from her mind's eye and turned her attention to Chance watching the campsite below. She dreaded returning to the white man's village. She felt him slip away there in the web of the white woman's ways. She knew she must find a way to make a place for herself in that world if she wished to hold him, but how? The ways of the whites were strange to her. She could not match the fire-hair's ways. She could only try to hold him with the whole of her spirit. She pulled her blanket around her shoulders against the night chill and moved a little closer.

Chance wrapped an arm around her and pulled her head to his chest. He chided himself for leading her on that way, but she was cold and he knew her heart was heavy. He would wipe her pain away if he could. He would always hold dear the gentle good-ness of the woman who'd nursed him back to health. She'd left her people, her village and the warmth of her lodge, and for what? For him, and for that he must be fair and honest with her. She gave him warmth and comfort against more than the night chill, but what did that mean? It meant he needed to be honest with himself first, and that seemed the hardest part of all.

The sun came up over the red rock cut. Pink and orange fired the dawn of a new day. A cloudbank built in the west, heavy with the prospect of spring rain. Chance and Dove came down from the butte to collect Salute and Sage for the ride back to Cheyenne. They found Westfield hitching Ned to the wagon in preparation for the return trip.

"Mornin', Jon."

"Mornin', Lucky. Quiet night."

"Best kind. We'll be ready to head out when you are."

They had a little hardtack and coffee before Westfield climbed onto the wagon box. "Yee ha," he called, slapping old Ned into a jog with the reins tracking the rail bed back east. Chance and Dove gave him his lead before trailing out behind, keeping a sharp eye peeled for any sign of movement.

There wouldn't be any sign of movement either, at least not right away. Spotted Hawk and five of his Dog Soldier brothers hid in the rocks at the east end of the cut's north butte, watching them go. This day he would count coup on the white eyes. This day he would feed his bullets on the white man's blood. Mourning Dove would see him for a warrior. He would hang the white eyes' scalp on their lodge pole to remind his wife of how he had won her. This vision would carry him to battle. They mounted up and rode north by northeast, trailing Jon Westfield's escort and leaving almost no telltale sign of their presence.

Clouds built in as the day wore on. A cold wind came up out of the northwest ahead of a darkening bank of thunderheads. Chance checked the gathering storm clouds on the horizon with resignation. *Watching over Westfield is dull doin's in the best of circumstances. Cold and pretty soon wet aren't gonna do anything to improve the situation.*

The plodding cold and impending storm fit Dove's mood. Every step of this trail led her away from the lands of her people and back to the stifling confines of the white man's village. She'd spent the night in the crook of his arm, feeling warm and comforted there. Back in the loft the vision of fire hair loomed over her like the storm building at her back.

Spotted Hawk tracked his query east, north of the iron horse trail. At midday he determined how they would strike. He sent Young Bull and two others south across the iron horse trail behind the white eyes and Mourning Dove. They would trail them from the south and attack from their back while Spotted Hawk and the others struck from the north. The old man in the wagon would be too far in front to interfere and more likely to run than fight. They could easily run him down when they finished with the white eyes.

As the afternoon wore on, the wind intensified. It whipped the sea of sage and scrub prairie grass. Sage and Salute became restless and unsettled. Chance credited the disturbance to the storm building in. Dove wondered if the horses sensed something else, but she saw no sign other than the storm clouds and the distant flashes of lightning followed by rumbles of thunder.

Spotted Hawk pressed his band forward. Using a low ridgeline for cover, they passed the white eyes and Mourning Dove to the north. With the band in position to strike, he crawled to the crest of the ridge and waited. He watched the slow-moving wagon plod its way east along the rail bed. The white eyes and Talks with Buffalo's daughter were barely visible tailing behind. He saw no sign of Young Bull and the others, but he knew they were out there. Soon his prey would ride into his trap.

The wind kicked up harder in advance of the storm. Lightning flashed in the distance, followed seconds later by rumbles of thunder growing closer as they rolled across the basin. It'd be a cold wet ride into Cheyenne for sure. Chance wished Westfield would pick up the pace, but he showed no sign of hurry. Chance decided they should close up with him and push the pace a little. If Taggert hadn't shown by now, it seemed unlikely that he would.

"Let's catch up to Jon, Dove, and see if we can move us along a little faster ahead of the storm."

Chance had just squeezed up an easy lope to close the gap on the wagon, when war whoops broke over a rumble of thunder off to the left. Chance counted three by the muzzle flashes and rifle reports. The big App in the lead told him one of them might have a score to settle.

Chance picked out a stand of rocks on the south side of the tracks maybe a half a mile further east.

160

"Come on, Dove," he yelled, stretching Salute into his run. "Head for those rocks up yonder." He checked Salute and waved her on ahead of him. He drew his left-hand Colt and lay down on the neck of the big Morgan, looking back for the chance at a shot.

Their pursuers threw up rifle fire from the backs of their galloping horses. The shots went wild, though the whine of hot lead overhead never made for a comforting sound. Sage and Salute set a fast pace that did not allow their pursuers to gain on them. Chance figured to make it to the rocks and make a fight of it. That way Dove could keep going and get away.

The next challenge loomed dead ahead. How would Sage react to crossing the tracks? It didn't take long to answer that question. Dove angled south as they approached the rocks. Chance watched the little mustang gather herself as they came to the tracks. She took the ribbon of rail and ties with a graceful leap that never missed a stride. Dove held her seat with the skill of one born to the saddle. Salute followed her lead with a powerful jump. The rocks were won.

Dove shot past the rocks just as Chance had hoped she would. He pulled Salute up as he rounded the rocks. He spun out of the saddle and came up under cover with both guns in hand. He held his fire, letting his pursuers come into range. That's when the whooping and rifle fire started out of the south.

Dove heard the rifle fire coming from the south. She checked Sage and turned to see Young Bull lead his two brothers in a hard charge toward the rock formation where Lah Kee faced Spotted Hawk and the others. She guessed he meant for her to get away. With warriors attacking from both sides, they had him in bad trouble.

She wheeled Sage and raced back to the rocks. She leaped down from her pony and drew her pistol. She took cover at Chance's back, ready to fight.

Chance heard her come back. While he'd intended for her to get away, he was damn happy to have her at his back given the turn this fight had taken.

The storm hit in full force, pelting them with wind-whipped rain, punctuated by violent lightning strikes and thunder claps so powerful they rattled a man's innards.

Spotted Hawk and his warriors had charged up the roadbed just west of the rocks when the lightning bolt hit the tracks in front of them. A huge flash of white light blinded man and horse. The bang that followed might have been a dynamite blast. Blue light arced across the rails. It hissed as it steamed down the tracks faster than any runaway train.

The Dog Soldier's war ponies wanted no part of crossing those tracks. They broke into a rearing, bucking melee that took all the fight out of Spotted Hawk and his warriors. Chance got off a couple of shots, dropping one Dog Soldier with a lung shot that would finish him soon enough.

He heard Dove light up a couple of rounds at his back as Young Bull and the others came in with their charge. Chance took advantage of the confusion on his side of the rocks to turn next to Dove and get off a couple shots of his own as Young Bull and his warriors swept by, firing from beneath the heads of their galloping horses as they hung off to the side. Chance's first shot hit the second pony in the shoulder, sending the terrified animal leaping into the air and its rider flying into the sage. Young Bull wheeled his paint to pick up his fallen brother. He pulled him up on his horse and galloped south out of pistol range.

Chance spun back to the north, ready for more. Spotted Hawk had enough to convince him to regroup. He collected his spooked App and headed off to the north. It looked like they would get a break to wait out the storm, but they were still in a plenty tight spot.

"You shoulda kept goin', Dove. You could have got away, maybe gone for help."

She studied his profile with the rain pouring off his hat brim as he searched the gloom through the downpour for any sign of hostile movement. *Men, all war and no wisdom.* "Lah Kee no fight many Dog Soldiers alone."

She could have gotten away, but she'd come back. She'd saved his backside again. He was grateful for that. "You covered my back, Dove. I appreciate that. I just wish you'd have gotten away."

She said no more. They were in this together, as it should be.

THIRTY

As soon as the storm blew through, Young Bull and his two warriors crossed to the north side of the roadbed west of the rocks and joined up with Spotted Hawk. The doubled-up warrior took his fallen brother's pony, making them five riders.

Spotted Hawk crawled to the top of the ridge to consider his next move. The storm had saved them this time. His anger burned with frustration. His bullets could not kill this white man. He wondered if the white eyes possessed evil magic. It seemed so. Still, he had them in range of his rifle. They had nowhere to go without giving him a killing shot. He had his vision. Soon he would cut the white eyes' scalp from his head. Mourning Dove would regret her disrespect of a warrior honored by the blood of the white man. She would learn to respect the husband who took her. She would serve him as an obedient wife, if the beatings didn't kill her first. That would be for her choosing. From the ridge he could see his plan of attack.

Spotted Hawk rejoined his brothers. "Young Bull, lead attack on the white eyes. Spotted Hawk take She Bear there," he said, pointing east along the ridgeline. "Give us time to get behind the white eyes, then attack. We will ride down on them from behind."

Young Bull nodded. Spotted Hawk and She Bear started for their ponies.

Spotted Hawk swung up on his war pony. "Young Bull, Spotted Hawk wants Talks with Buffalo's daughter taken alive."

Young Bull nodded. Spotted Hawk wheeled away to the east at a lope with She Bear trailing behind.

Things were quiet once the storm had passed through. Too quiet, by Chance's reckoning. *They're out there, but where?* They'd have regrouped, most likely behind the ridgeline to the north. *They'll attack again, but probably give the ponies a wide birth of the tracks.* He and Dove didn't have many options. If they tried to make a run for it, they'd be easy targets in open country. If Jon Westfield had gotten away, maybe he'd come back with help. Then again, maybe there were more than six of them. The last remains of Jon's hair might already be decorating some Dog Soldier's war shirt. Not a comforting thought.

With the storm cleared away the sky brightened, but that only underscored another problem. Afternoon would pass into evening, and when darkness fell it would be real hard to keep track of that many hunters. The ridgeline to the north stood gray-green and quiet. They were sitting ducks with no place to run.

Joe Clark thought he might be in for a ribbing from Jack Stubbs and Iowa Barnes for having dragged them off on the boss's trail on account of thinking he could smell Indian trouble. It had started bothering him the moment the boss rolled out of camp. Try as he might, he couldn't shake the feeling. Finally he'd rounded up Jack and Iowa and started out after the boss. His suspicions were confirmed when he saw the thin cloud of dust moving south toward the rail bed.

When he heard the rattle of rifle fire in the distance right before the storm broke, he knew they were needed. The storm blew up such a fury they had to stop to wait it out. As soon as the storm passed, he got the boys up and moving cautiously, on the lookout for trouble.

Young Bull led his warriors west behind the ridgeline before turning south toward the iron horse trail. He would attack the rock formation from the west with Brother Sun slanting his afternoon rays at their back. They would stay far enough away from the iron horse trail to keep the skittish ponies under control. They lit it up from a quarter mile off, whooping and firing as they stormed out of the sun to attack Chance and Dove's position.

Chance held his fire, counting three attackers. That left two un-accounted for. "Keep an eye peeled behind us and over yonder," Chance cautioned Dove, indicating an approach from the east or the south. "There's two more of 'em out there somewhere. If I was Spotted Hawk, that's where they'd be comin' from."

Dove nodded. She turned her attention to the lookout as Chance opened fire on the attackers thundering by their position. The Dog Soldiers fired wildly from below the necks of their ponies, giving Chance precious little to shoot at. Bullets whined off the rocks, showering them with rock chips as the attackers raced past their position.

Young Bull led his warriors in a tight circle away to the north. They turned back to the west, out of pistol range, preparing for another pass in the attack. The country boy from Missouri took a lesson. He needed a rifle to handle situations like this. Wisdom that didn't help wasn't worth much.

Jon Westfield circled back in his wagon at the sound of the first firefight. The storm hit before he could deliver any help from the plodding wagon. Like everyone else, he took cover until the storm blew over.

Now, by the sound of it, the renegades had launched another attack on Chance and Dove. Westfield pushed his wagon back toward the sound of the gunfire, hoping to hit the attackers by surprise.

He pulled Ned up short when two Indians broke cover from behind the ridgeline to the north less than a hundred yards in front of his position. He grabbed the old single-shot Sharps rifle he carried in the wagon boot along with his Winchester. He raised the long rifle to his shoulder and dropped the muzzle on line. He fixed the second rider in his sights. He took an easy breath and let it out slowly with a gentle squeeze. The Sharps roared with a powerful kick that rocked the wagon box. The .50 caliber slug ripped She Bear between the shoulders, all but taking his head off.

Spotted Hawk glanced back at the rifle report in time to see the bloody mess that had been She Bear spill from the back of his pony. He bent over the big App's neck and continued his charge, riding down on Chance from behind. The old white eyes in the wagon couldn't keep up if he struck swiftly. He would be there for the taking when they finished Mourning Dove and her white eyes.

Young Bull and his Dog Soldiers rounded off their circle to the west, ready for another run on Chance and Dove. Young Bull expected to draw their fire away from the fatal blow Spotted Hawk would deliver from behind.

As it happened, the people swinging the blow from behind were Joe Clark, Jack Stubbs and Iowa Barnes. Old Joe used the setting sun too. He and his men rode down on Young Bull and his warriors from behind as they launched their charge on Chance and Dove's beleaguered position.

Clark and his men opened fire on the three attackers from behind. His first round dropped Crooked Stick just as Chance opened up from the rocks. Young Bull looked back when Crooked Stick fell to find himself caught in a crossfire. Filled with rage, he reacted instantly, breaking off the attack to the north.

Spotted Hawk galloped in from the east. He saw Crooked Stick fall to the white eyes attacking Young Bull from behind. When Mourning Dove's white eyes opened fire on Young Bull, Spotted Hawk had him in his sights. This time his bullet would feed on the white man's blood.

The booming report of Westfield's Sharps drew Dove's attention up the iron horse trail to the east. She saw Spotted Hawk riding down on them from behind.

"Lah Kee down!"

Spotted Hawk fired.

Chance ducked under the whining shot that glanced off the rocks where he'd stood an instant before. The ricochet showered him in rock splinters. Dove got off two quick shots as Spotted Hawk galloped by.

Spotted Hawk caught Young Bull's turn to the north over the muzzle flash of his failed shot. He wheeled his pony away from Dove's fire, following the remains of his band to the north and the safety of the ridgeline.

Joe Clark and his men rode up to the rocks as the smoke drifted away on the breeze.

"Afternoon, Marshal, glad to see you're all in one piece."

"Afternoon, Joe, you're not half as glad as we are to see you boys."

"Where's the boss?" As if to answer his own question, Joe looked up the line to the east. "Well, looky yonder, I guess that'd be the boss."

Jon Westfield pulled his wagon to a halt a few minutes later. "Sorry I couldn't get here sooner, Lucky. The storm sorta held me up. That might have been for the best, though, 'cause otherwise them two that come in behind you might a got me too."

"Two?" Chance asked.

"Yeah, the other one met his maker courtesy of Mr. Sharps here."

"Good to see you haven't lost your touch with that old girl, boss," Joe Clark offered with a good-natured grin.

"Well, we're much obliged to all of you for savin' our skins," Chance said. "We were supposed to be doin' that for you, Jon."

"Don't think nothin' of it." Joe Clark spoke for all of them. "Now I'm tellin' you, you'd best turn that wagon around and make tracks for Cheyenne before that buck has a chance to come back with more of his friends. You won't make it by dark, but you'll be close enough to be in familiar country before nightfall."

"Good advice, Joe," Jon Westfield approved. "You and the boys take care goin' back to the cut. We'll see you in Cheyenne in a few days once you've cleaned up. And Joe, one more thing. I'm pleased to see you ain't lost your touch either."

The two men exchanged a look of mutual respect. The kind born of the trust that comes with long friendships gone through good times and bad.

It has to be magic, evil magic. How else to explain it? At every turn the white eyes finds ways to escape Spotted Hawk's bullet. Frustration and anger boiled to blood feud. He would not rest until he killed this white man.

THIRTY-ONE

Chance kept them close to the wagon for the remainder of the ride back to Cheyenne. It had been quite a day. Joe Clark's instincts had probably saved them. Jon Westfield had displayed real grit, coming back to help out against the odds, and with enough skill to blunt the attack Spotted Hawk had mounted at their back. More than that though, he thought about Dove.

She'd come back when she could have run. She'd held their left and watched his back and never flinched when the lead started flying hot and heavy. A man had to respect that in a partner. She might be a woman, but she more than held her own. He didn't feel right about having her shot at, but she'd stood up to the test. Riding along in the moonlight, following the rail bed back to Cheyenne, he felt the need to tell her how much he appreciated what she'd done. He cocked his head and studied her silhouette under the brim of his hat.

"Thank you."

She turned her head toward him, showing the whites of those big dark eyes in the pale light of the moon.

"For comin' back and coverin' me the way you did. They'd have got me sure if you hadn't."

Dove gave a slight nod of acknowledgement and returned her profile to shadow. *Wisdom finds this man. Soon maybe the gift of the spirit finds him too.*

They rode into the yard between the Stage & Rail office and Brady Cain's livery just before midnight. Chance and Dove stepped down from their saddles and loosened the cinches. Jon Westfield backed the wagon into the company shed and unhitched old Ned. He led the horse across the yard, following Chance and Dove as they led Salute and Sage into the stable.

Victoria came running across the moonlit yard to greet her father. "Oh, Daddy, I've been so worried. You should have been back hours ago. What happened? Are you all right? Why are you so late?"

"There, there, little girl," he said, wrapping her up in a great bear hug. "We had a little Indian trouble. Nothin' serious. Your Marshal Chance done a real good job of takin' care of me."

"More like the other way around, Victoria," Chance offered, pausing with Salute at the stable door. "Your daddy covered Dove and me when we got crossed with some of Roman Nose's renegades."

"Well, I'm truly relieved you're both back safe and sound," she said, flashing a smile that brightened the stable yard more than the moon.

This last Dove missed, climbing the ladder to the loft after consigning Sage to her stall.

Chance spotted it the next day as he passed the window of Gohram's Emporium. The blue and white gingham shirt would be perfect for Dove and a fine replacement for the bloodstained old shirt of his she'd been wearing. He knew she'd be surprised and hoped she'd like the color as he hurried back to the loft with the parcel tucked under his arm.

Dove accepted the gift of the shirt all right, and it looked real pretty on her too. But she did a real good job of keeping whatever excitement she might have had for the gift to herself. Chance made it one of the mysteries about women that men would never understand.

Dove thought the shirt looked pretty enough, but it looked like Victoria Westfield. A Cheyenne woman could never be like the fire-hair white woman. Could he not see this? Sadly, the differences between her and the fire-hair kept finding ways to confront her.

Jake Gelb sat in his plush office as the bustle of the financial district quieted at day's end. He watched the late afternoon sun paint Wall Street in long blue shadows. He poured himself a cognac and lit a favored Cuban cigar as he reflected on Diamond Jim Trask's proposal. He liked the idea of a play in gold, particularly if they could hedge their positions against the risk of Treasury intervention.

He stroked his waxed moustache. It would take some time to arrange the letters of credit they would need to finance the contracts, given the serpentine web that separated him from the operational realities of his businesses, but no matter. He would put the time to good use by sending Burnswick to California to buy contracts on future gold production.

Burnswick could stop in Cheyenne on his way to shore up Taggert's ineffective effort to close the Stage & Rail acquisition. That deal appeared to be unraveling at every turn. Burnswick could certainly help the situation. He'd turn Burnswick's New York duties over to young Slane.

Gelb liked Davis Slane. He might be a junior man in the firm, but the bright young Harvard-educated lawyer had already demonstrated the kind of blind ambition and ruthless greed Gelb respected. Slane had come up with the idea of buying future gold production directly from the mines. It would build their initial positions at fifty cents on the dollar and tighten the gold supply before trading operations even got underway. Brilliant, really, the kind of money-making genius Gelb admired above all.

Burnswick's muffled knock at the office door announced his arrival.

"Come in," Gelb called over his shoulder without bothering to rise.

Burnswick crossed the plush office carpet and stood in the shadows beside Gelb's desk. "I've heard from one of our Washington friends. It appears President Grant has ordered a Treasury audit of the Union Pacific project and a Justice Department investigation. Our friend doesn't understand what all that might mean, but he doesn't much like the sound of it either."

"No, I'm sure he doesn't." Gelb blew a cloud of blue smoke and examined the white ash beyond the glowing tip of his cigar. "All it really means is that some of the frock-coated sons of bitches we've been paying so handsomely are going to have to earn their money now."

"I'm afraid the news out of Cheyenne isn't good either, Jake."

"It never is these days." Gelb scowled.

"Taggert reports that the Indian raid on the Stage & Rail crew did more damage to Roman Nose and his band than it did to Westfield's crew. They were waiting for the raid, probably tipped off by the U.S. marshal Taggert's got on his trail."

"U.S. marshal? That would be the Justice Department end of our President's little investigation. It seems our Mr. Taggert has attracted a rather high profile in law enforcement circles."

"How quaint, first the administration plays paymaster to the Union Pacific and now they're overseeing railroad construction. Who the hell's running the country? Doesn't the President have anything better to do than worry about railroad problems? And of course, those problems would be us."

"So what do we do now, Jake?"

"I need you to go to San Francisco to represent the company in the matter of purchasing gold production later this summer. I think you should leave now. Take that lovely little railroad we're building. I want you to stop in Cheyenne and personally deliver Mr. Taggert's next set of instructions."

"And what are those instructions?"

"It seems to me that it would be easier to deal with Mr. Westfield's estate than with the old man himself. Don't you agree, Mr. Burnswick?"

"Got it, boss."

"Oh, and while he's at it, you might suggest to our friend Mr. Taggert that he finish the job on that marshal. They can't connect Taggert to us in any way, but I do so despise loose ends. Stay in Cheyenne to make sure that Taggert carries out his orders successfully this time. The railroad should be ready to take you the rest of the way to San Francisco by the time he's finished."

Burnswick nodded. "Now tell me about these gold contracts."

THIRTY-TWO

Grant sat at his desk in the Oval Office wreathed in cigar smoke. The halo of a single kerosene lamp surrounded him in an island of light amid the gathering gloom of evening. He pored over a staff brief describing legislative options for reforming Indian policy and, ultimately, according them the protections of citi-zenship. It promised a politically unpopular fight, but a noble cause worthy of the undertaking.

Past and present Indian policy amounted to a travesty. One broken treaty followed another. The discovery of gold in Colorado had brought a rush of gold seekers and opportunists to Indian lands, forcing the tribes to move north and west.

The railroad, for all its importance to the nation, cut its path through Indian lands. The Indian lived off his hunting grounds and the great buffalo herds that roamed there. The herds competed for grazing land. They stood as a barrier to the railroad and continued westward expansion. The herds were thinned in the name of progress. The Indians' ability to feed and clothe themselves was disappearing with the herds.

Everywhere the pressures of white westward expansion encroached on Indian lands. The miners and settlers relied on the Army to drive the Indians out of the way. No wonder they fought. Those that went to the reservations suffered from the abuses of the reservation system.

One injustice piled upon another until the very foundations of the plains Indians' way of life were threatened. Seated in the Oval

Office in the shadow of the Lincoln presidency and all that had been done to right the wrongs of slavery, Grant felt he could do no less than right the wrongs done the Indian. He would make it a defining goal of his presidency.

A soft knock at the door broke his concentration. "Come in," Grant summoned absently, absorbed in thought as he studied the report.

"Mr. President, a telegram just arrived from Colonel Dodge," Horace Porter said, handing him the yellow sheet of transcribed telegraphy. "I thought you would want to see it right away, sir."

"Thank you, Horace. What are you still doing here? Time for you to be home having dinner with the misses."

"I thought you might need me, sir."

"Nothing further tonight, Horace. You go along home. I'll be heading up to the residence to have dinner with Mrs. Grant in just a few minutes."

Horace let himself out as Grant turned to the telegram.

Promontory Point, Utah
May 10, 1869

Dear Mr. President,

Today the Union Pacific and Central Pacific railroads joined their tracks, completing this historic venture. Our nation stands united by a transcontinental railroad. May God bless America!

Respectfully,
G. Dodge, Col.

Grant sat back in his chair and took a long, thoughtful draw on his cigar. Historic news deserved a drink. He poured himself a stiff bourbon at the sideboard and opened the doors to the gardens. The soft warm sounds of the spring evening filled the dark corners of the office around its halo of lamplight. He sat on the comfortable settee at the side of the office and loosened his tie.

It had taken nearly six years to complete, and at a dear price when measured in the human terms of lives lost and national resources expended, but the force of will and indomitable spirit that made America great had prevailed in the end. By any measure Grant counted, history would record it a worthy investment. While the nation still struggled with the reconstruction of the south and recovery from the wounds of rebellion, it would now be bound together by a union of commerce never to be shaken again.

Each and every great achievement of this nation, he reflected, going back to its founding, had been realized in sweat and blood. Courage and sacrifice defined the character of the people building a great nation of these United States. This transcontinental railroad would be recorded as another such achievement. For this sense of history, he felt profoundly privileged to serve this great nation as her president. Raising his glass in salute, he tossed off the drink in his own private toast. *May God bless America indeed!*

Taggert rode into Cheyenne Sunday afternoon and checked into the Rawlins House to wait for the Betchers. It felt good to be back in the familiar surroundings of the Rawlins after the limited comforts he'd found hiding out in Central City. He threw his saddlebags in his room and headed down to the hotel saloon. He found his favorite corner table and let Smitty pour him three fingers of the cut above bourbon he favored. He'd just finished his first drink when White's telegram arrived with instructions for him to meet Burnswick at the noon train on Monday. *Burnswick*, he thought. *Haven't seen him in more than two years. Wonder what brings him all the way out here?* Given all the trouble with the Westfield deal, it couldn't amount to no good.

Victoria's invitation to Sunday dinner came as a surprise when it included Dove. It struck Chance as a neighborly thing to do, considering the two women had made plain that neither one of them appreciated the other's interest in him. So once again, just to keep things even, he never saw it coming.

Cold discomfort hit Dove like a blast of icy winter wind from the moment they arrived. She had no experience with the furnishings of a white man's lodge. Chance and Jon Westfield had a drink before dinner in the small sitting room. Dove opted to kneel on the floor, sitting on her heels. The meal came next, with the stiff straight-backed chair that hurt to sit on. She'd worn the blue gingham shirt to please Lah Kee, only to find Victoria wearing gingham too in a very pretty white way. They were different. They could not possibly be more so. Wearing the same fabric only made the differences that much more obvious. The gift of her spirit guide could not help but notice.

Victoria served the meal at a table set with an array of eating utensils bewildering to one accustomed to eating with a bowl, a horn spoon, or most often, nothing more than her hands. Dove watched Chance eat and took her leads on using the utensils from him. The dull knife they gave her would not cut the chicken, and the new peas would not stay on her fork. She knew too late that she'd played into Victoria's trap the moment she drew her sheath knife in place of the pointless dull table silver.

She could not taste the food. It gathered in a hard ball in the knot of her stomach. She did not understand the use of napkins and could not comprehend the delicate facility with which Victoria negotiated the serving and eating of the meal. By the time the meal ended with the pie made of apples, Dove could scarcely conceal her embarrassment and hurt in the pride of her people. Her simple ways were lost in the cultivated manners affected by the white woman. Lah Kee seemed not to notice, but how could he not? The fire-hair woman made her way in his world, and she most surely did not. It seemed as though the pain of this meal would never end, until at last Lah Kee dabbed his chin with his napkin.

"That was a fine meal, Victoria. Your chicken is fit to write home for."

"Why, thank you, Lucky. What a nice thing to say," Victoria said, blushing with the compliment. She gave the downcast Dove a sidelong glance, privately congratulating herself on her victory. It had been a perfect plan. The little savage had stumbled into her trap at every level. There could be no doubt that Lucky would see her for all her shortcomings after this.

"If you'll excuse me, I need to make my rounds over to the Rawlins House," Chance said, pushing back his chair.

"Do come back for another piece of pie when you finish, Lucky." This invitation made no mention of Dove.

Dove pushed back her chair with a mumbled "Thank you" and followed Chance to the door. She made a hasty escape across the alley and scrambled up the ladder to the privacy of the loft. Her heart ached with humiliation and hurt.

THIRTY-THREE

Chance looped Salute's rein over the hitch rail in front of the Rawlins House and climbed the silvered step to the boardwalk. Kerosene lamps gave the deserted lobby a soft glow in the gathering gloom of early evening. The muted hum of quiet conversation spilled out of the saloon through the swinging door. Chance crossed the lobby to the registration desk.

"Evenin', Mr. Bickford. Any new arrivals?"

The mousy, balding desk clerk nodded. He'd been expecting the marshal's nightly rounds, and he didn't appreciate the position it put him in. The marshal had come by looking for Mr. Taggert every evening for a couple of weeks now. Bickford didn't know why and didn't care to. Mr. Taggert was a regular guest. He minded his own business, even though by the look of him, Bickford suspected that some of his business might be carried out with a gun. He had no interest in getting in the middle of whatever might transpire between Mr. Taggert and a U.S. marshal. No, he'd just do his job and stay out of the way. He spun the register around and pointed to the entry for room 210. He didn't say anything about the two hard cases who'd come to see Taggert earlier in the evening.

Chance read the entry the clerk indicated and nodded his thanks. Finally he'd caught up with the man. As he strolled across the lobby to the stairway, he wondered if he should take time to call out Sheriff Teet for backup. He'd already started up the stairs by the time he dismissed the thought.

He quietly made his way to the second floor. Chance could feel it. Taggert would crack the Union Pacific case wide open. He would give up the conspirators responsible for the railroad's troubles. The general would have the justice he wanted, and Chance could finally figure out the future he wanted. It would be over before long.

Chance found room 210 halfway down the hall from the second floor landing. He flattened against the wall next to the doorframe and drew a Colt. He gave the door a sharp rap. In seconds he heard movement on the other side of the door as Taggert moved to answer it.

"Who is it?" a muffled voice called from the other side of the door.

"Bickford, Mr. Taggert. I got a telegram for you." Chance heard scuffled movement in the room. The door clicked opened and Chance pushed through, driving Taggert back at the point of his gun. Taggert raised his hands and backed away from the door toward the window at the far side of the small room.

"Who are you?" Taggert demanded in mock surprise. "What's the meaning of this?"

"J.R. Chance, U.S. Marshal. I'd like to talk to you about the Drainsville train robbery, among other things."

"Well, you've come to the right place." Rank Betcher pressed the muzzle of a six gun to the back of Chance's head from behind the door. "Now drop the gun."

Chance let his pistol fall to the floor, flooded with anger at his own stupidity for having walked into a trap without backup. It was a stupid mistake and likely a costly one. That thought went black under the butt of Betcher's big Colt as the gunman turned his lights out.

"Get his guns and tie him up," Taggert ordered.

Matt Betcher took Chance's rig with an admiring look at the tooled leather and the easy feel of the modified rim fire pieces. He tied Chance's hands behind his back as ordered and then strapped on the pistol belt, figuring Chance would have no further need of it.

"The marshal is probably riding a big sorrel you'll find hitched out in front, Matt. Fetch the marshal's horse around back of the hotel while Rank and I bring him down the back stairs. Then you boys take him out to the old line shack northeast of town and take proper care of him. I'll join you there tomorrow after I meet my company man at the train station. My guess is we'll be takin' care of Westfield after that, with some bonus money in it for the work."

At the front desk Bickford mopped his brow with a thin handkerchief. He was sweating heavily despite the cool temperature of the early evening. He half expected to hear the second floor erupt in gunfire at any moment, but it didn't. Instead the young tough who'd come to see Mr. Taggert earlier in the evening came down the stairs and went out to the street.

Bickford paused, wondering if he had done the right thing. Judging by the distinctive natural wood handles of the pistols the young shooter wore, he guessed they might be the marshal's double rig. He watched through a part in the curtains as the hard case took the marshal's horse from the hitch rail and led it down the alley t oward the back of the hotel. He wondered if he should go for Sheriff Teet. He wondered, but he didn't move.

Mourning Dove sat in the loft feeling more alone and out of place in the white world of Victoria Westfield than she had ever felt before. Sister Eagle may have given her Lah Kee, but the ways of the whites were not the ways of the spirits or her people. The spirits were lost to her here, and she feared the gift of her spirit guide might be lost with them. Her heart ached at the thought of losing him, yet she could only wonder at the last if the differences between their peoples were too great to bring them together. Perhaps the spirits were telling her to give him up to a life with his own people. Perhaps they were telling her to return to hers.

Suddenly these hapless thoughts were interrupted by a soft scratching sound coming from a dark corner of the loft. She became aware of a small presence and listened intently to find the source of the sound.

Brother Rat stuck his head out of the shadows into the last beam of setting sunlight filtering through a chink in the wooden slates of the stable loft. Straw dust haloed his dark fur fired orange in the bright shaft of light. Brother Rat's eyes glittered as he chattered animatedly. He exposed himself in an unusual display he would never risk if Sister Cat were about. Dove felt a strong sense of alarm.

The world turned upside down. A sharp pain sliced through Chance's head from behind his right ear. They'd bent him over his saddle and tied him hand and foot. One of the two dark riders ahead had Salute on a lead rope as they headed out of town. Chance had a hunch they might be the men who had helped Taggert with the Drainsville train robbery, but he couldn't make out much from where he hung over the saddle. *Hell of a way to ride,* he thought as his gut turned. He lost the best Sunday dinner he'd had in a long time before they were even out of town. He didn't know where they were going, but he guessed they planned a short ride for him. He worked the ropes binding his wrists. His best chance would be to surprise them if he could get loose. The prospects of that didn't feel too good. The ropes cut his wrists, rubbing them raw in short order.

His captors drew rein in what looked like the middle of nowhere. He could make out the silhouette of an old line shack. His captors dismounted. Chance figured he didn't have much time left.

They untied his feet and pulled him off Salute. Chance wobbled in a bandy-legged stagger that forced them to half carry him into the shack. He wanted them to think he still suffered the effects of the blow to his head even though his fogged mind had cleared around the ache in his head.

Creaking porch boards and a musty smell told him the old shack must be abandoned. The dilapidated log structure had once sheltered track laying crews from the foul winter weather in the passes. With the passing of the line it served no useful purpose to anyone, unless someone happened to need a quiet place to dispose of something or someone.

Matt Betcher struck a match and found an old coal oil lamp with a little light left in it. Rank dumped Chance into a dusty wooden chair against the far wall of the shack. Chance lolled his head to one side, making a quick sweep of the room looking for anything that might become a weapon or offer some way of escape. The shack offered little beyond a rusty potbelly stove, a table, a bed frame and a couple of broken chairs. One of those chairs might make the best weapon if he could get his hands loose, and that effort showed only the barest sign of progress.

Matt Betcher pulled one of Chance's Colts with the dull-witted half smile of a killer who enjoyed his work.

"Not much call to drag this out, is there, Rank?"

"Not as far as I can see," the older brother said with disinterest.

Matt spun the cylinder of the Colt, checking the loads, as Chance quietly worked the ropes behind his back with the intensity of a man facing his last. The rope cut. He could feel warm blood slick his wrists.

"Won't do no good, Marshal," the young killer drawled, lifting the pistol and drawing a bead on Chance's forehead. "Tied them knots myself. They're real good 'n tight." He drew the single action hammer back with its distinctive click as a round rolled into place and locked.

"Drop gun." The order came with a fine edge of steel determination running through the quiet tone.

Matt Betcher paused. He raised the pistol in mock surrender and turned toward the door behind him with a crooked grin on his face.

Dove hid in the shadow of the doorway with her pistol pointed straight at the young killer's head.

"Now put that thing down, little lady, afore someone gets hurt," Betcher drawled as if waiting for her to give up at the sound of his voice. When she didn't, he dropped his pistol onto a firing line.

Dove lit the doorway with muzzle flashes twice as the little Colt spit lead. Matt Betcher's eyes glazed in disbelief as if fixed on the holes that opened above the bridge of his nose and over his left eye. The back of his head blew into his hat. The young gunslinger was dead before his body hit the floor.

Chance came free of his bonds in the commotion just as Rank Betcher reached for his draw. He came up out of the chair and caught the older Betcher with a kick that dislocated the elbow of his gun arm with a sharp crack. The big .44 cleared leather and clattered harmlessly to the floor.

Betcher spun around with a vicious cut from a boot knife that appeared out of nowhere in his left hand. Chance sidestepped the cut and delivered another booted kick to the side of Rank's knee. He dropped like a sack of flour, unable to support himself on the ruined limb.

Betcher rolled over in pain, but when he came up again he held a pepper box derringer that also came out of nowhere. The little pistol never came into play. Dove stepped through the door and cut loose a third shot with a flash that blew through Betcher's temple and dropped him dead.

They stood there looking at each other through a blue haze of gun smoke hanging in the small shack by the light of the oil lamp. Chance couldn't help thinking, *Her shootin's come a long way from a couple a prickly pear ears.* He thanked his stars for that for the second time in just a few days.

"I owe you my life again, Mourning Dove. If you hadn't come along when you did, I reckon I'd be a goner by now."

Dove lowered her eyes, mixing his gratitude and her relief with the leftover pain of the Sunday dinner.

"How'd you know where to find me?"

"Brother Rat tell Mourning Dove bad man make trouble. Mourning Dove see bad men ride out of town with Lah Kee. Mourning Dove follow here."

"Brother Rat, you say? I'm not sure how to take that, but I reckon I owe you both a debt of thanks," Chance said, bending to retrieve his gun belt from Matt Betcher's body.

Thanks. She had plenty of that. She wanted more. Could he not see? He could not. *His white eyes remain blind to the gift of the spirit. He has eyes only for the fire-hair. Women are for making pies with apples, not shooting bad men.*

"You're takin' to marshalin' so good I might have to deputize you," Chance said with a twinkle in his eye as he wiped the blood off his wrists.

"What is this 'dep-u-tize'?"

"Raise your right hand and repeat after me," Chance said, holstering her Colt and raising her hand for her.

"Do you solemnly swear to uphold the law to the best of your ability so help you God? Say 'I do.'"

"I do."

"There. That's all there is to it. Now you're a properly sworn deputy marshal," Chance said, wrapping an arm around her in an appreciative hug.

The hug felt better than the deputizing, Dove thought.

Victoria Westfield wouldn't be shootin' my way out of any tight scrapes, Chance thought, but then he guessed there wouldn't be many tight scrapes in the construction business.

Dove helped Chance tie the Betchers' bodies over their horses. When the bodies were secure, they mounted up and rode back to Cheyenne. They dropped the bodies off at Ned Martin's blacksmith shop. Ned would take care of the undertaking and see that the bodies found a proper resting place on the hill behind the white church in the morning.

THIRTY-FOUR

Cheyenne Sheriff Jess Teet had just finished his evening rounds when Chance and Dove rode up to the jail. A tall, wiry reed of a man, Teet's once bushy brown moustaches were shot through with gray. He looked a little gawky and scarecrow-like, except for the clear blue eyes that belied the weatherbeaten features surrounding them. Those eyes looked like they could see right through a man. What the sheriff lacked in physical presence he more than made up for with the quiet air of a competent man you'd want at your back in a tight spot. Instead of taking a load off his feet at this hour and getting some sleep after a long day, Teet would get a visit from a U.S. marshal.

"Evenin', Sheriff."

"Marshal. What brings you by this late?"

"Had a little run-in with a man I'm after earlier this evenin'. A couple of hard cases who work for him knocked me out and carted me off to that line shack northeast of town. They'd have done me in if Dove here hadn't followed me."

"Where are they now?"

"Ned Martin's got the bodies. Their boss is over at the Rawlins House. I'd be much obliged for your help in bringing him in. I'd have saved myself a lot of trouble tonight if I'd come for your help earlier."

"Well, Marshal, I expect we ought to head down there and round him up then," Teet drawled. He took a sawed-off shotgun down from the rack behind his rolltop desk. He cracked it open

188

and gave it a double load from a box of shells in the desk drawer. He stuffed four more shells in his shirt pocket and adjusted the .44 on his hip. Teet led them out of the office and they all trooped down the street to the Rawlins House.

Bickford dozed behind the registration desk at the end of his day. He woke with a start when the sheriff and the marshal came in armed to the teeth, followed by an Indian squaw who also packed a gun. Bickford masked his surprise at seeing the marshal. He didn't let on that he might have known he was in trouble earlier that evening. This looked like the trouble he'd been fearful of for sure.

"Bickford, I need the key to room 210," Teet demanded.

Bickford handed the pass key over without question, deciding he'd best take cover from the showdown he feared would end in gunplay.

Chance and the sheriff headed for the stairs. They climbed to the second floor and made their way quietly down the hall to the door to room 210. Dove dropped into a back-up position on the landing covering the hall. Chance and the sheriff took positions on either side of the door. Chance drew his right-hand Colt and nodded to the sheriff, who knocked on the door with his shotgun barrel from the left of the doorframe.

No answer.

The sheriff knocked again, louder this time. "Open up, Taggert, it's the law," Teet boomed.

Room 210 remained silent.

Teet fitted the key to the lock, taking care to stay outside the doorframe. He exchanged glances with Chance before turning the key, confirming that he would go in high with the scattergun while Chance went in low with his pistol.

He threw the door open on a darkened room covered by the lawmen's collective firepower. The room was empty. The sheriff scratched a match on his jeans and lit the coal oil lamp on the bedside table. The bed was rumpled, like someone had left in a hurry.

The smell of cigarette smoke hung in the air, and the stubbed-out butt in the tin cup on the bedside table was still warm.

Chance retrieved his hat from the corner where someone had kicked it during his earlier visit. He left the sheriff in the room and ran down the hall to the back stairs with Dove on his heels. They reached the doorway that opened onto the second floor landing. The back stairs descended to a deserted stable yard dimly lit by a sliver of moon.

Chance and Dove quietly descended the stairs to the yard fronting the stable. They crossed the yard, guns drawn, moving cautiously toward the inky blackness beyond the open stable doors. As they approached the stable doors, the darkness inside exploded in two rapid-fire muzzle flashes.

Chance and Dove dived left and right. They rolled up against the sides of the barn as Taggert's big black gelding shot through the doors and wheeled hard left into the alley. Taggert blasted two more pistol shots along his line of escape.

Chance jumped to his feet and ran down the alley. He got off a quick shot at the back of the horse and rider pounding away, eating up ground as they headed north out of town. They'd left the horses tied out front of the sheriff's office. That fact spotted Taggert a big lead. Trying to track him at night would be no small chore, but they had to give it a shot.

"C'mon, Dove, let's git after him," Chance shouted, running up the alley toward Sixteenth Street. He whistled up Salute, who pricked up his ears and pulled away from the hitch rail. The big sorrel came galloping up Sixteenth Street with Sage hot on his heels.

Chance caught Salute's saddle horn as the big Morgan wheeled around the corner of the hotel and headed up the alley toward the stable. He vaulted into the saddle in a fluid Pony Express mount as they flashed through the yard past the stable and out into the night.

Sage checked one stride for Dove to make her vault to the saddle, and they were off at a dead run, stretched out after the plume of Salute's tail disappearing into the night.

Taggert had disappeared into the cover of darkness by the time Chance broke into the open behind the stable. He had a pretty good head start. Chance checked Salute. Speed wouldn't help if it were going in the wrong direction. They needed to find Taggert's trail and use the moon to track him as best they could.

Dove drew up beside him. She seemed to sense his mind, and in a matter of seconds she had the sign. "This way," she said, sliding off to the northwest at a lope.

Chance wasn't sure what she'd seen, but she seemed very sure she had the right trail.

Taggert hightailed it out of town heading northwest to throw off the sense he was headed for Indian country. He used the terrain, dodging and weaving around low hills and washes. He used a stand of trees here and a rock formation there to complicate his trail. These tactics would slow any pursuit that might follow. Tracking him at night would not be easy. He had the advantage of deception, so he could set a pace his pursuers could not match without risking losing his trail. With all that in his favor, he still needed to take care of his horse. When he was sure he'd put enough twists and turns in his trail to slow down anyone trying to follow him, he slowed the big black to a lope he could hold over a longer distance.

Dove managed to cling to Taggert's trail over the next two hours. Taggert used every trick of the terrain to cover his trail. At times they were forced to circle one sign to find the next. Chance knew their agonizingly slow pace had them falling farther and farther behind. Taggert might hole up somewhere, allowing them to catch up with him, but Chance doubted it.

Bitter frustration ate at him. He'd made a foolish mistake and almost paid for it with his life. On top of that, the man had somehow managed to slip through his fingers again. If anything happened to Jon Westfield after this bungled opportunity, he'd never forgive himself.

Taggert drew rein on the banks of a fast-flowing stream spilling out of the northeast. A low bank of clouds rolled in from the west, drawing a dark blanket over the little moonlight that remained. He let the black drink as he surveyed the sky. The cloud cover would make it near impossible to track him. The stream gave him the perfect line of escape. Streams didn't leave any trail at all.

Taggert let the black drink his fill before turning him into the stream, angling upstream to the northeast at a trot. A mile upstream he turned back to the south, doubling back toward Cheyenne. Satisfied that he'd cleared his trail, he turned southeast and headed for the abandoned line shack.

Good thing he'd seen the marshal and the Indian ride up to the sheriff's office, or he'd be in jail by now. How could the Betchers have bungled such a simple job? He'd damn well give 'em what for as soon as he caught up with 'em.

Dove hung onto the trail until the cloudbank left them without light. Chance couldn't figure how she'd been able to stay on it as long as she had. If they camped here to wait for first light, Taggert would be long gone on a trail they might yet lose. If he doubled back to Cheyenne, he could get to Jon Westfield while they were out here chasing his shadow.

"C'mon, Dove. Time we get back to Cheyenne. We best make sure Taggert don't double back to do Jon any harm."

THIRTY-FIVE

Taggert drew up on the trail just below the hill where the dark line shack perched. He saw no sign of the Betchers or their horses. It looked like the marshal had done more than simply give them the slip. If he and the Indian had turned the tables on the brothers, they'd have brought them in to the sheriff. The fact that they had come in alone suggested the Betchers might have bigger problems than the cussin' he had planned for them.

Taggert drew his Colt and reloaded the four spent chambers before easing the big gelding up to the shack. The shack was eerily quiet. The soft groan of saddle leather sounded like a clap of thunder as he stepped down at the rail. He could see the sign of an unshod Indian pony among the tracks in the soft dirt at the rail. His boots hit the step up to the front of the shack loud enough to wake the dead.

Inside the shack he struck a match and lit the coal lamp. Two large, fresh bloodstains on the plank floor told the story. The bodies that had made them had been dragged out the door. He had all he needed to frame the picture. The Indian with the marshal at the sheriff's office must have followed the brothers out here, and by the look of it neither one of them would be taking any abuse from him over the bungled job. They'd both already paid for their carelessness.

Victoria Westfield lay wide awake in her bed. Chance hadn't come back for his pie and coffee. She worried that perhaps she'd overstepped herself in exposing the Indian for her shortcomings in polite society. No, she steeled herself with her own resolve. Lucky needed to see his little Indian for what she was. She would never fit in polite society. She needed to make that perfectly plain for him. He'd never appreciate the kind of life he could have with a genteel woman like her until he understood. The little savage could never manage life back east the way Victoria could, let alone survive in the society surrounding presidential service. *The man simply must be made to understand.*

The clatter of horses riding up to the livery next door roused her near midnight. She sat up in bed and looked out the window. She could see Chance and Dove pull up across the alley. She slipped out of bed and made her way quietly out to the porch, taking care not to wake her father.

The clouds had cleared and moonlight washed over her as she stood on the porch watching them step down from their horses. She knew she must make a scandalous display standing on the moonlit porch in her flannel nightdress. Scandalous perhaps, but carefully calculated scandal for the effect she expected to have on one U.S. marshal from Missouri.

Chance saw her silhouetted in the pale moonlight as he stepped down from Salute. He remembered the offer of pie and coffee that had gone unaccepted in all the commotion of the evening. Without thinking he handed Salute's lead to Dove and walked across the alley. Victoria crossed the yard to meet him at the gate.

Dove watched him go for a bitter moment before she led the horses into the stable.

"Lucky, I worried sick when you didn't come back," Victoria said in her best voice of concern for his safe return.

She looked beautiful. Her eyes were dark liquid in the low light of the moon. Soft shadows touched the bow of her lips, while the night breeze tossed the mass of her auburn curls let down for the night. Chilled berry points stood out against the bodice of her light flannel shift. The vision hit Chance hard in his jeans.

"Sorry I didn't make it back, Victoria," he breathed around a catch in his throat. "We had a little run in with Taggert tonight."

"Oh, Lucky, are you all right? Did you get him?"

"I'm fine, though sorry to say, he got away again."

"Shall we never be done with the man? First I couldn't sleep for worrying over you, and now I shall worry over Daddy."

"Now don't fret yourself none. Dove and I will keep a real close watch over the place, so there's nothin' for you to be afraid of."

"I do feel better with you about," she said, lowering her eyelids and looking vulnerable as a newborn kitten. "But wouldn't you be more comfortable here in the house? I know I'd feel safer if you were inside."

The young marshal from Missouri completely missed the underlying invitation.

"Oh no, Victoria, we got a real good lookout from the loft over there. Taggert won't be no trouble to you tonight. Now you best get back inside before you catch your death." *Or I ketch mine from the look your chill's a givin' me.* When she looked up and nodded, he could feel the expectant hesitation in the upturned bow of her lips. He could almost taste the sweetness he knew he would find there for the taking. One member of this little party made a powerful vote for taking that kiss, though he knew that wouldn't settle his conflictions. He tipped his hat. "Good night, Victoria."

By the time he got to the stable Salute and Sage were unsaddled and turned into stalls. When he scrambled up the ladder to the loft, he found Dove rolled up in her blanket already asleep, or so it appeared. Chance couldn't tell for sure. Her face was turned into the shadows with no possibility of his noticing the crystal tear that slid slowly down her cheek. It looked like he'd be taking first watch.

As he settled himself in the shadows of the loft door, he noticed a lamp burning brightly in a window at the back of the Westfield residence. Suddenly Victoria appeared in the window. She bent over the lamp, the lush curves of her body perfectly silhouetted in the glow before she extinguished it.

Now what's a feller supposed to think of that? Chance wondered, feeling all the tender possibilities of Victoria Westfield tug at the notion of settling down to the comforts of a normal life. No more running around in the middle of the night being shot at by the likes of Taggert.

Dove stirred in the straw behind him. Chance looked at her dark form shadowed against the straw. She meant a lot to him too. Maybe more, deep down inside. The confines of the hayloft closed in on him like one of Jess Teet's jail cells. The two women had him trapped with no good way out. He needed to get this Taggert mess settled and get on with the business of sorting out his life and his feelings where both women were concerned.

THIRTY-SIX

Taggert rode into a stand of aspens east of the Union Pacific Station at five minutes of twelve the next morning. The distant whine of a whistle announced the approach of the noon train from Omaha. He didn't like the idea of coming to town with both the sheriff and a U.S. marshal looking for him, let alone do it in broad daylight, but his orders from White were to meet Burnswick at the station. He stepped down and tied the black to a sapling, then fished a sack of Bull Durham out of his shirt pocket. He peeled a paper from the pack inside the sack and shook tobacco into it. Rolling his smoke with the practiced fingers of one hand, he looked for any sign of either lawman in the crowd on the depot platform. He fitted the cigarette in the corner of his mouth, struck a match, lit his smoke, and settled back to wait for the train out of sight of the depot.

The Omaha train rumbled into Cheyenne on time, belching clouds of steam and grinding its brakes as it coughed to a stop. It would be a thirty-minute stop, long enough to discharge and take on passengers, mail and freight. Burnswick would use the time to take care of his business with Taggert in the commotion that swirled around the depot platform.

Burnswick stepped down from the coach to the rough-hewn platform planks. The heat of early summer midday hit him with a hot, dry gust of wind. He searched the surge of people and freight hurrying up and down the platform, looking for his contact. He spotted a tall man dressed in a black frock coat with a low crowned hat like he remembered from his first meeting with Taggert in the

Denver saloon. He leaned against the corner of the depot at the east end of the platform, well away from the bustle of servicing the train.

Burnswick casually strolled down the platform toward the east end until he was certain he'd found his man.

"Afternoon, Taggert."

"Afternoon, Burnswick. What brings you to Cheyenne?"

"Just passing through on my way to San Francisco."

"That's a long way to travel. What takes you way out there?"

"Business," Burnswick replied, dismissing Taggert's question as none of his. "Now we've only got a few minutes here, so let's get to the point. We haven't had much success in bringing your current assignment to a conclusion. Mr. White feels that we need to take a more direct approach."

"Oh, how's that?"

"It might be easier to negotiate with the owner's estate than the current owner, if you take my meaning."

Taggert nodded. "I figured."

"And while you're at it, you might want to take care of that marshal you've got on your trail."

"I almost got him last night. If it hadn't been for that Indian ridin' with him, I would have. That one cost me two good men and then they almost got me."

Burnswick's eyes hardened. "I hope you're not losing control of the situation out here, Mr. Taggert. We've had such a long and successful association it would be a shame to see it come to, shall we say, an unpleasant end."

"Don't threaten me, Burnswick. I'll take care of it."

"See that you do, Mr. Taggert. Mr. White expects improved results from your operation, and soon."

"I'll take care of Westfield and the marshal real soon. Now if you'll excuse me, I'm gonna get outta town."

Burnswick found Dodge in his small office off the depot's passenger lounge.

"Afternoon, Colonel Dodge, thought I might find you here."

"I'm sorry, sir, I don't believe I've had the pleasure."

"Burnswick's the name, Right of Way Development, Colonel. I happened to be passing through Cheyenne and thought I'd stop by to discuss a small securities transaction. Did you receive the share certificates we sent you?"

"Why, yes I did, though I don't feel as though I should accept them—conflict of interest, you understand."

"We don't see any conflict, Colonel. Right of Way Development is your biggest and most successful contractor. It's only natural you'd want to own shares in a company like that. Now that the line is finished, there's good money to be made laying the spurs and building the things the railroad will need to operate. There's no reason you shouldn't benefit by being a friend of the family, now is there?"

Dodge shook his head. It sure could add up to a lot of money.

Sheriff Jess Teet watched the big man in the black suit walk up from the depot carrying a valise and wondered. He hadn't gotten a very good look at the feller they'd been after last night, but this feller fit Lucky's description close enough to arouse the sheriff's curiosity. He watched the stranger cross Sixteenth Street and turn east. He walked at a leisurely pace, like a man with nary a care in the world. Few men could claim that luxury. It was enough to rouse Jess Teet's curiosity further.

Teet waited for the man to get a block or so down the street before he fell in behind him. He exchanged pleasantries with the townsfolk he met as he strolled along, keeping an eye on the stranger. The sheriff meant to see where he went and who he might meet, and find out who the man was if he could.

The man headed straight for the Rawlins House. Teet watched him enter the lobby. Teet crossed the street to the Rawlins boardwalk and paused at the lobby window. The stranger was talking to Bickford at the registration desk as he checked in. Teet waited outside until the big man left the desk and headed upstairs before entering the lobby.

Bickford looked up when the sheriff came in.

"Afternoon, Sheriff, what can I do for you?"

"The feller just checked in, what's his name?"

"Signed the register Ripley, says he hails from New York."

"He's not that Taggert feller we chased outta here last night then?"

"Oh, no, Sheriff, Mr. Taggert's been a regular guest here off and on most of the last two years. I've never seen Mr. Ripley before."

"I see. Well, much obliged, Stanley, you've been a big help. If Mr. Taggert comes back you be sure to let Marshal Chance or me know right away then, you hear?"

"Sure will, Sheriff." Bickford thought, *No chance of that.*

Keeping watch at the Westfield place settled into the familiar routines, with the exception of Chance's nightly rounds at the Rawlins House. He didn't figure Taggert would show up there again. He'd lay low somewhere. Looking for him would be like going after that needle in the haystack. Waiting for Taggert to come to him still seemed to be the best plan, but the tensions of waiting ate at him with no end in sight.

Victoria seemed perfectly delighted with the arrangement. She made her daily visits to Old Ned and engaged Chance at every opportunity with any little invitation she could dream up. It seemed she always had something fresh baking in the Westfield kitchen for him to taste, or something cool to drink by way of an evening's refreshment.

For all the strain of his conflicts, Chance never tired of Victoria's attention. He remained pleasant and sociable as ever, answering her endless questions about Washington and the society that attended the inner circle in service to the President. He knew that if he ever asked her to take the train back east for a visit to Washington she'd go in an instant, without a single thought to the appearance of propriety.

Dove, on the other hand, suffocated in the white man's village. Cooped up in the loft, keeping watch over the safety of the fire-hair woman, couldn't have been any more painful. She felt powerless to hold Lah Kee in the world of the whites. The land of her people and the comfort of her spirits called to her.

Chance couldn't help but notice the change in her mood. He took it for homesickness and the tedium of the daily watch. It never occurred to him that his apparent infatuation with something she could never be crushed her under the weight of her feelings for him.

THIRTY-SEVEN

Jon Westfield hunched over his ledgers and rubbed the throbbing ache in his temples. Another payroll loomed at the end of the week, and old Dodge had yet to pay the last of his billings. *Damn Dodge for a tight-fisted skinflint*, he thought as he sweated over his ciphering. The hour grew late. He should go to bed, he told himself. He couldn't do much here other than worry, which was why going to bed made no sense.

Dove kept the watch up in the loft across the alley. Her mind wandered. The quiet night sounds of Brother Cricket and Brother Owl drew her thoughts to the land. Far off in the distance the lonely bark of Brother Coyote called her home. Her Cheyenne ways could not overcome the wiles of the white woman. She knew Lah Kee for the gift of her spirit guide, but sadly, only if he would be given. Her spirit grew restless with a growing sense of loss. The fire-hair would take him away.

The soft clop, clop of a lone horse brought her back from her troubles. She could make out the dark shape of a lone rider coming up Sixteenth Street from town. The rider turned north on Cody just west of Gorham's Emporium and disappeared between the buildings. Moments later he reappeared in the alley behind the Westfield residence and drew rein. The tall, dark figure stepped down from the saddle and looped his reins over the yard fence.

Dove shook Chance awake. He scrambled to the loft door, instantly alert to the possibility that their long wait might finally be over. The dark figure below looked around for any sign of movement. He flicked away the glowing butt of a cigarette and moved off up the alley toward the office at the front.

"Taggert," Chance whispered, scrambling to the loft ladder. He covered the distance to the ground in two leaps.

The door to the office burst open. Jonathon Westfield came up short, staring down the long barrel of Taggert's Colt. His own weapon lay in the desk drawer under his right hand. He kept it there to avoid alarming Victoria. Now he knew it might as well be a hundred miles away for all the good it would do him.

"Evenin', Westfield." Taggert flicked his eyes around the office.

"Evenin', Taggert. Little late for a social call, ain't it?"

"This ain't no social call. I'm here to close our deal."

"We ain't got a deal."

"Oh, we will, soon as you're out of the picture." Taggert crossed the office cautiously to the door to the living quarters. He listened for any sign of movement on the other side, all the while keeping a sharp eye and his gun trained on Westfield.

"Drop it, Taggert," Chance ordered, stepping through the office door with a .38 in each hand.

The words were scarcely out of his mouth when Victoria Westfield came through the residence door between Taggert and Chance. She stepped right into Taggert's clutches, flannel nightdress and all. Taggert held her fast in front of him. He pressed the muzzle of his gun to her throat, tilting her chin with the pressure. "Looks like you got it wrong, Marshal. Drop your guns or the girl gets a hole in her pretty little head."

Chance dropped his guns with an ominous clatter on the plank floor.

Victoria's eyes went wide with terror. She knew she'd put them all in danger. Her knees turned watery. Her head grew light.

"Real nice of you to drop by, Marshal. Saves me the trouble of havin' to go look for you. Now I can take care of both of you.

Too bad about the girl here, but I cain't be leavin' any witnesses. You understand."

He released Victoria with a shove toward the two men on the other side of the office. He leveled his pistol at Chance. As Victoria crossed the room she passed between Taggert and her father. Westfield seized the moment. He blew out the kerosene desk lamp and plunged the office into darkness.

Chance caught Westfield's move in the corner of his eye and knocked Victoria to the floor as Taggert blindly fired two quick shots. The muzzle flashes lit the darkness, filling the small office with the roar of pistol reports. Chance found his pistols in the dark and fired a quick shot into the dark void where Taggert had disappeared through the door to the residence. Chance could hear him running for the side door to the yard.

"Jon, Victoria, you all right?"

"Fine, Lucky," Westfield replied, his voice tight with emotion. His hand trembled as he scratched a match to relight the lamp.

Chance ran to the door to the residence. Moonlight filtered through the open door to the porch, bathing the empty parlor in dark shadows to the yard beyond. Chance reached the door in time to catch sight of Taggert running for his horse. He fired again, trying to bring the gunman down with a shot in the leg that would leave him alive. The shot kicked up a puff of dust in the alley.

Taggert reached his horse and returned fire. The shot forced Chance to duck back inside the residence. Dove opened fire from the barn door across the alley. Taggert swung into the saddle. He spun the black on his heels and lit out of town, headed northwest into open country.

Chance ran across the yard as Dove led Salute out of the stable saddled and ready to ride. She'd guessed he might need him if Taggert managed to slip the trap. Chance dashed across the alley. He grabbed the saddle horn and sent Salute off at a gallop with a two-step vault into the saddle from the Morgan's right side.

"C'mon, Salute! We cain't let him get away like he done the other night." The big sorrel stretched out his full burst in response.

Dove ducked back into the barn for Sage. Victoria ran into the yard in time to see Chance ride off after Taggert. Dove led the little mustang across the alley to where Victoria stood trembling like a leaf.

"Vic tor ria hurt?"

"No, no, I'll be fine. You go now. Lucky'll need your help."

Dove nodded. She swung up on Sage bareback and kicked up a flat-out run, chasing the plumes of Salute's dust rising in the moonlight.

Taggert had a head start on a good horse that held his separation for more than a mile before Salute's Morgan breeding began to assert itself, closing the gap.

Chance measured the ground they gained. He guessed Taggert could feel it too when he turned in the saddle. Chance gave Salute a cut to the right just before the flash and puff of white smoke charged from Taggert's pistol.

Salute knew the drill, checking left and right in response to Chance's knee pressure, giving Taggert no steady target to hit from the back of a galloping horse. *Four*, Chance counted the whining round. *Five rounds*, he calculated his bet. Nobody with any sense wore leg iron on a loaded chamber. Salute closed the gap on the laboring black, slowly but surely coming back to him. *Five*, now "Go!"

Chance bent over Salute's neck and asked the big Morgan for all he had. Salute responded with an explosive hind stride. He stretched the pull of his front drive with all the strength in his powerful chest. The gap closed quickly as they pounded down on the black. Salute drew up on the black's left flank close enough for Chance to make the leap that spilled Taggert off his horse and sent both men tumbling down a steep embankment beside the trail.

They hit the ground hard. Chance landed on top of Taggert as they rolled down the hill in a cloud of dust and a spill of small rocks.

Taggert came up fast for a big man. He caught Chance with a solid right cross that snapped his head back and sent him reeling. Stars crossed his eyes as he tripped over a rock and sprawled on his back. Taggert drove a vicious kick at Chance's head that he barely stopped with both hands. He gave the boot a violent twist that wrenched Taggert's knee. The gunman flipped sideways and hit the ground hard again.

Chance sprang to his feet. He caught Taggert on his knees with a left cross and a right uppercut that grazed the big man's chin and shattered the bridge of his nose with a sickening crack. A dark splatter of blood poured out of his nose onto his moustache and chin. Staggered by the blows, Taggert pitched sideways. He came up with a handful of dirt he pitched into Chance's eyes.

Blinded, Chance took the full force of Taggert's charge. The gunman drove a shoulder into his chest that knocked the wind out of him. He hit the ground hard on his back with Taggert on top of him. They rolled in the dirt. Taggert tried desperately to gouge Chance in the eye as he fought to regain his breath. Chance caught Taggert's hand, but not before his thumb nail sliced across the bridge of his nose, opening a wet, sticky gash.

Chance kicked free with an all-out effort and rolled up on his feet. Taggert answered the move by coming up with a rock in his fist. He took a vicious swing with the rock that grazed Chance in the temple as he ducked to avoid the punch. The wild swing staggered Taggert. Chance stepped into the opening, landing a knee in the killer's groin. The air rushed out of him in a groan. He doubled over and sank to his knees. Chance caught him with a roundhouse right cross that snapped his head hard left with a sharp crack. The whites of the gunman's eyes rolled up in their sockets. He toppled over cold and still.

Dove slid Sage to a halt as Chance cuffed the unconscious Taggert's hands behind his back. Taggert didn't look too good with his bloody broken nose mashed across his face. Chance didn't look much better with a face full of dirt, a gash across his nose and a swollen eye that had the makings of a fine shiner. Dove shook her head with a small smile at the mess both men had made and rode off to collect Salute and the blown black for the ride back to town.

Chance and Dove rode to Cheyenne with Taggert. The company man had regained consciousness. The combination of his injuries and incarceration had him in a foul mood. He spit blood, venom and defiance every step of the way back to town. Chance was anxious to get him locked up and catch a little shuteye. The strain of the long wait, the demands of the capture and the relief at finally getting his man had released a flood of tension. Suddenly he felt very tired.

Lights still burned in the Stage & Rail office as they rode into town. Chance drew up and stepped down at the hitch rail. He was anxious to get Taggert locked up, but he felt the need to let Jon Westfield know he'd gotten his man.

"I'm gonna let Jon know we got him, Mourning Dove. If that skunk so much as moves, shoot him."

Taggert spit derisively.

"Mind your manners, Taggert, or I'll shoot you myself."

Jon Westfield sat at his desk with no thought of sleep after the harrowing events of the evening. All the worries of his business problems were swept aside by his brush with the gunman and the thought of how Victoria might have been hurt. He'd just poured himself a stiff bourbon to settle his nerves when the doorbell clanged. Chance came in dirt-stained, swollen eye and all.

"We got him, Jon. Taggert won't be no trouble to you after this."

"That's mighty good news, Lucky. I don't mind sayin' I'm relieved."

Victoria Westfield heard the muffled voices coming from the office. She tiptoed to the door connecting the residence to the office. When she recognized Chance's voice she burst through the door and ran straight into his arms.

"Oh, Lucky! I'm so glad you're safe."

"It's all right, Victoria, we got him. Everything'll be fine now," Chance said, holding her tightly and stroking her hair in the relief of the moment.

"I'm so grateful. How can I ever repay you for all that you've done?"

"No need," Chance said, stepping out of her embrace. "All in a day's work. Now I gotta get Taggert over to the jail."

"But you're hurt," she blurted out, noticing his swollen eye and the gash over his nose. "Come in and let me clean that up."

"It's nothin', Victoria. It'll have to keep for now. I got business to finish."

Dove watched the scene play out in the Stage & Rail Office with the stony heart of one resigned to her fate.

THIRTY-EIGHT

The banging at the front door finally roused an irritated Sheriff Jess Teet from his bed. "All right, all right, I'm comin'," he shouted as he pulled on his britches and tucked in his nightshirt. Somehow he knew his visitor would be Marshal Chance. A man just couldn't get a decent night's sleep with that man around.

"What's all the ruckus about?" Teet demanded through the door.

"We got a prisoner for you, Sheriff."

Teet recognized the voice, confirming his suspicion. He opened the door and stepped out on the porch. "So you got him," Teet observed, sizing up the prisoner. "Well, if you're gonna drag a man out of bed in the middle of the night again, at least this time it's to lock up the culprit to a passel of recent local trouble."

Judging by the look of both Taggert and the marshal, it must have been a hell of a fight. Taggert wasn't any too pretty to start with, Teet reckoned, but with his nose making a crooked turn to the left side of his face and his eyes already starting to blacken, he looked a mess. The marshal didn't look much better with a bloody gash on the bridge of his nose and a swollen eye.

Teet went back inside long enough to pull on his boots and strap on his gun for the short walk over to the jail. Teet walked beside the horses as the mounted party made their way up the street to the jail. He unlocked the office door while Chance pulled Taggert off his horse. The sheriff led the way to the cellblock and locked Taggert away behind bars.

"Formal charges can wait until morning, Lucky. With what we know or suspect, we got more'n enough to lock this one up for a good long time. More likely we got enough to hang him."

"Thanks, Jess. We'll take Taggert's horse down to Brady Cain's with us."

"Much obliged. That'll save me a trip."

"See you in the morning." Chance and Dove stepped into the saddle and jogged up Sixteenth Street. They made it back to the loft well past midnight. They were both exhausted by the strain of the evening's events, but for different reasons. Chance would handle his by an untroubled night's sleep. Dove would face the bitter knowledge sent by her spirits as she lay wide-eyed in the white man's straw.

Chance woke the next morning well past sunup. Bumps and bruises reminded him of what he'd done the night before. But underneath the pain he felt a deep sense of satisfaction. With Taggert locked up, Jon Westfield was safe and Chance had a link to those responsible for the Union Pacific troubles. The general would be pleased. All he had to do was sweat Taggert to get to the bottom of the case. He saddled Salute and headed over to the jail to question the prisoner and write the report he would send to Bryson.

Dove watched him ride away from the shadows of the loft.

Chance stepped down at the rail in front of the sheriff's office and clumped up the boardwalk. The office smelled of fresh-brewed coffee.

"Mornin', Jess."

"Mornin', Lucky. Good lookin' eye you got there." Teet smiled, blowing the steam off a hot cup of coffee.

"Thanks for noticin'. How's our boy?"

"None too sociable, that one. Coffee's fresh. Pot's on the stove."

"Thanks, Jess, maybe later. I'd like to talk to our prisoner first."

"Suit yourself. You know where to find him."

Chance grabbed a bent wood side chair from the office and carried it into the tiny cellblock. Taggert occupied one cell, the other stood empty. Chance drew his chair up beside the cell and straddled it. Taggert slouched on the bunk, making no secret of his foul temper. He was in no mood to cooperate. A night's rest had done little to improve the condition of his nose. Dried blood caked his moustache and stained his chin and the front of his shirt. A splinter of white bone protruded from one nostril. Blood sprayed a fine mist when he breathed.

"All right, Taggert, let's see what we got here. We gotcha charged with robbery, murder, runnin' guns to the Indians, abduction, three counts of attempted murder, resistin' arrest and interference with a peace officer in the performance of his duties. I reckon we can take our pick of offenses to hang you for."

Chance let his words sink in. A fat black fly circled the prisoner's hat, its buzz the only break in the silence. The air in the cellblock hung warm and heavy with the smell of sweat. Conditions weren't likely to improve as the heat of the day built. Taggert stared straight ahead. He gave no sign that he'd heard anything Chance had said or that any of it mattered to him in the least.

"I guess you're a real hard case. I cain't rightly figure how the man you're workin' for'd be worth dyin' for. Now if you was to cooperate, we might work somethin' out. It'd put you away for a good long spell, but we could probably save you from gettin' your neck stretched. Think about that awhile. I'll have Sheriff Teet send for Doc Daily to have a look at that nose. I'm gonna have a cup of coffee. You want some?"

Taggert looked at Chance and nodded.

Chance sauntered into Teet's small office and headed for the coffee pot on the potbelly stove. He picked two tin cups off the sideboard and filled them with steaming java.

Teet lifted a bushy eyebrow. "Makin' any progress in there?"

"Nah. He's a hard case, that one. Maybe he'll come around when he gets the idea we got him on hangin' charges."

"He best get that notion. Old Judge Crockett ain't bashful when it comes to hangin' a sidewinder like him."

"Hear that, Taggert?" Chance called. "Sheriff says Judge Crockett'd be right pleased to hang the likes of you." Chance paused at the door to the cellblock with the two cups of coffee. "Jess, you mind sendin' for Doc Daily to have a look at his nose? He looks so ugly I can hardly talk to him."

Teet nodded and left the office.

Chance walked back into the cellblock. "Here, Taggert, have a little of this. It'll make you feel some better."

Taggert eyed the steaming cup. He rolled off the creaking bunk and took the cup through the bars.

"You think about what Judge Crockett's gonna make of those charges. It might make a difference if I was to speak up about how you cooperated with the investigation. We'll talk again after Doc Daily's got you patched up."

The town hummed with talk of the shooting at the Stage & Rail offices the previous night. It didn't take Burnswick long to piece the picture together. Taggert had failed to get Jon Westfield, and worse, he'd managed to get himself caught. The sheriff had him in custody over at the jail. Jake would not be happy about either circumstance. Taggert couldn't do them much real harm, though he did know him for his contact if he talked. He'd let Jake know what had happened, but he didn't need the boss's order to know that Taggert had to go.

He coded up a telegram for Gelb and took it over to the Western Union office at the depot right after breakfast.

Doc Daily snapped his black bag shut as he walked out of the cellblock. He was a small man in an ill-fitting, rumpled black suit. He had a white fringe of hair and gentle brown eyes behind wire-rimmed spectacles. "He'll be good as new in a few days," he said as he headed for the door.

"Much obliged, Doc," Chance said, pouring himself another cup of coffee.

Chance had just finished his coffee when he heard the bunk springs squeak in the cellblock.

"All right, Marshal, let's talk."

Chance walked back into the cellblock and pulled up his seat. Taggert sat on the edge of the bunk, his nose plastered, the damaged nostril packed with gauze.

"Now that's more like it." Chance smiled. "Who do you work for?"

"Feller by the name of White."

"Where do I find him?"

"Good question. I got a St. Louie address for him, but all my orders come from New York."

"What's he look like?"

"No idea, I've never seen him."

"You work for a man you've never seen?"

"That's right. All my orders come by coded telegram."

"Coded?"

Taggert nodded. "Yup, they use numbers for words in the Webster book."

"The one I found in your saddlebags."

"That'd be the one. I use it to send White telegrams too. You'll find the St. Louie address written inside the cover."

"So how did you come to work for a man you never met?"

"A man name of Burnswick come to see me two years back."

"What did he look like?"

"Big man, black hair, scar on his left cheek."

"Where is he now?"

"No idea. Last time I saw him was about a week ago. Said he was passin' through on his way to San Francisco. He stopped here to give me the order to kill Westfield and you."

"So you say he was on his way to San Francisco. Any idea why?"

"Business, was all he said."

"So this Burnswick feller hires you two years ago, to do what?"

"Take care of the competition as Mr. White directed."

"What happened to the loot from the Drainsville train robbery?"

Taggert scowled. "You'll find what's left of my share in the safe over at the Rawlins House."

"What happened to the rest of it?"

"You'll have to ask the Betcher brothers, though I expect they won't be doin' much talkin'.

Once he got to singing, Taggert spilled more of his activities over the last two years. What he said confirmed what Chance had suspected. Most of the Union Pacific contractors who'd failed had help from Taggert and Right of Way Development. Everything had been aimed at eliminating Right of Way Development competitors. Somebody at Right of Way had a lot of explaining to do over the cost overruns and the appearance of fraud that concerned the President. That started with Mr. White, whoever he was.

Taggert couldn't or wouldn't make a connection to Grenville Dodge. He swore up and down he didn't know Dodge and had never known him to have anything to do with White or Right of Way Development. Dodge had had opportunity, all right. Maybe even motive, but Chance couldn't find any evidence that tied him to

Right of Way Development or the attempt to take over Stage & Rail Construction. The only things he had to go on were an address in St. Louis for the unknown Mr. White, a code and somebody named Burnswick, who might be anywhere between Cheyenne and San Francisco. Still, his suspicions about Dodge wouldn't go away. He had reason enough to see if there might be a money trail.

THIRTY-NINE

If Chance found a money trail that involved Dodge, it stood to reason it would pass through the City National Bank of Cheyenne. That's where Taggert had gotten paid. Chance ambled into the sleepy bank lobby early that afternoon. The heavyset man at the big desk next to the vault looked to be in charge.

Blanton Collier recognized the badge at once. He'd heard that a U.S. marshal was in town. Rumor said it had something to do with the Drainsville train robbery. Collier wondered what would bring him to the bank. He didn't have to wait long for his answer.

"Afternoon, sir. J.R. Chance, U.S. Marshal. I'm lookin' for the cashier."

The big man stood, extending his hand across the desk. "Blanton Collier, President and Cashier, at your service, Marshal. What can I do for you?"

"I understand you hold an account for a man named Taggert."

"Taggert, Taggert… hmmm, that does sound familiar. I believe we might. How might that be of interest?"

"I got Taggert locked up over at the jail, charged with the Drainsville train robbery among other things. Was there any unusual activity in the account around the time of the robbery?"

"Have a seat, Marshal." Collier gestured to a pair of wooden chairs across from his desk. "I can't show you the account records without a court order, but let me have a look."

Collier crossed the lobby and walked around behind the teller line to an open file filled with cards recording depositors' accounts.

The banker bent over the file and thumbed through the cards. He plucked one out and held it up to his spectacles. He returned to his desk in a few moments, studying a card he'd selected from the file with a furrowed brow.

"Small personal account, it appears. Benefit of a monthly draft drawn on a New York bank. Doesn't seem to be any unusual activity in the past year, though I suppose that's not much help, is it, Marshal?"

"No, it's not. You wouldn't happen to hold accounts for Right of Way Development or Grenville Dodge, would you?"

"Why yes, we do, for both, as a matter of fact."

"What can you tell me about them?"

"Right of Way Development is a commercial account. Maintains a small balance most of the time, other than the occasions when we take in their Union Pacific payments. Those deposits are drawn down pretty fast by transfer to a bank back east."

"That wouldn't by any chance be to the same bank Taggert's drafts come from?"

Collier glanced at the card. "Why, yes, as a matter of fact, it is. Merchants Bank of New York. My, that is a coincidence."

"And Colonel Dodge's account, are there any transactions between the colonel and Right of Way Development or the Merchants Bank?"

"I don't know the answer to that question without checking the records, Marshal, but I'm afraid I'll have to ask you for a court order before divulging that kind of information."

"Well, thanks for your help, Mr. Collier. If I need that information, I'll be back with a court order. Have a good day." Chance shook Collier's hand and headed across the dimly lit lobby toward the bright sunlight pooling on the floor in front of the door.

Collier watched him go, curious now about why the marshal might be interested in a connection between Grenville Dodge and Right of Way Development or the Merchants Bank of New York.

The marshal had more on his mind than the Drainsville train robbery. Under other circumstances he would have reported this sort of information to Mr. White, but given the nature of the marshal's inquiry, Collier thought it best to keep his distance from the Right of Way Development accountholder for a time.

Davis Slane picked up the telegram at the storefront blind on Second Avenue where communications for Mr. White were delivered. This one was from Burnswick in Cheyenne, and while Slane did not fully understand the state of affairs in Cheyenne, he knew they were having some sort of trouble with the law because one of their operatives had been arrested. He hurried back toward Gelb's Wall Street offices. Mr. Gelb would want to see this right away.

Slane had good instincts for the things that were important to the business and important to Gelb. He'd picked up Burnswick's responsibilities with relative ease, earning him Gelb's approval and increasingly, his confidence. Slane liked the increased responsibility and the opportunity to work more closely with Gelb. Gelb meant power and money in this organization, and that was what mattered to Slane. He hurried up to Gelb's office with Burnswick's message and knocked softly before letting himself in.

"Telegram from Mr. Burnswick in Cheyenne, Mr. Gelb," Slane said, handing the transcription across the desk.

Gelb scanned the page, his brow furrowed beneath the cool shine of his head. Taggert had bungled the Westfield job and had gotten himself caught in the bargain. He could implicate Burnswick, and that could lead to Gelb. The Taggert situation took no thought at all. The man was a cutout, completely expendable. Burnswick knew enough to take care of that, but that still left Burnswick exposed. With Burnswick in Cheyenne, he could be apprehended if Taggert talked. Gelb didn't like the risk created by a loose end. Something needed to be done.

Gelb wasn't concerned about the hayseed Cheyenne sheriff. The U.S. marshal bothered him. The marshal's interest clearly rested on the larger case of their dealings with the Union Pacific. He probably accounted for Taggert's arrest. That investigation needed to be brought to a dead end, which meant taking care of Taggert and getting Burnswick out of Cheyenne fast.

That left the question of what to do about Westfield and the Stage & Rail contracts. Much as Gelb hated the thought of losing, it might be time to cut his losses on that one, at least for the time being. Westfield had proven stubborn, and with the marshal involved, it would be even harder to take over his business by force without added risk of exposure. Unfortunately, in this case it was time to cut his losses and move on. He still might take over the Stage & Rail contracts by working on Dodge to squeeze Westfield out of the business, but for now Burnswick needed to get out of Cheyenne and get on with the business of the gold purchases.

"All right, Slane. Get these instructions to Burnswick right away."

Chance spent the rest of the afternoon working on the charges he would file against Taggert in Judge Crockett's court and writing the report he would send to Bryson. Late that afternoon he handed Teet the charges to hold for the circuit judge.

"Thanks for all your help, Jess."

"Glad we finally got that skunk locked up."

"I gotta get a move on. Get this report over to the depot in time to catch the morning train east."

"What'll you do then, Lucky?"

"I expect it will be awhile before I get my next set of orders. I'm gonna use the time to take Dove back to her people."

"I'll hold the fort here 'til you get back," Teet assured him.

"Thanks again, Jess. Much obliged."

Riding up Sixteenth Street to Brady Cain's livery stable, Chance had a hunch there might be a trip to San Francisco in his future. That made it important to get Dove back to her people while he had the opportunity to do it. A trip west would give him the time he needed to sort out his feelings for the two women tugging at him like two dogs fighting over the last bone in the barnyard.

Stepping down in front of Brady Cain's, he led Salute into the barn. The sense that something had changed hit him almost immediately. The stall next to Salute's stood empty. *Where is Sage? Maybe she went for a ride.* The long days of watching the Westfield place had worn on her too. He'd seen the change in her mood. She had seemed more at peace in the cold rocks of the south butte at the red rock cut than she did in the loft. She'd been even more troubled after the Sunday dinner when he thought about it. Who could blame her for wanting a little fresh air? He knew he needed some.

He turned Salute into his stall and climbed the ladder to the loft. What he saw there stopped him dead in his tracks. The truth hit him like a punch in the gut. The blue gingham shirt lay rolled up in place of Dove's blanket. She was gone. Left him and run off to who knew what trouble.

Suddenly all those confusing feelings he couldn't seem to sort out fell into place. He'd come to a fork in the path of his life. The two choices couldn't be clearer. All the indecision and uncertainty melted away in that moment. He knew the path he would follow.

FORTY

He knew where to find her. Other times he might have thought it a hunch, but not this time. This time he knew. He needed to go after her, but first he had some shopping to do.

He bought a new '66 model Winchester, three boxes of cartridges and a saddle boot down at Gorham's Emporium. Walking back to the stable with his purchases under his arm, Victoria called to him from the porch of the Westfield residence.

"Lucky, do come to dinner tonight. I'm making a roast with all the trimmings to thank you for all you've done for Daddy and me."

Pretty as a picture, Chance thought, walking over to the gate where she'd come out to meet him.

"Dove's gone," he said simply.

"I know," Victoria said. "I saw her go this morning. She said she was going back to her people."

"I'm goin' after her. It's not safe for her travelin' alone."

"Oh, Lucky. Don't you see it's for the best? She's not at home here, and the two of you couldn't be more different. Now be a dear and come to dinner tonight. In a few days you'll see that I'm right about this."

Chance studied the intense pleading in those green eyes for several moments. She might be right. Maybe he and Mourning Dove were too different. Maybe the gulf between their peoples was too wide to bridge. Maybe he belonged here, in the company of this beautiful woman who so obviously cared for him. Maybe, but if all that was true, why didn't his heart agree?

Victoria had offered an easy choice from the beginning. He could have the settled-down life he thought he wanted with her. They wouldn't have any divides to bridge between different peoples. She gave him an easy choice, all right, but that didn't make her the right choice for him.

He hadn't felt right about leaving Dove up on the north platte when he did. He'd carried feelings for her with him all the while they were apart. Those feelings cast a shadow over whatever feelings he might have had for Victoria. The realization that she'd left hit had him so hard it surprised him. It hurt like someone had ripped a hole in his heart.

Chance took off his hat and leaned across the gate. He gave Victoria a light kiss on the cheek. "Sorry, Victoria, I gotta go."

Victoria watched him walk away. She'd lost. Bested by something she could neither see nor understand. By any measure of her imagining she offered him more, much more. Yet somehow it would not be enough.

She watched him strap the rifle boot on Salute's saddle and step up. He gave her a final wave and squeezed up an easy lope to the north without looking back. She watched as he faded to a dark speck in the last light of sunset. Brushing a tear from her cheek, she turned back to the house. Dinner with Daddy would be lonely tonight.

He rode out to the north with the sun disappearing over smoky purple peaks that faded to darkness in the distant west. If he'd looked back he'd have seen Victoria Westfield silhouetted in the yard, her hair aflame in the lingering rays of the setting sun. He didn't look back.

Riding at night made good time for thinking. Mourning Dove had brought him to a fork in the road, all right. The sight of the blue gingham shirt had hit him with the choice. The hard choice forced him to confront himself. It forced him to decide the direction he would take on the path of his life.

Victoria loved the life he'd left in the east. She saw him as a way out of Cheyenne to the glamorous life he'd left behind. He saw her for a settled-down change from the dangers of the life he now led. A life free of violence and death, though last night had taught him that wasn't foolproof either.

Mourning Dove, on the other hand, simply accepted him. In her own quiet way she did whatever needed to be done. In that they were alike. He'd been doing the same thing ever since he'd joined the army of the Missouri. The things he found that needed doing ran to the dangerous side. Victoria Westfield would take no part in that the way Dove did.

The frontier would be settled. It would be hard work full of risk. The people building this nation needed men like him. Men trained to deal with danger. He'd been doing it for a long time. Taggert's bullet had shaken him, but in the end it hadn't changed him. Deep down he knew he would soon grow weary in the quiet routines of a settled-down life. Dove had forced him to confront that fact with a blue gingham shirt. She'd forced him to choose one life or the other. Their peoples might be different, but they were very much alike. Together, if he could convince her, they would make that enough.

Burnswick came down the stairs to the hotel lobby on his way to Delmonico's for a drink and some dinner.

"Oh, Mr. Ripley," Bickford hailed him from behind the registration counter. "Western Union just delivered it a few minutes ago. Thanks for saving me the trouble of bringing it up to your room," he added, handing over the sealed yellow envelope.

Dinner would have to wait. He headed back upstairs to his room to decode the message. It would confirm his own sense of what Jake wanted him to do.

Spotted Hawk and the hunting party he led crossed the trail heading north toward Platte River country early that morning. Spotted Hawk drew to a halt and dropped to the ground to study the sign. *Fresh pony sign*, he read. *One rider, shoe like pony soldier*. Spotted Hawk knew this sign. This trail held more interest than the small herd of buffalo the hunting party followed. It spoke of the white eyes passing this way so recently he must have ridden all night. Spotted Hawk felt the hot surge of vengeance rise in his blood. He left the hunting of four-legged game to the others and took up this new trail.

Burnswick walked up Sixteenth Street at a brisk pace, thinking about his instructions from Gelb. He'd devised his plan over dinner the night before. He passed the jail on his way to Gorham's Emporium, where he purchased a few sundry items he would need later that morning.

Back in his room at the Rawlins, he completed preparations for his meeting with Taggert and checked his watch. He'd need to time his visit precisely, arriving at the jail promptly at eleven-fifteen. He settled in to wait.

The small stand of cottonwoods grown up in the willow breaks along the slow-moving creek came into view. They'd camped there that first night after he rescued her from Spotted Hawk, or maybe she'd rescued him. He squeezed Salute into a lope. His heart quickened in the hope of finding her there.

Sage interrupted her grazing with a snort of recognition as she caught Salute's scent on the morning breeze. Dove came up from the bank of the creek where she sat among the willows, watching the slow-moving waters and listening for the guidance of her spirits.

She saw the lone rider coming toward her. She recognized him instantly, but wondered if her eyes played tricks on her. She had given him up to Victoria. Why had he come? He drew rein in the cottonwood grove. She stood stone still in disbelief, watching him step down from his horse. A shadow of doubt shaded her soft brown eyes as she watched him walk toward her through patches of sunlight splashing between the trees. She thought he might be a vision, little more than patches of light and shadow. Then he wrapped his arms around her and covered her lips with a kiss that brought the ancient land of her people and all its spirits to a standstill.

They held each other there for a long time, neither of them having anything to say, neither of them needing to say anything. They were together, and that seemed enough. At last Chance broke the silence.

"Why'd you run away?"

"It best. Mourning Dove not woman of white ways like Vic-tor-iah."

"Well, 'It not best.' Mourning Dove and Lah Kee are more alike than Lucky and Victoria. I see that now. Your spirit guide gave us to one another. I see that too. That's mighty strong medicine to just up and walk away from. It's so strong I think we could come together as one."

Dove looked up at Chance with wide eyes, not believing the sound of his words in her ears. The Cheyenne wedding custom spoke of coming together as one. That he could feel it too made her heart sing.

The whine of a heavy caliber bullet nearly cut a sapling in two barely a foot over their heads. The rifle report cracked the silence, breaking the mood.

Chance pulled Mourning Dove down beside him and stuck his head up through the trees. The rifle cracked again as he ducked back, but he'd seen all he needed to see.

"Spotted Hawk," he whispered. "He's sittin' out there in the open on that big Appaloosa of his, havin' a fine time with his rifle out of pistol range."

Another shot rocked a nearby tree.

"Guess he thinks we're sittin' ducks here. Well, I hate the thought of usin' another man's property without askin' first, but I guess under the circumstances I'm to be forgiven."

Dove flashed a quizzical look. Sometimes the man made no sense even for a white man.

Chance gave a low whistle that pricked up Salute's ears. "Come here, boy." Salute walked over to where Chance and Dove had taken cover on the bank of the creek.

"Good boy. Now hold steady a minute." Chance eased the new Winchester out of the saddle boot and fished a box of cartridges out of the saddlebag. Another shot raked the creek bed, spraying mud where he stood.

"Now get back to Sage," Chance ordered and eased back to the creek bed beside Dove. He loaded the Winchester and handed Dove one of his .38's.

"Use your guns to keep him busy. You cain't reach him, but it'll hold his attention while I work my way up the creek bed. This'll give him a little surprise he ain't countin' on."

Dove nodded, pulling out her own Colt. She cracked off a shot as Chance slipped away. He worked his way down the creek bed, keeping his movements below the bank under the cover of the willows.

Spotted Hawk laughed at the return fire. He could toy with them now. The white eyes could not escape. He had them. "The white man will die," he called to Dove in Cheyenne, levering another round into the chamber and paying his respects with another shot. He could wait patiently here until he had a killing shot. He could feel the blood rush when the white eyes fell. He would take his scalp and bind Talks with Buffalo's foolish daughter to her rightful place as his bride.

Chance reached the edge of the cottonwoods north of Spotted Hawk's position. He levered a round into the chamber and set himself up, supporting the Winchester on the rise of the creek bank. The shot would carry something over a hundred yards. *Light breeze,* he thought. *It shouldn't be much of a factor.* He took careful aim, lifting the sight a little bit high. *Just get the trajectory right.* He took a slow breath, easing it out as he squeezed the trigger.

The Winchester charged, the recoil kicking his shoulder at about the same instant Spotted Hawk pitched off his horse and disappeared into the long prairie grass. *He's down, but is he out?* Chance had learned from years of hard experience you never took that outcome for granted. The first order of business was to get back to Dove.

Crouching low, he ran back down the creek bed to where she held her position. By the time he got to her, they had their answer. Spotted Hawk pulled himself up on his pony and high tailed it northwest, holding on to his mount with the look of a man who'd been pretty well shot.

FORTY-ONE

"Secretary Hoar and Chief Marshal Bryson to see you, Mr. President." Horace made the announcement quietly, as if reluctant to interrupt the President's concentration.

"Send them in, Horace," Grant replied absently. He shook his head as he set aside the Bureau of Indian Affairs report on the question of Indian citizenship. *It'll be a hell of a fight on the hill.* Footfalls at the door to the office reminded him that he had visitors.

"Good afternoon, gentlemen. What have you got for me?"

"A report from Marshal Chance, Mr. President," the attorney general said, crossing the office and taking a seat in one of the wing chairs across from the President's desk. Bryson took the other. "He got the man who's been trying to run Stage & Rail Construction out of the Union Pacific bidding."

Grant brightened at the news. "Good man, Lucky. I knew he'd get the job done."

"I'm afraid it's not clear that the job is done, sir," Bryson said with a field commander's attention to detail. "Marshal Chance reports that the man in question, a Mr. Taggert, is no more than a hired gun. He works for someone back east by the name of White. Taggert's never met him. He gets his orders by coded telegrams that come from New York."

"A man named White from New York," Grant mused, biting the tip off a fresh cigar. "Not much help there." He spit the tip in a crystal ashtray.

"There's more," Hoar continued. "Taggert worked for Right of Way Development. Right of Way is the largest of the Union Pacific contractors. It turns out Right of Way is based in St. Louis. The general manager there is a man named Hauser. When our field people checked him out, he said he'd never heard of any Mr. White and had no record of employing anyone named Taggert."

"Marshal Chance decided to see if he could follow the money trail," Bryson continued.

"Money trail." Grant raised a bushy eyebrow. "What the devil is that?"

"A very interesting line of investigation, Mr. President." Bryson leaned forward, intent on his report. "Taggert got paid every month by a draft drawn on the Merchants Bank of New York. Marshal Chance found out that's the same bank Right of Way Development uses. Lucky figured that if we looked into who controlled the Merchants Bank of New York accounts, we might get some idea of who was behind Taggert."

"Clever." Grant nodded, striking a match. "Very clever. You can always count on Lucky to figure things out." He lit his cigar, drawing the match flame to rich aged tobacco.

"It turns out Taggert's drafts were drawn on a Right of Way Development account." Hoar picked up the report as he closed in on the important part of their discovery. "We found out from Hauser in St. Louis that profits from the Right of Way contracts were also sent to an account at Merchants Bank of New York. The transaction records tell us the profits were then transferred to the account of a company called Credit Mobilier. From there they were paid out to the owners as dividends. When we got into the Credit Mobilier account and corporate records, we struck it rich."

Hoar removed his spectacles and rubbed his eyes. "Credit Mobilier owns Right of Way Development and a number of other companies. It isn't much of a company, no more than a street address in Pennsylvania, really. What makes it interesting is the list of shareholders and directors. That list includes Union Pacific directors and a handful of influential congressmen and senators." Hoar handed Grant the list of Credit Mobilier directors and shareholders.

Grant's expression darkened as he scanned the names through a cloud of blue smoke. "It looks as though the Union Pacific favored firms owned by its directors in letting contracts for the construction of the line. The congressional owners were paid to head off the possibility of any investigation of the project." He scanned the list a second time, looking for one name in particular. Not finding it, he turned to Bryson. "What about Senator Carswell, any sign of him?"

Bryson consulted his notes. "The senator owns shares in a company called Right of Way Holdings. It is controlled by Credit Mobilier, though the senator does not appear among the owners or directors of that company. The stock ownership may be on questionable ground ethically, given the senator's seat on the Oversight Committee, but I doubt that it rises to the level of an indictable offense."

Grant fumed to himself. *Damnation! One could only hope.*

"As to the chief marshal's point, Mr. President, Senator Carswell did approach George Boutwell to express his personal concerns over the cost overruns before any of this broke. He expressed full support for the audit and investigative actions you ordered."

All that proves is that the slimy bastard manages to stay one step ahead of the hangman. Grant handed the list back to Hoar. "What have the rest of these people got to say for themselves?"

"We're trying to get to the bottom of that now, sir," Bryson answered. "It's pretty clear that Credit Mobilier had a big hand in the Union Pacific's financial troubles. It's not clear that the owners and directors knew about the rough stuff."

"If they didn't, then who the hell did?" The more he thought about the situation, the angrier Grant became.

"We don't know yet, Mr. President." The chief marshal could feel Grant's anger and frustration build. Hoar was happy to report the big news and just as happy to leave the unpleasant parts to him. Bryson hoped the general in the President would understand that he was only the messenger. "We can account for all those involved with Credit Mobilier except for the largest shareholder. Profits on those shares were sent by standing instruction to a numbered account at a bank in Switzerland."

"Switzerland! Somebody went to a hell of a lot of trouble to bring that trail to a dead end." Grant locked his eyes on Hoar. "Is that all you've got, Rockwood?"

Hoar stared back at the President, not knowing quite what to say. Bryson picked up the answer to the question for his boss. "There's a little more, sir. Both Taggert and Hauser were hired by a man named Burnswick. Taggert hadn't seen Burnswick for two years until he showed up in Cheyenne a couple of weeks ago."

Grant turned his attention to Bryson. "Where is he now?"

"Marshal Chance doesn't know. According to Taggert, Burnswick passed through Cheyenne on his way to San Francisco."

"It doesn't sound like there's much to go on, other than trying to track down Burnswick," Grant said in disgust.

"Marshal Chance has one more idea, Mr. President," Bryson continued. "Taggert communicated with White by telegram using a code based on the Webster Dictionary. The wires were sent to a rooming house in St. Louis. Marshall Chance thinks we might be able to smoke out White using one of those coded wires. If White doesn't know that Taggert's been arrested, Chance figures he could send him a message from Taggert. Our people in St. Louis can watch the rooming house to see who receives the wire and follow the trail to Taggert's handler."

"Leave it to Lucky." Grant squinted into a cloud of smoke. "Sounds like it's worth a try. Damn little else we've got to go on."

"I agree, Mr. President. We'll run the operation as soon as I can get my St. Louis people in place," Bryson said as he stood, preparing to leave.

"One more thing, Rockwood," Grant interjected. "I want the people responsible for this brought to justice. The taxpayers deserve nothing less."

The big appaloosa war pony picked his way toward the picket line at the back of the village. Spotted Hawk slumped over the horse's neck. Both rider and horse were smeared with blood from his wounded shoulder.

Autumn Snow felt a presence. It rang with alarm. She looked out her lodge flap and recognized horse and rider at once. She ran to take the horse's bridle, her heart caught in her throat. If he would not come to her lodge from his heart, he would come to her lodge in need.

Talks with Buffalo and Standing Elk helped her take him down and lay him in her lodge, where she would tend his wound. She put a kettle of water to heat on the lodge fire and cleaned the wound. The bullet had passed through. She would sew it closed with sinew and bind it. His body would heal with time. She wondered how his heart would heal. She wondered if her heart would heal with him.

FORTY-TWO

Burnswick paused on the boardwalk outside the sheriff's office. He drew his gold watch out of his vest pocket and flicked the cover open. *Fifteen minutes past eleven o'clock. Perfect.*

Sheriff Teet glanced up from the wanted poster that had just come in. He recognized the tall dark stranger he'd followed coming up from the depot the other day.

"Mornin', stranger. I'm Sheriff Teet. What can I do for you?"

"My name is Ripley. I'm an attorney. I've been retained to defend a Mr. Taggert I believe you have in your jail. I'd like to see my client."

"I see. Well, if you re carryin' any firearms or weapons, you'll have to check 'em here," Teet said, rising from his desk and taking the key ring down from the peg beside the rifle rack.

Ripley held his coat open to show he was unarmed. He followed the sheriff into the small cellblock. Taggert was stretched out on the bunk in his cell with his hat pulled down over his eyes.

"Wake up, Taggert. You got a visitor," Teet announced, unlocking the cell to admit Ripley.

Taggert looked up from beneath his hat brim as Ripley entered the cell. As he locked the cell door behind Ripley, it struck Teet that Taggert seemed to recognize his visitor. He didn't make anything special of it at the time.

"Just give a holler when you're finished. I'll be right outside." Teet returned to his desk, leaving them alone.

"This wouldn't be the improved performance we were expecting, Taggert," Burnswick hissed, his soft-spoken words creased with a hard edge. "Judging by the look of you, I'd say you more than met your match."

Taggert replied with sullen silence.

"Well, I can't blame you for being surly under the circumstances," Burnswick continued in a low, confidential tone. "The important thing is that we're going to get you out of here. Mr. White doesn't want to see you come to trial. I've sent for a couple of associates to help me spring you. You can expect us tonight after midnight. Be ready."

Taggert shifted his demeanor to a more hopeful expression. "Much obliged. Gettin' out of this shit hole cain't come soon enough."

"We'll take care of everything. Now just relax until tonight." Burnswick turned to go and then, as if it were an afterthought, he turned back to Taggert. He reached into his coat pocket and pulled out a fine twist of chewing tobacco. He tossed to Taggert. "No sense suffering here without the comforts of home."

Taggert caught the twist with an appreciative nod.

"Sheriff," Burnswick called.

Moments later Burnswick stepped out of the office and checked his watch. Forty-five minutes past eleven. *Right on schedule,* he thought as he crossed Sixteenth Street and headed for the depot.

Molly brought the dinner trays over to the jail from the diner across the street at five o'clock that afternoon.

"Roast beef and mashed potatoes, Sheriff," she said, setting the trays on Teet's desk. "Got some red beans too, and apple pie for dessert."

"Much obliged, Molly." Teet smiled. The gravy looked rich and smooth with all the other fixin's. "Smells good enough to get a man's mouth to waterin'."

Molly smiled. "I'll be back to pick up the trays later," she said on her way out.

Teet picked up Taggert's tray and carried it into the cellblock. "Dinner's way better'n the likes of you deserves, Taggert," Teet drawled at the cellblock door. Inside Taggert lay sprawled out on the bunk. He'd torn the bandage off the bridge of his nose. His hands clutched his throat, the bandage caught in the crush of his fingers. Unseeing eyes bulged out of his head. His face twisted in a grotesque death mask.

Teet put down the tray and opened the cell. Taggert had fouled himself in death. The stench hit the sheriff hard, but something else scented the air. He picked up the half-bitten twist of tobacco and gave it a sniff. The light hint of almonds seemed strangely out of place.

Teet had Taggert's body hauled off to Ned Martin's blacksmith shop. *Seems like Ned's doin' a land office business in undertakin' these days,* he thought. He did the required check at the Rawlins House, confirming his suspicion. Ripley had checked out that morning.

He'd been smart, all right. He's walked the murder weapon into the jail right under Teet's nose and left. Taggert and his bad habits had taken care of the rest. A quick check of the depot confirmed Teet's other suspicion. Ripley had waltzed out of the jail, gone down to the depot, and thirty minutes later was highballing his way out of town. By now he could be almost anywhere. The best the sheriff had was wanted on suspicion of murder and a description that wouldn't pick him out of a crowd.

FORTY-THREE

Chance and Dove made the ride to Talks with Buffalo's village on the banks of the North Platte by evening. Dove's heart sang and her eyes glowed at the sight of him riding comfortably beside her. It filled her heart with joy and took her spirit to soar with Sister Eagle. Such a day it had been. One day she had hurt for the decision to leave him to the fire-hair woman. Loneliness and misery had followed her after that. The next day came with the sight of him stepping down from his horse in the sun-splashed willows. She'd thought it a dream until he filled her with the feeling of love, the feeling of home.

Chance felt peace on the path he'd chosen. He would walk the path of life with this woman. The path would lead them wherever it would. He found freedom in this choice and knew all would be right as long as they were together. He must make Talks with Buffalo see the right of their path together.

The camp dogs greeted their arrival with their usual noisy reception. Curious villagers interrupted evening meals or talk around lodge fires to watch Talks with Buffalo's daughter come home with the white eyes she had nursed back to health.

They drew rein before Talks with Buffalo's lodge and stepped down. The old chief came out to greet them.

"My daughter is welcome at her father's lodge. She returns with the Great Father's law. Did she find the path to her heart in the wisdom of her spirit guide?"

Dove flushed at his question and lowered her eyes. Talks with Buffalo nodded.

"You are both welcome. Come sit by our cook fire and join us in our meal."

Sweet Medicine roasted strips of buffalo steak on sticks over a cook fire set before Talks with Buffalo's lodge. She served it with corn cakes and a sweet paste made of choke cherries.

As they ate, Talks with Buffalo asked Mourning Dove what she had done in the weeks since she'd left the village. Mourning Dove told of her experiences, her rescue from Spotted Hawk and capturing Taggert. She did not speak of the struggle with the fire-hair woman for the gift of her spirit guide. They spoke in English so that Chance would understand.

When she finished, Talks with Buffalo said, "My daughter has learned to speak in the white man's tongue."

Dove gave her father a satisfied smile. "I have learned much of the white man's ways." She held her father's eyes, letting her simple words speak for her heart.

When the meal finished, Mourning Dove and Sweet Medicine busied themselves clearing away the dishes and scraps.

Talks with Buffalo remained seated before the fire, filling his long stemmed pipe. Chance stood up and went off to collect the Winchester in its saddle boot and the three boxes of ammunition, one missing one round. He returned to the fire and resumed his place, setting the Winchester across his knees. Talks with Buffalo cocked an eye at the rifle as he lit his pipe. Chance started to speak, but the old chief caught him with an arched brow.

"Smoke first, then talk."

Chance felt those bright black eyes look into his heart again, as though Talks with Buffalo knew his deepest thoughts. He watched as the great chief lit the pipe and savored a long draw on the sweet smoke. He released the smoke slowly, offering its voice to the Great

One Above. Talks with Buffalo seemed to sense his purpose. This would be serious talk done with the guidance of the spirits.

Sweet Medicine drew Mourning Dove inside the lodge, leaving the men to their smoke.

"Spotted Hawk is here," Sweet Medicine warned Mourning Dove. "His horse brought him to the village last sundown. He is wounded. Autumn Snow nurses him in her lodge."

Mourning Dove nodded. She knew Snow's heart burned for Spotted Hawk. It would have been better had he seen it before this. He had not. His blindness had caused much hurt. She could do nothing but wait for Lah Kee and her father to talk. She would go to Snow's lodge. It would be better than waiting.

Mourning Dove stood at the flap of Autumn Snow's lodge. She did not go in. Snow sensed her presence and came out to her sister. She could see deep concern in Mourning Dove's eyes.

"How is he?" Dove whispered.

"He sleeps." Snow spoke softly.

"Mourning Dove is sorry Spotted Hawk was wounded. He shot at us before Lah Kee shot him."

"Spotted Hawk hurts from his own anger. His body will heal. Autumn Snow will care for him."

"It is good my sister cares for Spotted Hawk. Maybe then he will see what is in your heart for him."

Snow rested her weary head on Dove's shoulder. *If only he would.*

The moon rose over the fire, a brilliant orange ball tinting the darkening wisps of cloud purple before it. Evening quiet settled over the camp with the restful buzz of an occasional insect and the snap and pop of the fire sending showers of sparks into the night sky. Talks with Buffalo passed the pipe to Chance. He took his draw, letting the sacred smoke rise like a prayer for blessing on the work of this night.

"Why you bring Mourning Dove back to Talks with Buffalo village?"

He isn't going to make this easy, Chance thought. "After I found Mourning Dove, I had her ride with me until I could find a way to safely bring her to her people. After all you done for me, it's the least I could do to repay you. She was a big help to me too, saved my life a couple more times, I reckon."

"Mourning Dove brings honor to her father's lodge." Talks with Buffalo drew on the pipe, letting the smoke drift over his thoughts. "Sweet Medicine say Mourning Dove leave village to follow her heart. Did she find it?"

"We did." He said it with quiet conviction. He meant Talks with Buffalo to hear his commitment.

Talks with Buffalo arched an eyebrow and fixed Chance in his gaze over the crackle of the fire.

"Lah Kee bring good rifle to Talks with Buffalo lodge."

"I hope you'll accept it as the bride price for your daughter, Mourning Dove. I hope you will bless our coming together as one."

Talks with Buffalo took another draw on the pipe and passed it back to Chance. He let his smoke rise slowly as he opened his spirit to the will of the Creator.

"Coming together as one is hard for our two peoples."

Talks with Buffalo's words spoke more than the coming together of his daughter and the white man smoking at his lodge fire. Chance sat in silence, respectful of the wisdom and truth of his words.

"The Great One Above would not have it always be so." Talks with Buffalo paced his words, letting the sounds of the evening fill the quiet places between his thoughts. "This is a difficult path you choose to walk, my son. Many whites will see no good in this coming together. Your lodge will not rest at peace in the village of either people."

"Worse than that, Father, I have no lodge to offer your daughter. In my line of work I am always on the move." Chance saw no reason to make the situation they would face anything other than the truth, even if it didn't help his cause. The look in the old chief's eyes said he understood and respected him for this honesty.

"Mourning Dove chooses this life with the wisdom of her spirit guide." Talks with Buffalo pondered his statement as if he considered it a question.

"She says her spirit guide gave me to her," Chance said quietly. "I cain't rightly say so for certain, as I cain't say I know much about spirit guides." The truth of it was that Chance felt he'd met his spirit guide. He knew it when she'd led him to the fork in the path of his life. She'd led his spirit to Talks with Buffalo's lodge fire, though that wouldn't fit the Cheyenne concept of spiritual guidance.

Somewhere in the camp the trill notes of a flute offered its melody to the spirits of the night as Talks with Buffalo sat silent.

"Talks with Buffalo will accept this rifle, and bless this coming together in time, if that is the will of the Great One Above. First there is much you and my daughter must learn on this path of coming together. You must walk this path between your two peoples to know the truth of your hearts."

Chance wasn't sure what Talks with Buffalo meant by "bless this coming together in time if that is the will of the Great One Above." He waited to hear more, accompanied by the sounds of the fire and the flute.

"Mourning Dove has ridden the lands of the whites with you for a short time. This is good. In this you come to know the true meaning of coming together and the life it will mean for you and your children. Take more time to gather this wisdom and know the true meaning of the path you are taking. When you have this wisdom, then come for my blessing."

Chance nodded. The great chief's words were the words of a father. He and Dove would gather the wisdom of the life they had chosen on the trail together.

FORTY-FOUR

The people of Talks with Buffalo's village watched the next morning as Mourning Dove and her white eyes rode out to the land of the whites, the daughter of their chief dressed as a man in the company of the Great Father's white warrior. It was a sight strange to their ways. But with the whites, it seemed their ways were always strange.

Talks with Buffalo's decision disappointed Mourning Dove. She had wanted his approval. She'd felt certain he would give it. After the long days in Cheyenne she could accept the wisdom of his words. At best the whites ignored her. Others looked down on her, or worse, showed hostile feelings toward her and her people. Still Lah Kee had told her his heart. She would make that enough. She would ride with him. In time her father would see the path of their coming together in the strength of their hearts.

The early summer sun rose warm over gray-green sage alive with the colorful remnants of spring wildflowers. The small, delicate blossoms spread a carpet of blue and pink, yellow and white as far as the eye could see. The trail rode easy. Even the horses seemed content to be together again. Dove's heart felt full, and the spirits wrapped her in the beauty of the day. Here, away from the expectations of others, they were together as they should be.

"We go back Cheyenne?" She knew the answer, but she needed to prepare herself for whatever might lay ahead.

"Yep. I expect I'll be gettin' new orders from Washington after the report I sent in. They'll tell us where we go next."

"We go back stable?" She did not welcome the thought of moving back to the loft in the shadow of Victoria Westfield.

Chance hadn't exactly thought much about that. They'd need a place to stay, but where? The widow Murphy wouldn't approve of taking Dove into her rooming house, let alone if the two of them were together. The idea of camping outside of town for any length of time wasn't too appealing either. He could see where Dove might come back to the stable, though he sensed Victoria lurking behind her question. No. The stable wouldn't be a good idea.

"We won't go back to the stable," he said by way of reassuring her. *I'll have to think of somethin', though, before we get there, but what?*

The sun drifted toward the distant peaks in the west when it came into sight. Chance knew he didn't need to solve the lodging problem for tonight. They would camp as they should in the small stand of cottonwoods grown up in the willow breaks along the banks of that slow-moving creek. They'd camped here the first night they were together again. Dove had chosen this spot to search for the guidance of her spirits after she left him. And he'd found her there after choosing the path of his life. It might be the closest place to home they would find on the path that traveled between two peoples.

Neither spoke the decision to stop and make camp. Both of them were drawn to this spot. They unsaddled the horses and led them downstream. They picketed them on the bank of the creek where they could drink and crop prairie grass.

Chance gathered firewood while Dove took her saddlebag and walked off toward the creek. It wasn't long before he heard her splashing in the creek and guessed she must be taking a bath. *Not a bad idea,* he thought, picking up wood for the fire. *I could use a little cleaning up myself.* He carried an armload of wood back near the creek, where he built a circle of stones. *It might be right nice to join her.* The thought jumped into his head. He hadn't been skinny dipping since those warm summer days on the farm back in Missouri. Those were happy, carefree days, the kind of days he knew he would find in the future with Dove. Then again, the thought of jumping into a creek with her naked struck him in a way those playful sunny summer afternoons of his youth never had. He decided it might be best to concentrate on building a fire. He'd take care of his bathing later.

The mountaintops flared orange between deep purple shadows at last light when Dove came up from the creek. She was dressed in the simple buckskin dress she'd worn in the days when she nursed him. Her hair hung loose, damp from the creek. It sparkled like diamonds with black light where it caught in the firelight. She set down the bundle of her trail clothes and came to rest her head on his chest.

He wrapped her in his arms, savoring the soft warm feel of her against him. His heart thudded against his chest, beating like a ceremonial drum. He lifted her chin to a kiss that melted, moist and sweet like a blade of new spring grass. The quiet crackle of the fire seemed to spring from the warmth of her embrace.

When breathing became necessary, she rested her head on the drum beating in his chest. Chance stroked her hair and reminded himself that he probably needed a trip to the creek.

"If you don't have that big kettle with you, Dove, I reckon I'll have to take a dip in the creek myself," he said with a twinkle in his eye.

She looked up at him, her dark eyes shining. A small smile turned the pretty bow of her lips at the corners. She nodded.

"Mourning Dove make food while Lah Kee wash."

Chance dropped his gun belt and hat beside his saddle and ambled off to the creek. Dove busied herself in the food pack she'd brought from her father's lodge. He peeled off his shirt, boots and jeans and sat down in the stream, letting the water flow over his body, cooling the lingering urges of her kiss. The moon rose behind him, lighting the surface of the creek with the arrival of the evening star. It would be a beautiful night, he thought, listening to the quiet songs of the night as if for the first time.

He came up from the creek dressed in his jeans. He carried his shirt and boots. Dove knelt beside the fire and a meal of pemmican and corn cakes. She looked up as he came to the fireside. The moon lit crystal droplets of water clinging to the planes of his chest. She rose to greet him, her eyes alive with the joy of being together. She touched his cheek, turning his head to the light.

"Lah Kee's eye is much better," she said, tracing his cheek with the tips of her fingers.

Chance reveled in the gentle strength he'd felt in her when she cared for him. Now a deeper emotion he knew for love laced that feeling. The cooling effects of the creek slowly warmed to the fires banked within.

"Eat now," she whispered, pulling him down beside her and offering him a corn cake.

They ate in silence, accompanied by the gentle snap and pop of the fire. Alone with his thoughts, Chance felt a deep sense of home for the first time in a long time. When they finished their meal they sat together, quietly watching the moon climb as the fire burned low.

The silence was filled with unspoken promise. Dove saw the future stretched before them beyond the circle of firelight. She savored a swirl of sensations edged with the nervous excitement that comes of knowing things will never be the same again.

The fire burned low as a cool night breeze came up. Chance wrapped a blanket around them and put his arm around Dove. She rested her head on his chest. Her cheek felt soft and warm against his skin. She felt a part of him, as though the boundaries of being had blurred. He lost the feeling of where he stopped and she began. That seemed somehow as it should be.

"We are of two peoples, as my father said." Her voice was a gentle murmur, warm at his breast. "Mourning Dove hear only one heart."

"I hear it too, Dove. I heard it when I saw you'd left your shirt behind in the loft. I saw a fork in the path of my life. I saw the true path to my heart."

She lifted her head, giving her eyes to his. His words rang like a song in her heart. "The peoples will see we are one heart." She paused, listening to the quickened beat in his chest. "Then they will see us come together."

Night song wrapped them in tender embrace. Chance took her lips in his. He touched her tongue with a hunger turned molten. Feelings withheld released as they drifted slowly to earth. Tangled tremors tumbled, together slipping the bonds of buckskin and denim. The world dissolved soft, warm. Her heart pounded against his. Her breath caught hot and moist against his throat. The song in her heart escaped at the back of her throat. She wrapped him in her gift. An overpowering surge ignited the fire that would warm their lodge and welcome them home all the days of this path.

He held her in the ember-lit glow under a cascade of stars.

FORTY-FIVE

The first rays of sunrise pierced the quiet comfort of sleep. The blanket felt cold in that first foggy sense of coming awake. Then he realized he was alone. He bolted upright, jolted by doubt. Had he misread her feelings? Had she run off? Sage stood on the picket line with Salute, a quiet reassurance. His doubt drained away. She couldn't have gone far.

She came up from the creek dressed for the trail, but this time wearing the blue gingham shirt. She looked beautiful touched by the morning sun lighting the eastern peaks. She walked up to Chance and lifted her kiss to his. The new day started as the last with the feel of her filling his senses. Standing there naked, he made no secret of his feelings for her. He just didn't care. She drew her head back. Her eyes locked with his. They turned dreamy with some private thought. He could feel the warmth without knowing her mind. A small smile turned up the corners of her mouth.

"Lah Kee get dressed now. Dove saddle horses."

Chance figured out the problem of where they would stay late that afternoon riding into Cheyenne. It was simple, really. Why hadn't he thought of it before? All he had to do was convince Bryson. First, though, he needed to stop at the jail and check in with the sheriff to see how their prisoner was doing.

Sheriff Jess Teet sat at his desk beside a steaming cup of coffee. He'd just struck a match to relight a balky cob pipe when Chance and Dove came in.

"Afternoon, Sheriff."

"Afternoon, Lucky," Teet said, putting down the pipe. "I figured you'd be back before long. I'm afraid I got some bad news." Teet hit things head on. No sense in tiptoein' around the shit pile. "Taggert's dead."

"What?"

"Yup. And I reckon it's my fault," Teet offered without waiting for the obvious question. "Fellah callin' himself Ripley come in claimin' to be Taggert's lawyer from back east. I let him in for a visit. Everythin' seemed right enough when he left, but when I took Taggert his evenin' meal I found him stone dead. Best I can figure, Ripley left him a twist of poisoned chewin' tabacca. I went lookin' for Ripley right off, but he'd checked out of the hotel that mornin'. The stationmaster down at the depot saw him get on the noon train west. He must have gone straight to the depot from the jail. I'm real sorry, Lucky."

"Not much you could have done about it, Jess. I'll let Washington know and see what they think I should do next."

Out at the hitch rail Chance and Dove mounted up.

"What we do now?" Dove asked.

"I don't rightly know. I'll have to give it some thought. In the meantime we're gonna check us into a first-class hotel."

Dove raised an eyebrow as they wheeled the horses and trotted up Sixteenth Street to the Rawlins House. Chance stepped down at the rail.

"Wait here with the horses while I get us a room, Dove, then we'll stable 'em out back." Chance figured that would take care of any argument he might get over sharing a room with an Indian. The only other problem would be convincing Bryson that his voucher covered his expenses *and those of his deputy.*

Bickford didn't offer the slightest objection. He rented him a room no questions asked. They settled the horses in the hotel stable with buckets of fresh water, a scoop of grain and a fork of hay. They used the back stairs to get up to room 215. The problem of lodging solved.

Next he needed to get them something to eat. Remembering her embarrassment at Sunday dinner, Chance reasoned that bringing their meal back to the room would give him a chance to teach her about tableware without running the risk of a restaurant and somebody saying something about her being an Indian.

"Make yourself at home, Dove. I'll run out to the diner and get us somethin' to eat," Chance said, closing the door on his way out. All these arrangements plainly made the point. Talks with Buffalo knew the path they had chosen.

Chance found her sitting on the floor in her buckskin dress when he returned with dinner. She watched him lay out the place setting on the floor before her. He served her a plate of steak, mashed potatoes and a helping of those embarrassing peas. He knelt beside her and patiently showed her how to hold the unfamiliar eating utensils. He taught her how to use them while his own meal went cold. When she had the hang of it, he sat across from her and began eating himself.

"See, that ain't so hard. You'll never be embarrassed by that again."

The look of love in her eyes warmed him in a way he could never have imagined before choosing the path to her heart. She had more than a smile for him after the apple pie when he tucked her in bed with him.

FORTY-SIX

Chance left Dove to tend to the horses and headed down to the lobby bright and early the next morning. Sun splashed through the windows, lighting the room. The smell of fresh brewed coffee drifted out from the small dining room. The smell reminded him that a little breakfast would taste pretty good. But there was no time for that as he stepped out on the boardwalk and turned up the street toward the Western Union office at the depot. A fresh breeze blew out of the west, pushing small clouds of dust through the freighters, traders, townspeople and drifters thronging Sixteenth Street.

The Union Pacific passenger lounge was deserted, with no train due in for a couple of hours. The telegrapher at the Western Union desk handed him a telegram from Bryson as expected.

Washington, DC
June 10, 1869

Congratulations on Taggert arrest. Be advised St. Louis office ready to follow your wire by 12 June. Advise send date.
Bryson

Chance wrote his reply. He reported the circumstances of Taggert's death and the fact that he would send a coded message to the St. Louis address the following day. With his message rattling down the wire to Washington, Chance strolled across the deserted passenger lounge to the small office, looking for Grenville Dodge.

"Mornin', Colonel."

"Mornin', Marshal. Sorry to hear about you losin' your prisoner."

"Yeah, that's a tough break, all right. Though I think I got most of what he had to give before he died." If he had anything to hide, Chance wanted Dodge to sweat a little over what Taggert might have told him.

"Colonel, the last time we talked you said that Right of Way Development held some of the Union Pacific's biggest contracts. Is that right?"

"That's right, Marshal."

"You also said you didn't know Taggert."

"Yes, that's right."

"Seems odd that you wouldn't have had any dealin's with the local representative of your largest contractor, don't it?"

"I don't know what you're gettin' at, Marshal. All my dealin's with Right of Way Development went through Mr. Hauser in their St. Louis office." Dodge didn't like the tone of the marshal's questioning or the uncomfortable feeling that he might be a suspect in the Union Pacific's financial problems. He'd done his best to manage the railroad funding honestly even when he'd been given the opportunity to compromise himself. He needed to make that point in a forceful way.

"All of my dealin's were with Hauser and the foremen of the crews workin' on the line. I never met Taggert or anyone else from Right of Way Development until the other day when a feller named Burnswick came to see me."

The mention of Burnswick brought Chance up short. "Burnswick, you say? What'd he want?"

"He wanted me to take these," Dodge replied, tossing an envelope across the desk.

Chance found a certificate for ten thousand shares of Right of Way Development stock inside.

"What did you tell him?"

Dodge straightened himself up in his chair. "I told him I wouldn't accept them for the conflict of interest they'd represent."

Chance knit his brow. "Then why do you have 'em?"

"He told me to think it over."

Dodge said it with the level look in his eye of a man telling the truth. "Where is he now?" Chance asked.

"He took the westbound train the day Taggert was killed."

That seemed too much to credit to coincidence. "What did this Burnswick look like?"

"Big feller, maybe six feet tall, dressed in black, with black hair and moustache. He's got a scar on his left cheek, looks like it might have been a knife wound."

This put a different light on things. Dodge didn't have to tell Chance about Burnswick or the offer of the stock. Add to that the fact that Chance now had a description of Burnswick he could compare with the sheriff's description of Taggert's killer. Chance had a hunch they'd match.

"Mind if I take these?" Chance asked, gesturing with the stock certificate.

"Be my guest, Marshal. You think Burnswick might have something to do with Taggert's murder?"

"It's a possibility, Colonel. It surely is a possibility."

FORTY-SEVEN

The stable afforded an island of peace in the midst of the white world. The hay smelled sweet. The gentle sounds of the horses soothed Dove's spirit. She took comfort in the familiar tasks of tending each horse with a scoop of grain, a bucket of fresh water and a fork of hay. With both horses contentedly munching their hay, she settled herself beside Sage. She stroked the pony's neck and rested her head against the familiar feel of her powerful muscles.

The white man's lodge drowned out the sounds and senses of the spirits. She missed the quiet warmth of a tipi. The bed felt too soft. She rested better in the breast of earth mother. She missed the scent of wood smoke in the cook fire and the crackle of the lodge fire. She missed the feeling of family in the village of her people. In the white man's village she found these comforts only with Lah Kee. Still, that part alone filled her heart. She would find her way among the whites.

They were one heart. She loved him as she knew he loved her. He would teach her the ways of the whites as he did in the eating of food and the matters of lodging. She held fast to her Cheyenne pride. In this she would not change. He did not ask this of her, but what of his people? What would they accept of her? Would they accept her at all?

He came to her people as a white man. He would not find family in her village beyond the lodge they shared. Talks with Buffalo and Sweet Medicine welcomed him. In time she believed her people would be more tolerant of him than the whites would be accepting of her. Still, they were one heart of two peoples. Her father had said it. "Your lodge will not rest at peace in the village of either people." The wisdom of his words echoed in her thoughts.

Chance left Dodge and headed for the sheriff's office. His gut told him that Ripley and Burnswick were the same man, but he had to confirm it. If that checked out, he had a description to go on. Unless the coded message turned up a solid link to Taggert's handlers and Right of Way Development, Burnswick would be the only lead left. The coded wire was worth a shot, but this bunch had already proven to be damn slippery. He had a hunch that when the wire trail ended, he'd be on his way to San Francisco. He'd get to the coded message later. First he needed to talk to Sheriff Teet.

As he crossed Sixteenth Street on his way to the jail, a familiar voice brought him up in his tracks.

"Lucky, oh Lucky," Victoria called, hurrying down the boardwalk from Gorham's Emporium.

Chance braced himself. He knew he'd need to tell Victoria that he'd asked Talks with Buffalo for Dove's hand sooner or later, but he wanted some time to think about that conversation. Having it in broad daylight in the middle of Sixteenth Street just didn't feel right. *So much for thinking things over.* She hurried up to him, radiating that take-your-breath-away beauty of hers.

"Lucky, I'm so glad you're back." She beamed, giving him one of those smiles that seemed to make the sun fade a little. "When did you get in?"

"Dove and I got back late yesterday." Chance tipped his hat and then took it off altogether as he suddenly felt the need to give his hands something to do.

Victoria's sunny smile faded at the mention of Mourning Dove, but only for a moment. "Well, now that you're back you must come to dinner. We still owe you a debt of gratitude for all that you did for Daddy."

"Thank you for the thought, Victoria, but I'm pretty busy with my investigation right now." He shifted his weight to one hip, feeling the awkward turn the conversation would take before it happened.

"Yes, I heard about that dreadful business with Taggert. Busy as you are, though, you must take time to eat. You can even bring your Indian friend if you must."

"Mourning Dove is more than my friend. I asked Talks with Buffalo to bless our coming together as one." He tried to say this with real concern for her feelings, though he couldn't soften the import of the words.

Victoria arched an eyebrow. "And just what is that supposed to mean?"

"Coming together as one is the Cheyenne wedding custom." Chance thought he saw a flash of recognition, like lightning in those wide green eyes.

"Cheyenne wedding custom," Victoria stiffened. "Lucky, you can't be serious! She's a savage. You are nothing alike," she said, folding her arms across her chest as though the subject were closed.

"I am serious, Victoria. We are one heart. It's our people who are not alike." *Damn, there sure isn't any easy way to make her understand.*

"It will never work," she declared with determined conviction. "Civilized society will never accept such a thing." She softened her tone. "Surely you must see that. You must take some time away from her and come to your senses."

"You sound like Talks with Buffalo. He asked us to wait a spell for the same reason."

"Now that's the first sensible thing you've said in this entire conversation, and we owe our thanks to another savage. If he can see the truth of it, you must see it for yourself. I can help, Lucky," she pleaded. "I can help you see the kind of life you could have with someone of your own kind. Now be a dear and come to dinner tonight and we can start to make right of this."

Chance stood silent, absorbing her words, stirring them together with Talks with Buffalo's counsel. Her eyes were liquid with earnest sincerity in the shadow of her sunbonnet. "Thanks all the same, Victoria. I know you mean well, but there are feelin's here a man can't deny."

"Fiddlesticks, Lucky Chance," she bristled, looking him hard in the eye. Then she softened a little and her shoulders drooped. "The offer is there for the taking when you come to your senses." She turned on her heel and hurried back up the boardwalk toward home.

Chance watched her go. *Never an easy way to do hard things*, he thought. *She'll get over it. It just wasn't meant to be.* Victoria couldn't understand his feelings for Dove. How could she? She didn't know Dove. Like so many whites, she couldn't get past the fact that Dove was an Indian. Chance figured he was about to find out just how many of his people were like that. Talks with Buffalo knew. Chance had just never seen it before.

FORTY-EIGHT

It didn't take more than a brief conversation with Sheriff Teet to match Dodge's description of Burnswick to the man posing as Ripley. Chance headed back to the Rawlins. He kicked himself for relying on Taggert's story that Burnswick had passed through Cheyenne on his way to San Francisco. He should have checked to see if the man might still be in town. He'd let the man slip through his fingers. The mistake had cost him Taggert and another link to Taggert's Mr. White. Maybe he could use Burnswick to smoke out Taggert's handler. Someone had ordered Taggert's murder. It might be Burnswick, but Chance doubted it. Burnswick he figured for another hired gun, a cut above Taggert, but a hired gun just the same. With any luck, the coded message would find its way to the mysterious Mr. White and those responsible for the Union Pacific's problems. With any luck, but so far luck seemed in real short supply. He sure wasn't living up to his name.

The encounter with Victoria had upset him, as he'd expected it would. Her words echoed Talks with Buffalo's, calling out the differences between his people and Dove's and the enormity of the resistance they would face. These thoughts gnawed at the back of his mind as he turned into the dusty alley leading to the stable behind the Rawlins House. He found Dove alone with the horses.

She stood in the filtered rays of morning sunlight. Straw dust rose around her, giving a golden glow to her beauty. A sense of calm washed over him, quieting the turmoil of his encounter with Victoria. He only needed to look at her to confirm his resolve.

Sage turned a cool gray eye to Chance as he came into the stall and stood beside Dove. He put his arm around her. She turned to him, her embrace speaking a fierce determination he knew and understood. He returned the feeling, and in that moment their hearts beat as one.

Chance spent the afternoon thinking through the message he would send to White. The fact that Burnswick had killed Taggert gave a twist to the message ploy. Burnswick worked for White. He'd recruited Taggert and the general manager running the Right of Way Development office in St. Louis, according to Bryson. That might even make Hauser the link to White, though given the style of this bunch, going to the trouble of Swiss bank accounts and such, he guessed Hauser for another cutout in the game. If Burnswick worked for White, White knew where he'd gone. Chance decided the message should report Taggert's death, figuring that White had ordered the job done. He would then go on to ask for confirmation of his next move. Maybe he could get White to disclose Burnswick's whereabouts by return wire.

He coded up the message and headed back to the Western Union office at the depot. He sent a telegram to Bryson advising him that he would send the coded wire on the twelfth. He asked that the field people in St. Louis follow the pickup, but hold off on making an arrest until they had a chance to see if White would give up Burnswick.

Walking back up Sixteenth Street to the Rawlins, he came alongside a rough-cut mountain man strapping down a load of cured hides on an ox-drawn freight wagon. The old wagon had gone gray from the weather and dark from dried bloodstains. The hides weren't blue gingham, but it might be just what Dove needed. Riding around in open country dressed like a brave served a useful purpose, but here in town the disguise only went so far. A fine pair of leggings would dress her more respectably.

"Afternoon, partner." Chance approached him. "Any chance a small part of that load might be for sale?"

The old hunter looked up from the hitch he threw to tie down the load. A scruffy-looking old character, he had shoulder-length gray hair and a ragged explosion of whiskers. His eyes were shaded under a dirty slouch hat. He wore a long, heavy coat covered in a mixture of trail dust and grease. It hung on a lean frame, bent from the rigors of hunting, skinning and packing his livelihood out of the mountains. He looked Chance up and down with watery blue eyes. Casual conversation with a U.S. marshal wasn't something that happened every day.

"If you're talkin' cash money, Marshal, anythin' I got's for sale. Name's Skinner. What can I do for you?"

"I got a friend needs a pair a leggin's. Got a nice soft doe or antelope skin in there?"

Skinner scratched his chin thoughtfully. "I think I might have just what you're lookin' for. Now all I gotta do is find it. Gimme a minute."

Skinner hopped up in the wagon bed with a spry ease that belied his gawky frame. He rooted in the mound of hides for a couple of minutes before pulling out a pale yellow antelope skin.

"How's this?" The old hunter spread it out across his hands like a shopkeeper showing a customer a fine bolt of cloth.

Chance took the skin. The soft, supple feel told him the hide had been tanned and cured to perfection. It looked to be plenty big enough for the purpose. "How much?"

Skinner scratched his chin again. "That's a mighty fine antelope. Tanned it myself. I reckon you can tell that by the feel of it. I make it worth every bit of eight dollars."

Chance smiled to himself. *Who did the old bandit think he was dealing with?* "I'll give you three, cash money."

Skinner squinted hard, flicking his gaze between the skin and Chance, measuring the marshal's intent. "I might let it go for five, though I'd have a strong feelin' of bein' cheated. That'd be my final offer."

Chance reached into his pocket and counted out five silver dollars. Still too much, he thought, but Dove would put the fine skin to good use. Besides, for some reason Skinner seemed a likeable old cuss. "I think you got the best of me, friend, but you've got what I need and I haven't got time to do better. How about a beer to seal the deal?"

"Now you're talkin', Marshal. Seein' as how you're buyin', it's been a real pleasure doin' business with you."

They headed up the block to the Dusty Nugget Saloon. Skinner found a table in the corner while Chance ordered two beers. Sitting down at the table, they picked up the frosty steins and took a long pull on the nutty mellow brew.

"Leggin's makes it sound like your friend's an Injun," Skinner said, wiping foam out of his whiskers.

"Actually it's for my deputy." Chance nodded, setting down his glass.

"Never heard of deputizin' an Injun," Skinner drawled.

"Had to after she saved my life."

"She!" His blurted exclamation sprayed foam into his chin whiskers. "A U. S. marshal with a squaw for a deputy? Well, if that don't beat all."

"Rides and shoots 'bout as good as any man you'd want to have at your back," Chance said, taking another drink.

Skinner's curiosity piqued. "How'd you come by her?"

"More like she come by me. Patched me up after a hard case I was chasin' put a bullet in me. She found me half dead and nursed me back to health in Talks with Buffalo's village up on the North Platte."

Skinner brightened at the mention of Talks with Buffalo. "Good man, Talks with Buffalo." Skinner nodded. "I scouted for the Army when he signed on to the Treaty of 1861. T'wern't hardly a fair deal, but Talks with Buffalo took it for the good of his people. I'd known him for a few years by then already. He always made me welcome at his lodge, though I cain't say as I've seen him in recent years."

"Then maybe you knew his daughter, Mourning Dove."

"Sure did. Sweet Medicine used to let me bounce her on my knee when she weren't no more'n a pudgy papoose. She's probably all growed up by now, I reckon. Say, she's not your deputy, is she?"

"Saved my skin a couple of times already," Chance said with a smile.

"Well, I'll be…" Skinner's words trailed off in the crinkle of a stained-tooth grin that split the wild gray bush on his face.

"Come on down to the Rawlins and meet her."

"That all happened a long time ago, son. She'd never remember an ol' cuss like me."

And of course, she didn't.

"Have dinner with us at Delmonico's tonight," Chance invited. "You've probably got a story or two to tell Dove about her father."

Skinner chuckled. "Talks with Buffalo and one or two about a chubby papoose I remember. Tell you what, though, I ain't much for restaurants. I'm gonna camp southeast of town tonight. I'm signin' my load of hides to a broker for shippin' back east. I'll be headin' back to the front range in the mornin'. Why don't you and Mourning Dove ride out to my camp and I'll fix us a supper of open fire cooked venison?"

Dove liked the sound of that idea. Chance couldn't refuse the bright light the invitation brought to her eyes.

Skinner served roast venison, biscuits and beans. They ate on tin plates seated cross-legged around a merry campfire. Dove felt more welcome at this white man's campfire than anywhere she'd traveled among the whites.

Chance watched her handle her knife and fork with a smile. She caught him and smiled too.

Skinner watched her, turning over pleasant memories of days gone by. "You sure have growed up, little Dove," he said with a twinkle in his eye. Dove blushed a little and dropped her eyes from his admiring gaze.

"I was thinkin' about the last time I saw you whilest drivin' out here this afternoon," he continued. "Talks with Buffalo and me was sittin' around his lodge fire smokin'. We'd been hunting that day. Took a fair-sized grizzly, we did. Your daddy stuck him good with an arrow, and I finished him off with my Sharps. We skinned him for a rug, as I recall, and put in a good store of meat for the both of us."

"Mourning Dove remember this skin. It cover Earth Mother in my father's lodge," Dove said at the wistful reminder of home.

Skinner broke into a chuckle behind an explosion of whiskers and crinkled his eyes. "Yup, that's the last time I saw you. Your daddy and I was sittin' around the lodge fire that night. Your mama and the woman in the next tipi was fixin' to put you and your little friend to bed."

"Mourning Dove's spirit sister, Autumn Snow," Dove said, thinking of her friend caring for Spotted Hawk.

Chance watched Dove warm to the old man's story and the visions it gave her of home.

"That's the name I remember." Skinner nodded. "Your mama and Autumn Snow's mama must have been givin' the two of you a bath, 'cause all of a sudden the two of you come runnin' out of that tipi buck naked and drippin' wet. You was a pudgy little bundle, and Snow looked like a strip of a string bean. Your daddy and I laughed

262

till our sides hurt watchin' your mamas chase the two of you around the village."

Dove colored at the story, sorely embarrassed as the old mountain man had intended. Chance chuckled at her embarrassment. She let him know she didn't appreciate his humor with a good-natured rap on his knee.

And so they passed a pleasant evening listening to Skinner tell tales of hunting with Talks with Buffalo in the years before Sand Creek. The fire burned low. Dove enjoyed the stories, even the ones meant to embarrass her. They reminded her of the way the old ones told of such things in the circle of the village family.

"Well, Dove, I expect it's time we headed back to town," Chance said as the hour grew late. "We cain't thank you enough for the fine dinner and pleasant evenin'."

"Thank me? Hell, it ain't often I get an audience for the tellin' of my stories, let alone one as pretty as Mourning Dove. For that I thank her with the gift of that antelope skin Lucky brought you."

Dove blushed again. "Thank you for the warmth of your lodge fire and the stories of my family."

They bid Skinner goodbye and mounted up. They were almost back to the hotel when Chance remembered the old bandit still had the five dollars he'd paid the old man for his "gift." Still, he'd made a friend and Dove had found a welcoming fire among the whites. It gave her spirit a lift, and that made five dollars at least a fair price.

FORTY-NINE

Marshal Tom Taylor sat on a bench across the street and up the block from the rooming house. He pretended to read a newspaper to cover his interest in watching the address where the telegram from Cheyenne would be delivered. He could make out the carriage a block east of his position where his partner, Ed Benson, kept an eye on the back of the house and the alley behind.

Summer spread a steamy blanket over St. Louis, as though the Mississippi had risen above its banks and flooded the air. A man practically had to chew the heavy air before breathing. A bank of heavy gray clouds threatened to brew up a storm to add soaking wet discomfort to the heat and humidity.

The heat beat down as the day wore on. Sweat poured off Taylor, soaking his shirt. He envied Benson for the carriage top protecting him from the sun. It might not help the humidity, but even a little shaded relief would be welcome. Telegrams were supposed to be fast. This one seemed to be taking its own sweet time about getting here.

The sun and the sweltering heat had risen to high noon by the time the boy from Western Union came pedaling up the quiet, tree-lined residential street. Taylor watched him park the ungainly-looking velocipede outside the picket fence. The boy opened the gate and hurried up the walk to the door. He sounded the bell and waited impatiently. For all the time it had taken getting here, Taylor observed that telegrams still gave the appearance of being in a hurry.

An older woman dressed in dark widow's weeds came to the door. Her gray hair was pulled back in a tight bun. She took one look at the envelope the boy offered and stepped back inside. She returned moments later, scrawled something on the envelope and handed it back to the boy along with a tip. The boy hurried back to his cycle. He turned the bike around and hopped up from behind, pedaling back the way he'd come. Telegrams, it seemed, were always in a hurry.

Taylor collected his horse at the hitching post and mounted up. He kicked up a trot down the street following the messenger, or more to the point, following the message. They could come back to the rooming house for more answers as soon as they found their way to the final destination of the message.

Benson saw Taylor ride off after the boy. It seemed odd, but Taylor had the lead on this one. He giddy-upped the carriage horse to a brisk trot around the block and fell in behind his partner.

The telegram went straight back to the Western Union office. They sent it on to Mr. White at an address on Second Avenue in New York. Taylor got the address from the Western Union telegrapher and fired off a report to Bryson, along with an alert to the U.S. Marshals office in New York. The New York office promptly dispatched marshals to the Second Avenue address. Taylor's quick thinking had the address covered before Davis Slane made his daily trip to the blind mail drop.

Slane hired a carriage as he did each afternoon to make the drive from Gelb's Wall Street office down to the mail drop at the Second Avenue storefront. As they rounded the turn onto Second Avenue and picked up the staccato clop-clop of a trot, something struck Slane as odd. Over the next two blocks leading up to the storefront, Slane's senses prickled with an uneasy feeling he couldn't dismiss. He thought he might be imagining things until he spotted them. Three—no, make it four men in rumpled suits lounging on both sides of the street and on both sides of the store. Something didn't feel right.

"Driver," he called softly out the window. "Forget this stop. Take me to the Bowery Saloon." Shorty or one the string of couriers Burnswick had taught him to use would make this pickup. A man couldn't be too cautious in this sort of business.

An hour later Slane perched on the roof of the Bowery, straining his gaze up the street, waiting for Shorty to return. The last of the afternoon sun drifted below the skyline, casting the canyons of the city streets and walkways into deep blue shadow. If Shorty didn't show up pretty soon, there would be little chance of seeing far enough to know if he was being followed. Or maybe he just wouldn't show up at all. Maybe he'd already been picked up by the men watching the mail drop. The men he'd seen didn't look like city police. If they were the law, Slane guessed they must be U.S. marshals, considering that one of them had caught up with their man in Cheyenne.

The dark shadow of Shorty's stubby form rounded the corner two blocks up the street. He ambled along in no particular hurry through the lengthening shadows. A block later Slane saw them round the corner, two men keeping their distance without losing sight of their quarry. He would have to move fast. Good thing he'd arranged for the saddle horse tied in the alley behind the saloon rather than rely on the slower moving, less maneuverable carriage.

Slane climbed down from the roof to the second floor balcony at the back of the building. He let himself in through the window he'd left open and made his way down the back stairs to the Bowery's raucous, smoke-filled din. He took a position beside the door moments before Shorty came in.

Slane handed Shorty a twenty-dollar gold piece, dazzling him with the payment as he took the bundle of the day's mail. The pale yellow telegram envelope sounded an alarm in Slane's head. He hurried across the bar and disappeared out the back door to the alley.

Shorty headed for the bar, congratulating himself on his good luck. He ordered a drink, but unfortunately he wouldn't have time to enjoy it before the marshals swooped into the Bowery and his luck took a turn for the worse.

FIFTY

Slane left the alley behind the Bowery holding the bay mare to an easy trot. To a casual observer he looked the part of a successful young businessman heading home at the end of the day. He rode north and then west in the gathering gloom. Here and there street-lamps winked to life, islands of gaslight marking his progress. He changed direction frequently as he worked his way back up town to throw off anyone who might attempt to follow him.

The telegram from St. Louis meant Cheyenne, which meant Burnswick. Burnswick should be in San Francisco by now, so this telegram could only mean one thing—trouble.

Slane returned the mare to the livery where he'd rented her and made the short walk to the Wall Street offices that were the control center for Gelb's shadowy empire. He climbed the stairs two at a time and hurried to his small third floor office. He cleared his desk and set to work decoding the message. He'd deliver it personally to Mr. Gelb.

Gelb liked Slane's work. The boss had brought him into the gold futures project and used his training at law to prepare the contracts Burnswick would offer the miners in California. He'd also been involved in negotiating the lines of credit that would finance the gold positions they would take when trading operations began. His responsibilities had increased again when Burnswick left for California, and he'd earned additional respect by pointing out that the Denver gold market should not be overlooked in the futures operation.

The coded message from Burnswick reported that the Taggert matter had been successfully resolved and asked White if he should attempt to conclude the Stage & Rail acquisition before leaving Cheyenne. On the surface it sounded routine, but the surveillance on Second Avenue meant that the communication channel had been compromised, possibly even Burnswick himself. Slane hadn't waited around long enough to identify the men following Shorty. They could have been Pinkerton agents or the law, no telling which. But his gut told him they were U.S. marshals. With the telegram decoded, Slane dashed up two floors to Gelb's penthouse office suite.

Gelb sipped his snifter of cognac, savoring the warmth and aroma of the amber liquid blending with the mellow draw of his Cuban cigar. He listened to young Slane's report while his mind raced beyond the facts at hand to the next moves of the pieces arrayed on the board.

With the St. Louis channel compromised, it would have to be replaced. A minor operational inconvenience; it could easily be reconstructed. This time he would route it through Denver, considering the structure of the gold operation.

He didn't need to check his sources at Pinkerton to know that the people crawling over the St. Louis connection were not their agents. He'd have been warned if Pinkerton had an operation afoot. No, the people who'd shut down St. Louis were U.S. marshals. Taggert hadn't been able to take care of the marshal in Cheyenne, and apparently neither had Burnswick. That explained the bogus telegram.

Right of Way Development and Credit Mobilier were compromised. Their congressional friends were frantically trying to contact Burnswick to find out why the hell U.S. marshals were questioning them about their involvement in Right of Way Holdings or any of its many subsidiaries. Fortunately neither Right of Way Development nor Credit Mobilier could be linked to Gelb personally. It might not go so well for some of their "col-leagues"—or should he say, "former colleagues."

Credit Mobilier had had a good run, but now, with Right of Way Development and the investors exposed, Gelb thought it time to let things sort themselves out. The minority shareholders would pay whatever price justice demanded. Right of Way Development and its lucrative contracts would be put into receivership and reorganized. That was where Gelb would step in through his surrogates to buy it back. The river of profits would resume again, only this time with fewer shareholders to divide it. The Credit Mobilier affair would be little more than a temporary inconvenience.

That aside, operational security needed to be strengthened. Sadly, that meant taking Stage & Rail Construction off the table, at least for now. Gelb hated to lose, but he knew when to cut his losses. He consoled himself with the thought that Stage & Rail was small time money compared to Diamond Jim's gold scheme, and the game wasn't over. They still had the opportunity to work on Grenville Dodge.

That led him to Burnswick and the possibility that he too had been caught or compromised. That made for a disturbing thought. Not only could Burnswick make the connection back to him personally, he knew too much about the gold operation. Burnswick had definitely become too much of a risk. By the time Slane finished his report, Gelb had formulated his plan.

FIFTY-ONE

Chief Marshal Bryson ground his teeth in frustration, staring at the reports that had come in from St. Louis and New York. He had nothing to show for the operation but dead ends. He had a widow in St. Louis with a room rented to a man who seldom used it. He had a small-time thug from a bowery saloon in New York who didn't know much and said even less. Chance had constructed a good story that might have worked, but somehow the New York operation had been spotted before the telegram reached its intended recipient. Now he'd have to give the bad news to Secretary Hoar and likely the President too. Neither prospect would make for a good day.

Horace showed Secretary Hoar and the chief marshal into the Oval Office an hour later.

"Good morning, gentlemen. I take it you've got something for me on the Union Pacific business."

"That's right, Mr. President," the secretary acknowledged. "I'll leave it to the chief marshal to make his report."

So much for the secretary backing up the chain of command, Bryson thought as they dropped into the wing chairs across from the President's desk. He wondered privately who'd be delivering the report if the operation had produced a glowing success. Well, he knew the answer to that one too. At times like these he appreciated the

271

fact that the President had been a field commander first and not just another empty suit politician.

"I'm afraid we don't have anything good to report, sir." Bryson reverted to a still-appropriate form of military address and a subtle reminder that this report came from the President's field commander.

"Marshal Chance sent his message through St. Louis. We were able to follow it to a rooming house and the widow who received it. She sent it on to an address in New York as she'd been instructed by a man calling himself White. This White fellow has rented a room from her for more than two years, though he travels so much he's hardly ever there. He did get telegrams every so often, which she forwarded to New York according to his instructions. The whole arrangement struck her as odd, but it seemed harmless enough and provided her a good source of income. She couldn't give us much more than a description of the man, but it bears a striking resemblance to the descriptions of Burnswick we got from the Right of Way general manager in St. Louis and Colonel Dodge in Cheyenne.

"Thanks to quick action by the marshals in St. Louis, we were able to follow the telegram to an address in New York, where a small-time bowery hoodlum picked it up. We followed him to a saloon and arrested him, but the telegram had already been passed to the man who hired him. We can only conclude that the people we are after somehow spotted our surveillance and found a way to avoid it."

"That is very disappointing." Grant closed his eyes and rubbed his temples to beat back the frustration of a circumstance he couldn't control. "So where does that leave us?"

Silence attended the President's question, accompanied by a good deal of foot shuffling and careful examination of boot shines. Finally Bryson broke the tension.

"It isn't much to go on, Mr. President, but we do have a good description of this Burnswick fellow and his statement to Taggert that he was passing through Cheyenne on his way to San Francisco. He's also been mentioned by a couple of the congressional shareholders in the Credit Mobilier investigation. He's either the brains behind the whole scheme, or the only remaining link we have to the majority shareholder who got the biggest payday at the Union Pacific's expense. If we send Marshal Chance to San Francisco, maybe he can pick up Burnswick's trail. It's a long shot, but Chance seems to have a way of making something out of nothing."

"You're right, Chief Marshal, it is a long shot, a very long shot. Lucky is a good man, though. If anybody can make something of it, he'd be the one to do it. Get him his orders. Time's a-wasting."

"Yes, sir." Bryson felt the tension relax. *The President still has general's stars somewhere under that suit.*

FIFTY-TWO

Dove had almost finished her leggings. They'd found some beads she liked at Gorham's Emporium. She'd chosen blue for the sky, with some amber and green for Brother Sun and the land. Lah Kee had bought them for her, and she'd worked them into the fringes of the leggings and the headband she'd braided out of the remnants of the antelope skin. She liked the way they looked. She enjoyed doing the work. It kept her in touch with the ways of her people despite the unfamiliar surroundings of the white man's village.

Chance checked the Western Union office each day, hoping for a response to his wire or some report from Bryson on tracing the message to whoever controlled Taggert. He knew perfectly well that Western Union would deliver anything that came in for him, but the waiting wore on him. He was restless and anxious to move on to some new assignment. He had to admit that any thought of settling down probably wouldn't have worked out for long. He'd been in on the action long enough that he'd have soon gone out of his mind with boredom in some more peaceful pursuit.

The walks through town gave him an excuse to drop in on Sheriff Teet and pass the time of day. The life of a frontier sheriff wouldn't make a man wealthy or keep him from getting shot at from time to time, but a least the man had a place to hang his hat and a roof to go home to at night. Maybe he and Dove could find a town that needed a sheriff where they felt comfortable.

He managed to avoid any further encounters with Victoria, or maybe she managed to avoid meeting him. Who could say? That probably worked out for the best. She couldn't understand his feelings for Dove, and he couldn't see any reason she should. He didn't know how to explain it in a way that might make sense to her.

The telegram from Bryson arrived on the morning of the fifteenth. Bryson wasn't one for flowery explanations. Basically the message had ended in a series of dead ends. It all came down to the description of Burnswick confirmed by all those who'd had contact with him. They had a description of the man who'd hired the bowery thug, but that shred could have described half the male population of New York in their late twenties. Coming from a small-time crook, it wasn't likely to be much help.

Bryson's telegram put an end to waiting for his next assignment. The chief marshal had ordered Chance to proceed to San Francisco and use "all available means to find Brunswick and arrest him on charges of murder and fraud." *San Francisco*. That meant a ride on the new transcontinental railroad. That thought struck with a flash of new reality. *What about Dove?* The prospect of confronting the iron horse would be terrifying to her. The long train ride would be followed by San Francisco. She had no concept of a city that size. Chance had never been there, but he knew that gold, railroads and shipping trade to the Orient had turned San Francisco into a city the likes of which he hadn't seen since he'd left Washington. He could feel the terror of the experience for her in so many ways. It might be too much to ask so soon.

He found her in the stable sitting cross-legged in the straw between Sage and Salute's stalls, finishing her leggings. Her hair hung loose in the headband she'd fashioned out of the hide, drawing a curtain around her face as she worked the thongs closing the last of the seams. She preferred the quiet of the stable to the confines of the hotel room or the bustle of Cheyenne's streets.

As he stood in the stable doorway, sunlight cast his shadow on the hard-packed dirt floor before her. She looked up. A soft light lit her eyes. He never tired of discovering her beauty. In simple settings like this, he felt drawn to her like a bright light. He followed her eyes and dropped to his knees in front of her. He took her face in his hands and touched her lips with a kiss. She smiled and showed him that the leggings were nearly finished. The beadwork in the fringe and the rich golden tan of the skin would make a handsome addition to her man dress.

"Dove, I got orders to follow Burnswick to San Francisco. I'll need to take the train to make the trip."

She studied his face, letting the meaning of his words sink in. They would ride the iron horse that trampled the ways of her people. This would mean stepping into the belly of the great monster with the fire and smoke that had chased the buffalo from the land and crushed the spirit of her people. The thought ran dark with fear. She would need all of her strength to endure such a thing. Could she make herself do this?

Chance could see the uncertainty in her eyes. "That's a pretty big dose of white man's world. If you like, I'll take you back to your father's village. You can wait for me there until I return."

She gazed into his eyes with a faraway look. She knew he offered this out of concern for her. He knew the way of the path she did not know. She needed the vision of her spirits to see this path.

"Come, Lah Kee. We go to the land of my people. Mourning Dove must see this path in the wisdom of the spirits."

Chance didn't know what she had in mind, but it looked like they'd be checking out of the Rawlins House.

They rode north out of Cheyenne with Dove in the lead. She set the pace at a slow lope with a specific destination in mind.

Chance had a hunch he knew where they were headed. In the gathering purples of evening they reached the grove of cottonwoods grown up in the willow breaks along the banks of the slow-moving creek. Here she had found the spirits of the land and the feeling of home. Here they had found the fork in the trail that became their path of coming together. They would camp that night in sight of that path. The path they had traveled through the clash of white and Indian ways.

They picketed the horses along the banks of the stream and gathered wood for a fire. They settled side by side before the fire, watching the crackling flames pop showers of sparks that rose like prayers to the Great One Above. Dove produced the last of her supply of pemmican for their meal as the land settled into evening under a brilliant blanket of stars.

They finished their simple meal in silence, listening to the night sounds of the owl and the coyote. Chance knew Dove listened to her spirits here. He respected her need to be at one with them while she considered the path ahead. He waited patiently for her to see her way, unable to know her heart in this. He knew the iron horse for a powerful symbol of the clash between their peoples. The prospect of being swallowed by the beast must be terrifying to her. He couldn't blame her if she chose to return to the safety of her village rather than confront the monster that had changed her people's way of life.

The moon rose full and bright, illuminating the land in patches through low-running clouds. The land felt warm and at peace. Dove heard Brother Coyote call his brothers, giving voice to the spirits that surrounded her. Beyond the circle of firelight spirits walked the land. Here, away from the sights and sounds of the white man's village, she could feel them. She could see them. They would guide her. A ghost herd of buffalo, the great shaggy river of life to the old ways, flowed to the north, away from the steel and smoke of the iron horse and its trail. The spirits of her ancestors could follow the herd, but they could not bring them back. They could not bring back the old ways. Her father knew that. Here in her heart she knew it for herself.

In the dying embers of the fire she could see the path of coming together. Tomorrow this path would follow the iron horse trail. She would follow it and she would survive. She turned to Lah Kee and remembered the words her father had spoken. She looked into his eyes and spoke them again.

"You must come to know the true meaning of this coming together, and the life it will mean for you and your children. Take time to gather this wisdom. It will guide you on this path." She fell silent. She held him in her heart with her eyes. She could feel her heart beat. In that she knew again they were one.

"The path of coming together travels the iron horse trail. Mourning Dove will travel her path with Lah Kee."

He took her into his arms, there in the bosom of the land, in the presence of her spirits. This night they would take strength from each other for the days ahead. This strength would sustain them all their days on this path.

Case File:

BLACK FRIDAY

Jake Gelb needed no encouragement to take the meeting with Diamond Jim Trask. He'd done business with Trask before. Mostly railroad speculations Trask arranged when circumstances or politics favored the speculators. The ebullient womanizer had caught up with Gelb at the Exchange Club the night before. Trask said he had an idea he wanted to see him about. They'd agreed to meet at Gelb's offices this afternoon.

A quiet knock at the door announced Trask's arrival. Gelb opened the door himself to let him in. He'd never hired a secretary for security reasons. The fewer people involved in his business the better, though at times he found the lack of help inconvenient.

Diamond Jim Trask filled the office doorway with his bulk. He wore a dark gray suit with a green silk brocade vest that made a statement of his girth. A diamond stickpin the size of a man's thumb was stuck in a black tie between the points of his collar. His thinning dark hair was slicked back in oily strands. A fleshy red face with heavy jowls reduced his eyes to lively dark pinpoints.

"Come in, Jim. Care for a drink?"

"Hell yes," Trask boomed, lumbering across the richly appointed office to the seating area in front of the fireplace.

Gelb went to the sideboard and poured two generous snifters of cognac. Trask spread his bulk over the leather-covered settee at the center of the sitting group, where he wouldn't have to confine himself to one of the wing chairs. Gelb set the snifters down on

281

the table and retrieved his cigar and a crystal ashtray from his desk. He took the wing chair next to the fireplace and struck a match to relight his cigar.

"So tell me about this idea of yours, Jim," Gelb puffed around a cloud of blue smoke.

Trask swirled the amber cognac in his glass. "The play is gold, Jake."

Gelb arched an eyebrow in disbelief. He shook his head. "For a minute there I thought you said gold."

"That's what I said, Jake." Trask took a swallow of cognac.

"Don't waste my time, Trask. The gold market couldn't be in worse shape. All the smart money has gone short, and the price is going nowhere but down."

"That's what everybody thinks," Trask acknowledged, taking another sip of brandy. "That's precisely why the market is ripe to make us a fortune."

"If you're so bent on losing money, Jim, why don't you find yourself a nice high stakes poker game and leave me out of it." Gelb swallowed his cognac. He needed a drink just thinking about the risks of a play in gold.

"Now, Jake, before you decide I'm crazy, hear me out." Trask drained his glass.

Gelb refilled their glasses and settled back with a comfortable draw on his Cuban. He allowed the mellow blue cloud to draw a veil over his concentration. Traders who shorted the market borrowed gold and sold it on the expectation that prices would fall. The speculator could then buy back the borrowed position at lower prices to repay the loan and pocket the difference. Speculators, known as shorts or bears, had dominated the gold market since the end of the war. If Task saw opportunity in that mess, Gelb sure couldn't see it.

"You're right about the bears, Jake. Everybody thinks that gold is headed down. The smart money has gone short in the market, but sooner or later those shorts are going to have to cover their positions, and when they do, what do you suppose they are going to need?"

Gelb scowled. "Gold, of course. What's your point?"

"My point is the structure of the gold pool." Trask raised his glass in mock toast.

"What do you mean, gold pool?"

Trask turned professorial. "The gold pool is the supply of gold in circulation. The government owns ninety five million in gold, but only about twenty million of it is in circulation or in the hands of investors. If we can buy our way into the market to positions approaching the portion of the pool in the hands of investors, we can control the available supply and corner the market. If we don't sell, the price starts to rise and the shorts will have to cover their positions. Since we control the supply, they'll be forced to cover at prices we dictate."

Gelb furrowed his brow. "Interesting, but Treasury is certain to step in and sell gold to stabilize the market for the sake of the currency."

"Indeed they will, but we'll be out of the market before that happens," Trask said with a satisfied smile.

"How can you be so sure—" Gelb bit off the question. Trask was so cocksure of everything he became irritating at times. He always played with a stacked deck, so get to the point.

"Because our man at Treasury will tell us when they are ready to sell."

A slow smile replaced Gelb's perpetual sneer. He lifted his snifter to Trask. "Like I always say, Jim, I like the way you think. So where do we go from here?"

"I'll pull in a few of our Erie friends to put up the serious money. How could any of them resist the opportunity to take part in a Midas Compact?"

"Midas Compact. I like it."

"You need to arrange the financing for our share of the positions. We should be ready to go by early fall."